A DEADLY ABODE

AN OLIVIA WELLS MYSTERY

JANE McPARKES

A DEADLY ABODE

AN OLIVIA WELLS MYSTERY

NO EXIT PRESS

First published in the UK in 2026
by Bedford Square Publishers Ltd,
London, UK

bedfordsquarepublishers.co.uk

A CIP catalogue record for this book is available from the British Library.

ISBN
978-1-83501-530-8 (Paperback)
978-1-83501-531-5 (eBook)

2 4 6 8 10 9 7 5 3 1

Typeset in 11 on 14pt Adobe Caslon Pro
by Avocet Typeset, Bideford, Devon, EX39 2BP
Printed and bound in Great Britain by
CPI Group (UK) Ltd, Croydon CR0 4YY

FSC www.fsc.org MIX Paper | Supporting responsible forestry FSC® C013604

The manufacturer's authorised representative in the EU for product safety is Easy Access System Europe, Mustamäe tee 50, 10621 Tallinn, Estonia
gpsr.requests@easproject.com

For Catherine Teresa Harris
Without whom, Hallowe'en has never been the same

WHATSAPP GROUP – #FirstHomesOnly

@Homes4Locals: Who else is going to the beach clean on Saturday morning?

@NotJustForHolidays: I am. This is really important to KP and I think we should all help her out

@CornishCoastCustodian: Agree. She does loads for Penbartha and this is a really worthy cause. This data she's collecting is vital to the plastic free campaign

@CoastalCrusader: 👍

@PlasticFreePioneer: It's what we've been working towards for a year. A lot of our group are going

@Homes4Locals: There should be a good turnout. It's been well advertised

@PlasticFreePioneer: And it's a worthy cause

@PrimaryDweller: Cool. I think we should definitely show our solidarity and combine our efforts for the greater good. At least there shouldn't be many second-homers there as it isn't half term yet.

@NotJustForHolidays: Good. Can't imagine they'd help anyway. Why would they care?

@Homes4Locals: Think Treave School may finish this weekend

@KernowCurrent: How many of them have second homes here if their kids board there?

@BanSecondHomes: Quite a few. And more and more of them are looking to buy round here from what I've heard, for when they come down to see their precious darlings.

@NotJustForHolidays: Can't they bear to give their money to hotels or proper B&Bs even just for a weekend? 🤬

@Homes4Locals: Why would they do that? They don't care about the local economy. Or anything, apart from themselves and their own pockets

@KernowCurrent: Hmm. Doubt they'll dirty their hands at a beach clean then

@TheTyreQuencher: No, but they'll be driving their Chelsea Tractors badly and clogging up our lanes cos they don't know how to reverse.

@WanderWithoutWings: Bet they don't go anywhere near the beaches. Will be saving themselves for their next long-haul flight

@TheTyreQuencher: Do you reckon they ever give their carbon footprint a thought?

@WanderWithoutWings: Of course not. Too selfish. And self-obsessed.

@TheTyreQuencher: Agree. So let's see if we can focus their thoughts a bit.

@PlasticFreePioneer: Just be careful. And remember, we're doing this beach clean to help KP achieve Plastic Free Community status for Penbartha. No trouble please.

1

Olivia held her face up to the sun that was casting a low but bright glow over Penbartha beach, trying to glean some warmth from it despite the sharp breeze that made her glad of her woolly hat, and then sneezed violently.

'Remind me again why I'm standing on a windy beach, in the middle of October on a Saturday morning, with the worst cold of my life, when I could be tucked up in bed being waited on hand and foot by my fiancé? Who I haven't seen in two weeks, by the way.' Olivia blew her nose dramatically for added effect.

Kitten didn't look up from her iPad screen which she was tapping furiously, but waved vaguely in the direction of the groups of villagers spread out across the beach, armed with litter pickers and hessian sacks. 'Because it's the right thing to do. Look at all these people.' She glanced up briefly. 'And you love me like a sister.'

Olivia's laugh turned into a hacking cough, and Kitten looked at her more closely. 'You need to get Mum to prepare one of her potions for that, before it goes to your chest.'

Olivia grimaced. 'If I have to drink any more of her lemon, garlic and ginger concoction, I reckon Jago will be on the next train to London and still be able to smell me from there.'

Kitten went back to her iPad. 'No, he won't. The ginger counteracts the garlic. Thanks, Alice.' She looked up with a weary smile at the manager of the Goods Shed as she placed a sack brimming with empty plastic drinks bottles at her feet.

'Disposable cups over there where Paula is sitting,' she told the next person with an equally full sack, 'and takeaway containers over there with Lou, please.' Kitten sighed. 'The sea was rough last night because of the easterly winds, so there's more plastic being washed up than usual, but God knows how long this stuff has been festering in the water and the damage it's been doing to the marine life.'

'I don't understand why people don't just take their rubbish home with them, rather than thinking the tides will conveniently deal with it. Don't they realise tides don't work like that and it just ends up as someone else's problem?' Alice Greville – manager of the Goods Shed, the local coworking space for eco and creative entrepreneurs and the heart of the renovated and repurposed Penbartha railway station site and Olivia's right-hand woman – pursed her lips and glared at the sack of offending items.

'We need to educate people not to buy single-use plastic in the first place.' Kitten sighed again. 'But at least by documenting the worst offenders' – she poked an empty Coke bottle with a gloved finger – 'we can produce proper statistics and name and shame them properly.' She tutted as she dislodged it from the sack and bent to pick it up. 'Groups like us are collecting this information at beaches all around the country. When all the data is gathered and published, the hope is people will realise that it's their favourite drinks company that's responsible for a large proportion of the 40 million plastic bottles bought in the UK every day and think twice before buying them in future. That's my hope, anyway.'

'I reckon most people will probably only start taking notice when scientists have proved an actual link between microplastics and diseases like cancer and dementia. At the moment they just think it affects the oceans and has nothing to do with them. So they do nothing.' A girl who looked about eighteen, with dark cropped hair and the funkiest blue glasses Olivia had ever seen, and carrying a sack full of what looked horribly like disposable nappies and bathroom plastics, stopped for a moment as she walked past. 'I'm Mya Pascoe by the way. I live in Truro, but I heard about this beach clean last night in a group chat and wanted to come along to help. The beach is buzzin!"'

'It's amazing, isn't it?' Olivia seized on the change in subject, always eager to steer Kitten away from one of her passionate environmental monologues and welcome a new face. 'I can't believe how many locals have turned up to help. I don't recognise them all. Do you, Kitten?'

The three women gazed round the beach, busy with men, women and children all dressed in outdoor gear and woollen hats, cheerfully collecting their designated items and chatting to their friends and neighbours as they worked. Olivia smiled at Kitten, delighted for her that the beach clean was proving so popular and well attended. She knew how passionate Kitten was about the campaign against single-use plastic. She had achieved plastic-free status for the Waiting Rooms, the café she managed in the old railway station building, by slowly but surely eliminating the use of all single-use plastics in her business. Encouraged and emboldened by all her acquired knowledge on the subject, she had persuaded Olivia and Alice to do the same at the Goods Shed. That had been more difficult as there had been so many individual members based there, but Alice had embraced the challenge whole-heartedly and taken it upon herself to inform and educate everyone. And they had all been delighted when they achieved plastic-free status too. One by one, the village shops had got involved, as had the local school and several businesses. Kitten had not needed any further encouragement to set her sights on achieving the same status for the whole community. Today's beach clean was an important step in the right direction, and Olivia knew that to see that so many locals shared her vision really was a dream come true for her.

'There are lots of familiar faces,' Kitten confirmed, 'but quite a few new ones, too.' Olivia intercepted the nervous glance she sent in Mya's direction. 'Where did you say you read about it?'

Mya waved her litter-picker round in a vague way. 'Can't remember now. I belong to so many local groups that they all merge into one eventually. But everyone was very clear that we should support you.'

Kitten smiled. 'That's good to hear. You can sometimes get so caught up in a cause, you forget that everyone doesn't see things the same way.'

Mya laughed. 'Tell me about it. My best friend says I can bore for Britain on the subject of our oceans.' She spotted someone she recognised and rushed off with a cheery wave.

'Hey, look! Here come the boys.' Olivia pointed to Rocky's pick-up as it drove slowly onto the beach and parked up. A familiar tall, silver-haired and broad-shouldered figure climbed out of the double cab and helped Rocky remove a large trestle table from the open load bed. As they put it together and steadied it on the ground, the Old Bakehouse liveried van pulled up alongside.

'Great timing. It looks as though we'll be finished in record time and then everyone can be rewarded with fresh coffee and pastries.' Kitten grinned. 'I thought it was the least I could do to say thank you, so the Waiting Rooms have donated the coffee and Fraser offered me a good deal on the pastries.'

Olivia smiled. 'Fraser and Willow opening an independent bakery in the village has worked out really well all round, hasn't it?'

'Totally! We're so lucky we're able to claim that all our bread, cakes and pastries are baked within half a mile of the Waiting Rooms. It really supports our sustainability agenda.'

Olivia nodded. She'd always hoped that the Old Bakehouse and the Waiting Rooms café would be beneficial for each other, but the success of both ventures had already exceeded her expectations. Visitors to the café at the station site who tasted their delicious bread and pastries often popped into the Bakehouse on the way out of the village to buy more. And the staff at the bakery always pointed their customers in the direction of the Waiting Rooms.

'George would be proud of us, wouldn't he, Olive?'

Olivia felt a lump form in her throat. George Stevenson, her godfather, had been the original founder of the Goods Shed as a coworking space for eco-conscious and creative entrepreneurs who wanted to break free from more traditional ways of working and bring greener practices to their businesses. After his sudden death, Olivia had inherited his dreams and the station site and had thrown herself into fulfilling his legacy. It had been hard work, but now she was able to turn to Kitten with a smile, tinged with a little sadness.

'He would. But I wish he was here to see it.'

Kitten wiped a tear from her own cheek and waved her iPad in the air. 'He is, Olive. He is. Let's not be sad. He'd be thrilled.'

Rocky wandered towards them, wearing faded Levis tucked into scuffed builder's safety boots and a thick Arran sweater that always smelled faintly of a mixture of sawdust and salt. He dropped a kiss on Kitten's cheek. 'Hope you're happy, Kitti-Kat, because I'm beside myself with pride. You're amazing the way you've rallied all this support. Isn't she, Olive?'

'Absolutely.' Olivia felt the usual surge of happiness she experienced when she saw her two best friends together and then sneezed rapidly and violently. She fished a soggy cotton handkerchief out of her pocket and blew her nose noisily.

'Delightful!' Rocky pulled a face at her. 'I won't kiss you, if you don't mind. Jago said you were snoring like a Massey Ferguson tractor last night.'

'Charming.' Olivia couldn't help but laugh and peered up the beach to where Jago was leaning against the pick-up and chatting to a group of villagers. 'Is that why he's staying out of the way?'

'He's supposed to be helping Caroline unload the Old Bakehouse van.' He pointed to a pile of tied and labelled hessian sacks behind Kitten's chair. 'Are these to go?'

'Yes, they've all been sorted, recorded and labelled.' Kitten checked her iPad. 'It's the ones that aren't tied that we've still got to do.'

'I'll take some up with me then and come back for the others.' He grabbed two sacks in each hand, winked at Olivia and made his way back up the beach, calling out to the people he recognised as he went.

'It's good of Caroline to give up her morning off.' Olivia observed as a tall, thin woman with a greying pony tail and a black Bakehouse fleece started laying out insulated tea and coffee jugs, milk and platters of pastries. 'I don't know how she manages to juggle so many part-time jobs and still be active in so many community groups.'

Kitten shrugged. 'That's just the way many people make ends meet these days and' – a smile crept over her face and Olivia realised she hadn't seen Kitten smile much lately –'that's how she gets to hear all the best gossip in the village.'

Olivia shook her head in despair. Having been the subject of a great deal of gossip in the past, she now avoided it wherever she could and mentally added Caroline to the list of people to be careful around.

A shrill whistle pierced the chatter filling the beach and the waving arms by the table announced that refreshments were ready. Kitten signalled to the remaining people still collecting their specified items of litter.

'Just leave your sacks here and grab something to eat and drink. It won't take long to finish up here. Everyone's worked so hard.' She turned to Olivia, and handed her the iPad. 'Do you mind holding onto this for me down here while I go and thank everyone? I'll bring you a drink back.'

'That's fine. I ought to keep my germs to myself anyway.' Olivia sank down onto the beach chair Kitten had vacated and lifted her face up to enjoy the warmth of the sun on her skin again. She was just on the verge of dozing off when a deep, rich and familiar voice pierced her thoughts.

'I've brought you a little present.'

Olivia screwed her eyes tightly shut. 'If it's more lemon, ginger and garlic, you can give it to the seagulls,' she muttered.

'I thought I'd give more conventional medicine a go.' He handed her a thermos mug. 'A blackcurrant flu and cold remedy, made by the UK's finest pharmaceutical company.'

Olivia grabbed hold of it and shot an anxious glance up the beach. 'Just don't tell Kitten. That pharmaceutical company is probably guilty of a whole host of environmental sins, and I can't be seen to be supporting the enemy.' She took a large mouthful and then sighed happily.

'In Cassie's defence, the lemon, ginger and garlic does seem to be doing the trick.' Jago observed mildly. 'You don't look or sound half as disgusting as you did.'

She drained the mug and frowned. 'Thanks. I still feel fairly disgusting, and that shot of synthetic drugs could be just what I need.'

'Who's taking synthetic drugs?' A warm voice full of laughter interrupted and they both turned to see Jasmine, a part-time waitress at the Waiting Rooms. She was dressed, as usual, in dungarees, this time patterned with green jellyfish and other sea creatures, under a green fleece. She waved an iPad at them and addressed Jago. 'Rocky's asked for you to carry the rest of the tied bags up to the pick-up and help him with the table when everyone's finished.'

'Rightio.' He took Olivia's mug off her and hefted two sacks over his shoulder. 'Rocky and I'll make sure these are dealt with properly, and I'll see you back at home. The dogs will need letting out.'

A little thrill of pleasure ran through Olivia at Jago describing Tresillian House as home. She'd inherited it from her godparents and while it had always been home to her in many ways, she often felt like she was still living in someone else's house, rather than her own. Slowly, over time, she and Jago had made subtle changes to the house, and while she shared many of her godmother's tastes, she had succeeded in injecting a much more modern vibe while still retaining all of the original features.

She blew him a kiss and turned back to Jasmine, one of her favourite, and least gossipy, villagers.

'How's life?'

Jasmine's lovely round face broke into a big smile and her unusual pale grey eyes shone. 'Life's good now school's finished for half term. I don't know how the teachers do it! At least I'm only a lowly design and technology technician, but even I get fed up of the little darlings. I'm looking forward to spending more time working at the Waiting Rooms.' She looked around, making sure Kitten was out of earshot. 'I've never met anyone who supports local causes as much as Kitten does. Just spending time with her makes me more aware of my own convictions and gives me the encouragement I need to support her.' She turned back to Olivia. 'I'm hoping I can take some of the pressure off her. Do you think she's been herself lately?'

'Kitten?' Olivia frowned. 'I don't know really. I haven't seen that much of her. She's been so busy organising this, and I've been working silly hours trying to get the Old Foundry finished before November. Rocky hasn't said anything, or Cassie.' Guilt sliced through her. 'Am I missing something?'

'I'm not sure. Can't really put my finger on it.' Jasmine looked round the slowly emptying beach. 'At least it looks like this has been a huge success and her worst fears about it haven't come to pass.'

Olivia stared at her. 'What do you mean?'

'There were a lot of rumblings on social media between local groups about whose cause is the most important.'

Olivia felt a prickle of unease. 'What sort of groups?'

'Oh you know, all the usual suspects, but at the moment it seems that the anti-second homes lot are stepping up a gear, just in time for the half-term visitors. But it looks like they put their differences aside to support Kitten's campaign to get plastic-free status for the whole village, so that's good.' She frowned. "Do you really not look at social media, Olivia?'

'Not if I can help it.' She shuddered. 'Too much negativity, and with the speed at which gossip goes round this village, who needs it?'

Jasmine laughed. 'Fair enough. And talking of gossip, how are things going at the Old Foundry?'

'I'm not even going to ask you how— ouch!' Something heavy caught Olivia on the side of her face and her chair rocked violently, pitching her sideways onto the sand. Pain shot across her right cheek and nose. She lay, dazed, for a second and then through watering eyes watched as a heavy football bounced onto an open sack on the ground, dislodging its contents over the beach. A volley of braying laughter drew closer.

'Oi, you lot, watch what you're doing' Jasmine yelled as Olivia staggered to her feet, her right ear still ringing from the impact.

A group of teenagers, looking like they'd just stepped off the pages of glossy magazine advertising this season's look for preppie surfer dudes, sauntered up to them. Even to Olivia's watering eye, they oozed privilege.

'What's up, Miss?' one of the girls tittered. 'Nice threads. Did you make them yourself?' Her voice dripped with sarcasm.

Jasmine bristled. 'I did yes, thank you, Flora. I like to plough my own furrow.' Another titter rippled through the group, her own sarcasm completely lost on all of them. They were all wearing practically identical designer-labelled sherpa lined hoodies, relaxed cut jeans and Converse shoes, and hair artfully arranged around their woollen beanies. *They were probably the sort of teenagers who railed against having school uniform imposed on them as it stopped them expressing their individuality!*

Jasmine and Olivia exchanged a look.

'And as nice as it is to see you all so soon in the school break,' she continued. 'May I ask you to watch where you're kicking that football? A lot of people have given up their Saturday morning to pick all this litter up and sort it.'

'Haven't they got anything better to do?' The tallest of the boys sniggered. 'Carrot munchers.'

Olivia's hackles rose, not so much at the pure private schoolboy accent, but the attitude. 'You could always help us finish up here.'

'No thanks. We've got better things to do.' More sniggering.

Olivia's chin went up. 'Such as?'

'We'll think of something.'

She took a step closer, her cheek smarting. 'Let me think of something for you. How about starting with apologising for kicking that ball into the side of my face? And then help us finish up here. Doing something good for the environment might make you feel better about yourself.'

The ringleader looked around the beach. 'My dad says that

whatever you bunch of grungy carrot-munchers do in this poky little corner of Cornwall won't make any difference to anything.'

Olivia glared. 'Well you're wrong there. It only takes one person to start a change, then the community joins in and before you know it, the government is banning certain single-use plastics like straws, plastic cutlery and plastic bags.' She pointed at the pile of drink bottles on the sand. 'Those will be next, with a bit of luck.'

'Yada, yada'. He yawned loudly as his mate, shorter but rounder, spoke up. 'My dad says that there's no such thing as global warming. Look at how cold it was last winter.'

'So your dad knows better than the world's leading scientists, does he, Henry?' Jasmine asked. 'I think I might suggest that the teachers explain the difference between weather and climate in your General Studies sessions next year. Not to mention the effects of plastic pollution on climate change.' She turned to the girls in the group who were all busy pouting and taking selfies against the background of the beach. 'Don't you remember we had that session on fast fashion and microplastics, girls?' She was met with blank looks all round. She tried again.

'And how any plastic that ends up in the ocean, eventually breaks down and emits greenhouse gases that contribute to global warming and climate change? Don't you think that helping out here might slow that down a little?'

'I think you might have been wasting your time there, Jas,' Olivia observed. 'Which is a real shame as it's their generation who'll be the first one to really suffer. We might be lucky enough to die of old age. They'll probably all die of climate change.'

'I really don't think it's up to you to decide what we're taught, miss. Especially as you're not actually a teacher.' Another boy in the group spoke up, winking at his mates.

'And I thank my lucky stars every day that I'm not, Charlie.

But I still deserve some respect. Now, off you all go and play nicely.'

'Or what?'

Olivia stood her ground. Her head was thumping from the impact of the ball, but she was not intimidated. She closed her eyes briefly and when she opened them the teenagers had been joined by two others who were dressed completely differently. No designer labels for them, just sensible cold weather Cornish wear.

'What's up, Miss?' The two newcomers addressed Jasmine.

'Ah look, it's the bursary boys,' mocked Charlie.

Olivia looked again, recognising the boys as locals, but unable to put names to their faces.

'Piss off, Charlie,' the smaller lad said. 'What are you even doing here?

'We thought we'd come and check out where the bursary boys live. See if it's as drab as we thought.'

'Well, you're not wanted here.'

'Aren't we?' he sneered. 'Don't you lot need people like us?'

'People like you?' The other local lad was much taller and well-muscled.

'Yes, people who pay the full fees at school and subsidise the scholarship kids like you. And whose parents come down here and bring money into shitholes like this.'

The smaller, much slighter boy sprang forward, his face red with fury. 'People like you just add negativity and rubbish,' he spat. 'You buy up our homes so you can stay in them when you come down for a few weekends a year and stop local families from buying them. You're an entitled prick and—'

'That's enough, Alfie.' Jasmine warned, but it was too late. Alfie rushed at Charlie, and within seconds there were arms and legs everywhere. Flora picked up a half-full sack of litter and threw it at Alfie; another lad started kicking the rest of the open sacks until there was litter flying across the sand in all directions. Then a shout went up from the top of the beach, and all hell broke loose.

2

'So what happened then?' Jago watched closely as, still holding an ice pack to her face, Olivia poured boiling water into a glass bowl and then shook the contents of a brown paper bag into it. Her curls were tied up in their usual messy bun, her olive skin still tanned and glowing from the amazing summer they'd just had despite her rotten cold and slowly deepening bruise. But her usually warm and bright eyes were troubled. Jago's question had been on the tip of his tongue ever since he and Rocky had arrived back at the beach after the troublemakers had all been sent packing.

He'd taken one look at the large bruise forming all down the side of Olivia's face and started asking questions. But Cassie had intervened in her usual gentle way.

'Not now, my lovely. I reckon it's all a storm in a teacup, and she's still in a bit of shock. Why don't you take her home and make her a cup of tea, before you start your examination-in-chief or whatever it is you call it?'

And so he had, and for once there hadn't been loads of villagers hanging around, ready and willing to add their own opinion, spin, or little extras on what had just happened. How he missed London sometimes.

They'd driven the short distance home in silence and been given a rapturous welcome by their three affection-starved dogs.

Jago made tea while Olivia dispensed treats and only after they had empty mugs in front of them did he raise the question.

'Luckily Sam arrived with Cassie just as it all kicked off properly and put a stop to it all fairly quickly. But not before a few punches had been thrown on both sides.'

'And they took notice of Sam?' Jago stared at the bowl, intrigued as Olivia swirled what looked like sweepings from the garden round the bowl and added a few drops of something from a small brown bottle. Mylor and Zennor watched closely, their tails wagging expectantly.

'Well, once he'd whipped out his warrant card they did and scarpered pretty smartish. Those kids are smart enough to avoid getting into trouble with the police.' She paused. 'Although I think they were probably more scared of Cassie, who launched into mother tiger mode. I've never seen her so angry. For the first time I could see where Kitten gets her quick temper from.'

He chuckled and then sobered quickly as a horrible thought occurred to him. 'I'm not going to be eating the contents of that bowl later, am I ?'

Her laugh quickly turned into a grimace of pain and she swiped him with the tea towel she was holding and then carefully covered the steaming bowl with it. 'No, it's a herbal steam inhalation that Cassie made specially for me. She found Mollie's old book, the one where she wrote down the herbs that worked best for me when I was a kid.' She narrowed her eyes at him. 'Not all hers work the same way for all people, you know. So I've got dried eucalyptus, peppermint, rosemary, thyme and lavender, which all have immune-enhancing properties, and I've just added some tea-tree oil. I let it steep for ten minutes and then I inhale for ten minutes.'

Jago nodded, used to Olivia's firm belief in her godmother's herbal remedies. He just hoped it did the trick and also helped her throat. It had been her weak point ever since a murderer had attempted to strangle her the previous year, and her voice was often husky, but hearing it as hoarse as this brought back a whole load of troubling memories for both of them.

'So who were the lads who ended up fighting each other? You said the kids with the ball were from Treave School.' He glanced at Olivia's cheek where the bruise was already colouring nicely and wondered whether the herbs swilling in the bowl also had healing powers. Or was that arnica?

'Yes, arrogant little pricks. There's no way I would have got away with talking to adults like that when I was there, and even less so when you were. Can you imagine?'

'Not at all. I think we just had more respect for all adults, even if we did board,' Jago mused. In his line of work as a criminal barrister, his eyes had been firmly opened to what kids of that age were capable of. 'But what about the ones who turned up and joined in. Were they all locals? Did you know them?'

Olivia gave him a look as she carefully carried the bowl over to the refectory table in the orangery. It was the one that said, we aren't in court and you're not cross-examining me.

'I recognised Alfie who works weekends at the Waiting Rooms and Ned Roscoe, Pippa's son. They were already on the beach, helping out, and just came over when they saw the Treave kids talking to us, but I can't say I recognised many of the others who turned up after they started kicking the rubbish about. They just kind of appeared. Some were older, and perhaps some weren't from round here. Jasmine reckoned they might have been from the FHO group who had come along to support Kitten.'

He raised an eyebrow. 'The who?'

'First Homes Only, you know, the group that's campaigning against second homes being bought by people from upcountry and all the problems that entails.'

Jago's heart sank. He might not have known what the local group was called, but he was fully aware of their mission and how similar groups elsewhere in Cornwall were becoming more aggressive. A thought struck him.

'Is Jasmine part of that?'

'I think she's on some of the shared forums. But she did say that they'd all agreed not to cause trouble, for Kitten's sake.'

'But they couldn't resist joining in a scrap when they saw one starting?'

Olivia glared at him. 'Look, Jago, it's a highly contentious issue that brings out the worst in some people. And speaking as the only person who got hurt, I'd like to forget all about it, and get on with my steam inhalation.' She lifted the tea towel and a herbal scented steam escaped that very quickly made his eyes water. 'Would you mind taking the dogs down to the creek for a while so I can concentrate on my breathing?'

'Sure.' He recognised that tone and whistled to the dogs who were equally grateful to leave the strange, very undoggy-like smells that were filling the kitchen and escape into the garden.

Jago stood on the edge of the creek, trying to unpick the troubled thoughts chasing each other round inside his head, much like the dogs were doing on the shoreline. He'd come back from his most recent court case in London, determined to have an honest conversation about their wedding plans, which were still non-existent. He knew that he had messed up with his proposal. Presenting it as a legal contract had been a really bad idea. He also knew that Olivia wasn't into romantic gestures and might have laughed at him if he'd dropped to one knee and come out with any soppy stuff, so he'd gone too far the other way and she'd ended up doing the proposing. And of course, he'd accepted. It was what he wanted more than anything in the world, but they still hadn't bought a ring or done anything to arrange a wedding. Half of him wondered if Olivia expected him to carry on with their role reversal and turn into some sort of groomzilla and organise the wedding himself with the military precision that seemed to be the expected norm these days. But he very much doubted that was what she wanted, and he was pretty sure she would baulk at the idea of a big wedding. All he had to do was ask her, but he'd got his proposal wrong and was afraid of getting the next bit wrong too.

So James Trevithick KC and Deputy High Court Judge, one of the finest legal minds in London, who thought nothing of prosecuting some of the most high-profile criminal cases in the country, was in a quandary. He was used to, and happy, operating within the well-defined codes of the legal system. But when it came to matters of the heart, he was completely out of his depth.

And now, just when he'd built himself up to talk to Olivia about their future, this had happened. Despite what she said, it was obvious that the morning's encounter had rattled Olivia more than she would ever let on and now he was better at listening to his instincts, thanks to her, he too felt a prickle of unease. The resentment towards people from upcountry buying second homes in Cornish villages, leaving them hollowed out and soulless for much of the year, had been steadily growing. Jago could see both sides of the argument. *Audi alteram partem*, the Latin term for hearing both sides of the story, was the cornerstone of fair legal proceedings and had been drummed into him in his job as a barrister and a judge. Fortunately Penbartha had avoided many of the second home issues, but the village was becoming more well-known and popular, and Jago now wondered if Olivia felt partly responsible for that. Cornish folk came from miles around to shop for their baked goods at the Bakehouse and eat lunch at the Waiting Rooms. The two businesses had built up a mutually beneficial relationship. The customers who hadn't got the time or energy to get to the Waiting Rooms could taste the coffees and pastries on offer there at one of the American diner booths in the corner of the Bakehouse, usually occupied by a few of the elderly ladies of the village. The rise in popularity of coworking meant that the Goods Shed now had a waiting list for tenants and more and more artists wanted to join the Engine Shed collective, a space exclusively for creators and makers whose sustainability credentials aligned with its eco-friendly mission statement. And because of social media, word had spread. Penbartha was on the national sustainability map. Unfortunately, it was on another radar too, the sort of radar they perhaps didn't want.

Jago frowned, decided it was time to go home and whistled to the dogs, laughing as they ran towards him, goofy smiles on their faces. They made an unlikely trio. Olivia's dogs shared the same father – a famous French poodle nicknamed Romeo who, in addition to being a pedigree stud dog, enjoyed nothing more than escaping his kennel and indulging in unregulated love matches. Mylor's mother was an obliging black schnauzer and Zennor's an overambitious white chihuahua. Although unequal in size, the two dogs loved each other fiercely and had happily adopted Steren, Jago's black Labrador, as a surrogate sister even if she was too lazy to ever go out for runs with them.

As they made their way back down the lane a black Range Rover drove past them at great speed, forcing him and the dogs into the hedge.

'Slow down, idiot!' he yelled, but the car carried on out of sight. Then he heard a squeal of brakes, a familiar crunch of gravel and car doors slamming. He picked up his pace, his pulse quickening.

By the time he got to Tresillian's drive, he could hear raised voices. Once he'd rounded the curve, he had the perfect view of Olivia standing on the doorstep, hands on her hips, facing up to two men. Her American twang, stronger than usual and a definite sign of stress or anger, carried towards him on the breeze coming off the creek.

Mylor rushed ahead to protect his mistress, hackles up, and proceeded to add to the noise by barking and circling the two strangers. When Jago reached them, all three humans were talking loudly and all three dogs barking. 'Call your bloody mutts off!' the shorter of the two men demanded. 'Or I'm calling 999.'

'Go ahead,' Jago replied calmly. 'You're trespassing on private property and using threatening behaviour. The dogs are just being protective. Calm down, or I'll be the one calling the police.' Nevertheless, he whistled to the dogs and shooed them into the house, shutting the front door behind them. Then he stood firmly beside Olivia, slipped an arm round her waist and faced down the two strangers. He was taller than both of them and, from a quick estimation, probably fitter, despite being slightly older. They were casually, but expensively, dressed in clothes which immediately reminded him of the fathers of the lads he'd been at boarding school with, who had a uniform of their own. But there was something that didn't feel right about this pair and told Jago they were trying too hard to fit in with a social group they didn't quite belong to. Their tweed jackets looked brand new, their calfskin leather loafers pristine, their oxford shirts perfectly pressed. There was not a dog hair or a smear of Cornish mud anywhere to be seen. Even their signet rings were shiny and unscratched. *All just a bit too flashy*. Putting two and two together, and realising who these men were, he turned to Olivia.

'Is everything okay?' To his surprise, tears rushed to her eyes, but she brushed them away quickly. He decided to risk her wrath by intervening. Yes, she was a strong, independent woman, but this blasted cold had dragged her down and being hit on the head hadn't improved her mood. He turned back to the men, keeping his expression and voice neutral.

'How can I help?'

'We're here to find out why this woman verbally attacked our sons on the beach this morning.' The shorter of the two men pulled himself up to his full, not very impressive, height, his ruddy cheeks glowing with anger. He spoke with a smooth, almost arrogant air of confidence that Jago was used to back in legal London, but felt out of place here.

Jago felt his own hackles rise. 'But not to apologise for them kicking a ball into her face and causing her a significant injury?' He pointed to the bruise on Olivia's face which had spread and darkened even more in the time he'd been away.

'Our sons didn't do that,' the taller man insisted.

'So where did it come from then?' Olivia pushed the hair off her face. 'You can see the imprint of the ball and my right eye's swelling up. They were rude, arrogant and then kicked litter all over the beach after lots of people had spent the morning cleaning it up.'

The man waved her question away. 'They're just kids, having fun in their school holidays. But you called on the local hoodlums to come and sort them out, didn't you?'

'I did no such thing.' Olivia's American twang grew even stronger. 'I could hardly see what was happening, thanks to them. But it didn't last long. They were all sent packing pretty quickly. And now, I'm going to politely ask you and your friend to leave my property, Mr Burrows and if you don't, I'll call the police.'

'Just who do you think you are?' The shorter man blustered and then turned to his friend. 'Christ, I can see what you mean about this woman, Rafe.'

Jago felt Olivia stiffen beside him. *What on earth was going on?*

'Everyone here seems to have an advantage over me, so let me introduce myself.' He kept one arm around Olivia's waist and slid his other hand into his jeans pocket. 'I'm Jago Trevithick and this is my fiancée, Olivia Wells.'

'I'm Marcus Walker-Smith, and I own Walker Estates, an estate agency in London. My son Charlie is a boarder at Treave. One of the lads your fiancée denies verbally attacking.'

He held his hand out, but Jago kept his firmly in his pocket and just nodded. Rude, he admitted to himself, but he needed to make a point.

'And I'm Rafe Burrows, managing director of Burrows Prime Property Search in Truro. And my son, Henry, also boards at Treave. Olivia and I have come across each other several times in a professional capacity when clients of mine, for whom I've sourced the almost perfect second home, have sought her services and expertise to make some changes to the property, haven't we, Olivia?' Anger suffused the Burrows man's face as he turned to her. 'And you've refused to work for them every time, haven't you? Which has put me in repeatedly awkward situations.'

'I don't understand why you keep recommending my services to your clients, when you know I'll say no,' Olivia replied crossly. 'You're just wasting everyone's time.'

Rafe's lip curled. 'Unfortunately, you have one of the best reputations as an architect in this area. And an apparently very close relationship with the planning department.'

Rather than reacting to Rafe's unpleasant insinuation, Olivia seriously impressed Jago by just staring at the odious man. 'That's because I play by the rules and don't try to change them.' She drew herself up to her full height and pulled her shoulders back. 'All the proposals your clients have put to me have been totally inappropriate. I don't like cleaning up other people's dirty work. And quite often they've been downright illegal or immoral from the get-go. That proposal for that land in Mawgan Porth was utterly ridiculous. How can you think that building a house right on the sand dunes is a good idea? Did you even consider coastal erosion, never mind the impact that just the construction works would have on the site? It just wasn't sustainable.' Jago watched as her dark eyes flashed sparks.

An angry flush spread across Burrows's cheeks and he turned to his friend. 'Take no notice of her, she's making it up. People like her think they're better than us, and she's jealous of our success.' He looked back at Olivia. 'You like to think of yourself as Miss Sustainability, don't you? But we all know that you're just hiding behind all that eco claptrap you and your lot are always spouting. You just despise people who own second homes.'

3

Kitten sat for a moment, sipping a cup of tea and relishing the peace and quiet before she began the nightly ritual of closing up the Waiting Rooms. She had always loved the café when it was at its busiest and full of friends meeting up, chatting and making plans over coffee and food, and she could flit around, joining in and laughing with customers. Over the last few weeks though she had begun to prefer this time of the day, when the sun was dipping lower over the creek and the walkway, dappling the old building in golden light, warm and soothing on her face, until it disappeared altogether for another day. Now she liked to sit for a while, without any customers, and imagine the sounds of the old station, with steam engines pulling up and setting off, the guards' whistles and the low hum of chatter in what would have been the ladies' waiting room.

What the hell's the matter with me? she wondered. For some reason, a pain that had appeared behind her right eye a few weeks ago had got steadily worse, along with a numb right leg she had got from sleeping at a funny angle. Now her right eye was throbbing horribly and when she looked around, everything in the Waiting Rooms was decidedly blurred. *It's like the worst hangover ever. But without the alcohol. I need to ask Mum for some herbal stuff and see if that helps. Although, knowing her, that will lead to a whole load of fussy questions that will give me even more of a headache.* The locum GP she'd eventually seen hadn't seemed overly concerned. He'd just muttered something about stress and told her to come back if it didn't get any better. Well, she couldn't carry on like this, so she would have to go back. She sighed and went in search of regular painkillers.

Swallowing the two remaining tablets in the blister pack with a final gulp of tea, she forced herself to go about her usual tasks, promising herself a hot bath and an early night. Jasmine had already cashed up the till and the local food bank had been to collect the leftover food that couldn't be served the next day. Often, Kitten would end up driving to the Falmouth or Truro foodbanks herself, but not tonight. Brian had turned up early, beaming with gratitude. She wiped down the tables, took out the broom and began to sweep the stray leaves and lumps of cake and biscuits from the floor. It always amazed her how much mess parents allowed their children to make. Give her muddy pawprints any day.

As she was filling the mop bucket with hot water, a face appeared round the door to the back kitchen.

'You okay, Kitten?'

Another pain shot through Kitten's right eye, and her vision blurred again. She blinked rapidly and felt her way to a chair.

'That you, Alfie?'

'Yes, what's the matter?' She felt him move closer. 'You've gone a very funny colour. Are you sure you're all right?'

'Just give me a minute.' She pressed the palm of her hand against her eye and felt the pressure ease a little. She heard a tap being run in the main kitchen and something being placed on the counter beside her.

'Here, have some water. You sit there, and I'll mop the floor.'

'But it's your day off.' She pressed her hand against her eye again, praying that the painkillers would kick in soon.

'It's no problem.' She heard him heave the bucket out of the deep sink and then listened to the rhythmic sound of him moving tables and chairs, mopping the floor and putting everything back in its place. Only when she'd heard that he had tipped the water away, rinsed the mop and bucket and put them away, did Kitten try to open her eyes.

Alfie's concerned face appeared in front of her, blurry at first, but it soon settled into place. *Phew!* She let out a sigh of relief.

'How d'you feel now?' His sandy eyebrows were drawn together over dark eyes, and there was a deep line etched across his high, freckled forehead.

Kitten nodded her head and winced at the pain the movement caused. 'I'll be fine.' She took another sip of water. 'I just have the headache from hell.'

Alfie pursed his lips. 'I don't suppose what happened on the beach this morning helped. That's why I've come. To apologise.'

She peered closer at him; his thick dark-auburn hair was swept back from his face in curtains and cut short over his ears. Even the hair falling across his forehead couldn't disguise his look of genuine remorse, and she immediately felt sorry for him. He was a good lad and a hard worker.

'I saw it all happen from the top of the beach. And Jasmine told me the details. From what I hear, you didn't start it.'

He looked away. 'I shouldn't have retaliated.' He looked at her sideways through his fringe. 'Gran blames my hair colour.'

Kitten tried to smile, but pain turned it into a grimace. 'That's as good an excuse as any, I suppose.' Something Jasmine had said popped into her head. 'Do they give you a hard time at school?'

Alfie shrugged. 'Sometimes. They're not too bad individually, but when they're with the rest of their cool crowd, they really grind my gears, you know?'

This time before she smiled, she pressed three fingers against her right eye. She could just imagine the old-fashioned phrase coming out of his grandmother's mouth. Caroline Pellow, a proud local, was a right old busybody and was happy to share her opinions on a variety of subjects with anyone who'd listen. Kitten wholeheartedly agreed with many of them, but even she knew they wound up a lot of people. Still, that wasn't Alfie's fault.

'Is there much of a divide between the day and boarding pupils?'

Alfie rubbed hard at his left eyebrow. 'Not really. It's more between the ones who pay full fees and those on scholarships and bursaries. Guys like Charlie and Henry really like to go on and on about how their very wealthy parents are subsidising our places.'

Anger bubbled in her stomach. She hated the thought of this gentle boy being humiliated by revolting posh boys. 'What about Ned Roscoe? Didn't he win a scholarship too?'

'Yeah, but he's on a rugby scholarship and just look at the size of him. Being an art scholar doesn't have the same kudos, especially with the girls.' He peered through his fringe at Kitten, his freckled face colouring.

'Ned doesn't give you a hard time, does he?' She knew Ned's mum, Pippa, well. She'd recently been elected as Chair of Trustees of the Penbartha Station Heritage Trust, which ran the Goods Shed and oversaw the enterprises that took place in all the buildings on the old station site, including the Waiting Rooms, Engine Shed and the Signal Box, from where Jago ran the successful railway memorabilia business he had set up with George Stevenson. Kitten respected Pippa and was pretty sure she wouldn't tolerate her son making Alfie's life miserable.

'Nah. Me and Ned have been mates since nursery. He stands up for me a lot.' His young, worried face suddenly crumpled. 'It just all got to me this morning, when Charlie was shouting his mouth off. And although I love Penbartha, I wish I didn't have to go to Treave and that I could just live in Exeter with Mum and Dad and Bella. I really miss them.'

Kitten's heart melted as his voice cracked on his last words and she forgot her headache for a moment. 'Oh Alfie, I'm so sorry. I had no idea you were so unhappy.' She patted his shoulder. 'Have you spoken to your gran about it? Or your mum and dad?'

Alfie shook his head quickly. 'No. They all think it's the best opportunity for me.' His soft brown eyes filled with tears. 'And I suppose it is. But I'd still rather live with my own parents, rather than Gran. She does her best, but it's as though I'm a constant reminder that Mum and Dad had to move away to be able to afford somewhere bigger. Gran wanted them to buy the Old Foundry, but they just couldn't afford it, with all the work it needed. She sees Emily and Silas Hogan as incomers. It doesn't make sense but them buying it has given her so much fuel for her First Homes Only campaign. It's embarrassing!'

Kitten pulled a face. 'I really don't think the Old Foundry is the best example of incomers buying up our homes. It's an old industrial building that was empty for years and no one made an offer on it. Emily and Silas have been living in a caravan on their flower farm for two years while it's been done up.'

'Gran reckons you only defend the Hogans because Olivia's your friend and she and Rocky are doing the work on the Old Foundry.' His voice wobbled.

Kitten took a breath. She could easily imagine Caroline saying things like that too. 'I don't think your gran's being fair there, Alfie. She knows the Hogans bought the Old Foundry fairly and squarely. And it was entirely their choice to have Olivia and Rocky do the work. There's no conspiracy.'

'Gran says the owner should only have been allowed to sell it to a local.'

'Silas and Emily *are* locals now. Their only home is a caravan on their flower farm. They've had one baby while living in it, and they've got another one on the way. They've worked really hard to establish their business and they employ local people. How could they be more immersed in the village?' She kept her voice gentle, but inside she was fuming at Caroline. *Was she even aware how unhappy her grandson was?*

Alfie's face crumpled. 'I just feel I'm always caught in the crossfire. Gran winds me up and yet I can see your point when you explain it like that. If I was in Exeter, life would be so much easier.'

Kitten suddenly felt much older than her years. She was only ten years older than this lad and yet she wanted to mother him and tell him everything would be all right. She caught hold of his arm and he let her pull him into her side. 'I'm sorry things are so tough for you at the moment, Alfie. But I'm here for you, you know?'

He leaned into her for a moment and she could feel how slight he was. He pulled away and rubbed his eyes. 'Thanks, Kitten.'

'Any time. And I mean that—'

The loud roar of a powerful car engine and a sudden screeching of brakes at the back of the Waiting Rooms drowned out her words, and before Kitten could register what was going on, Alfie mumbled something she didn't hear and took off. She caught sight of a gunmetal grey BMW SUV out of the windows, glanced at her watch and hurried to the door, her mind still on Alfie.

She was just bolting the double doors when a man in his late forties, with sunglasses pushed up onto his head, appeared at the window. He knocked on the door with a single knuckle.

Kitten opened the door a fraction. 'I'm sorry, but I've just closed up for the evening.'

He gave an embarrassed smile. 'I'm sorry too, love, but could I use your facilities?'

Her vision blurred again and made it impossible to see his facial features clearly, but she reckoned he didn't look like the sort of person who needed to raid her till. Kitten didn't know, or care, much about high-end fashion, but the clothes he was wearing probably cost far more than her day's takings, not to mention the oversized watch on his wrist and the plummy accent.

Oh God, I've had enough of Hooray Henrys for one day. But the sooner I agree, the sooner he'll leave, she told herself and nodded to him.

'Through there.' She pointed to the far end of the main room.

Judging by the speed he moved at, his need was genuine, and she closed all the blinds and wiped down the counters as she waited for him to return.

'I say, those loos are absolutely amazing!' He reappeared with a bigger smile on his face and stood right next to her, gazing round the café. 'I like what you've done here.'

Hooray Henry really was launching a charm offensive now. She wasn't in the mood, but then remembered her hospitality manners.

'Thanks. They're genuine Great Western Railway lavatories, all restored to their original beauty. Most customers say how much they like them.' Kitten moved towards the door, still eager to close up, but Hooray Henry was scanning the chalkboard behind the counter which listed all their menus.

Her head was starting to pound again. 'Is there anything else I can help you with? Like I said, we're closed now, and it's been a long day.'

'This all looks healthily delicious. It's a shame you're closed. I'll have to come back another day.' He gave the board one last look. 'In the meantime, can you point me in the direction of the nearest pub, or somewhere I can get a good meal? My wife and I are meeting up with a few friends this evening, and I've been sent on a bit of a recce to find somewhere.'

'Sure, there's a pub in the village, on the left as you go up the hill. The Ship Inn.' She hesitated. 'Although a lot of tourists prefer the swankier restaurants in Falmouth.'

He laughed and touched her briefly on the arm. 'You've got me there. I'm sussing out the village a bit. First time I've ever been, but I like it. So I'm thinking about buying a place here. Expand my personal property portfolio to include Cornwall.'

Kitten's entire body stiffened. *Uh oh, this was not good.* 'You want to buy a house in Penbartha? To live here permanently?' She could barely get the words out.

'Not permanently, no. I just thought it might make it easier for us to see the kids more often. They're at Treave School. Two boys. And it would give my wife something to keep her occupied, you know.'

Kitten didn't know, but panic washed through her and her mind went into overdrive. *Think like Olivia. What would she do? Keep him sweet and put him off gently,* she told herself. *Don't launch into a hostile attack and get his back up.*

'It's really quiet here.' She moved away from him, suddenly realising how close he was. 'Mostly old people, you know. And there's nothing to do. Ever.' She managed a bright smile. 'You'd probably do better looking up in Rock. Or Padstow.'

'There's not much property available up there at the moment.' He smiled again. 'What about in the lane where that American woman lives?'

'American woman?' Kitten's mind went blank.

'You must know her. I thought everyone knew everyone else in these places. She's an architect.' His eyes narrowed. 'All the news, gossip, houses for sale, stuff like that, goes round like wildfire, doesn't it?'

Olivia. But her accent only gets noticeable when she's angry or upset. What the bloody hell is going on here?

She decided to play dumb, which wasn't her usual style, but

her brain was struggling to make sense of everything. 'Does it? Like I said. Penbartha's a very boring place to live.'

He gave her a look. 'I'd heard that there was a place that might be coming onto the market in that lane. An old house, bit of a wreck by all accounts. Owners have died, but they were old so it needs loads of work.'

Kitten swayed. She really didn't feel well. 'I've no idea, sorry.' Her phone buzzed and she snatched it out of her pocket. 'Yes, sure. I'm just locking up and I'll be on my way.'

She ended the call and held the door open. 'If I were you, I'd talk to the various estate agents in Truro. They're easy enough to find on the internet.'

He tried another smile. 'Well thanks for all your help. It's been nice to meet you.' He held out a hand. 'By the way, I'm Marcus Walker-Smith.'

WHATSAPP GROUP – #FirstHomesOnly

@CornishCoastCustodian: Thanks all for showing up 2day. Gr8 turnout

@Cornwall4Locals: Until those brats from Treave showed up

@BanSecondHomes:💩💩💩

@Homes4Locals: They're not all 💩. Just most probs.

@VeggieVibes: Felt sorry for Kitten

@CornishCoastCustodian: Me too. Shame she's not in this group. Can someone tell her?

@VeggieVibes: I will. Can we allow her in?

@Homes4Locals: We agreed not to. No need

@VeggieVibes: She looked awful this morning. Felt v sorry for her.

@Homes4Locals: Have some info re incomers for all

@PrimaryDweller ???

@Homes4Locals: Sniffing around for houses to buy in P

@CoastalCrusader: 🤬🤬 Who? Where?

@Homes4Locals: Can't really say yet. Pretty sure they're in The Ship this pm.

@BanSecondHomes: Anyone else up for leaving a them a msg?

@PrimaryDweller: Deffo. DM me.

@Cornwall4Locals: I'm in too

@NotJustForHolidays: 👍

@VeggieVibes: Don't be 2 extreme. Pls

@Homes4Locals: Leave it to us

4

'Well, it sounds like Marcus Walker-Smith was turning on the charm for you, Kitten,' Jago observed once she'd finished reporting on her encounter the previous afternoon. 'We certainly didn't see that side of him, did we, Liv?'

The weather outside mirrored the mood round the dinner table perfectly. The clouds hung so low over the garden at Tresillian that the fields on the opposite bank were invisible. Relentless mizzle blew up the creek on a sharp wind, enveloping everything in its thick, damp greyness.

'If you describe trying to winkle information out of people as charming,' Cassie huffed. 'And heaven only knows where he got the idea that Gillan Cottage might be going up for sale. That's total news to me. And I think I would have been told as I live slap bang between Gillan and here.'

As one of life's feeders Cassie always made too much food on a Sunday, invariably bringing it over to Tresillian to share with whoever was about. And hungry. Today, they were down to their core 'Sunday Group' of Olivia, Jago, Kitten, Rocky and Cassie. Sam had been called away on police business, but the rest of them had enjoyed a warming Spanish stew served with homemade crusty bread and a delicious Rioja.

Jago was still a little surprised by how much he enjoyed these gatherings, and how much he liked living at Tresillian. It really was a glorious house, with light pouring through the floor-to-ceiling windows, the familiar and welcoming smell of polish and lavender and the mixture of flagstone and wooden floors, all scattered with rugs and worn smooth by generations of feet. He had felt at home in it from the very first moment he'd visited George and Mollie there, all those years ago, and he was happy that he and Olivia were slowly making it their own. He gazed out of the rain-scarred window as they all listened to Rocky gently teasing Kitten about the effect she had on men, grateful that they were managing to keep the conversation light over dinner.

Unfortunately, Olivia was still feeling grumpy, even after her first run for a few days and another healthy dose of paracetamol. 'No, we didn't. He kept that side of his personality well hidden,' she commented crossly. 'Having said that his mate, Rafe, didn't let him get much of a word in.'

'Rafe Burrows has always been a complete and utter knob, in my opinion,' Rocky muttered. 'There's no way Olivia and I would work for him.'

Everyone was momentarily distracted by Sam letting himself in through the boot room door, dropping a kiss on Cassie's cheek and then turning to nod hello at everyone sitting round the table.

'Who's a knob?' he asked with a grin as Cassie filled a plate with Spanish stew and handed it to him.

Jago poured him a glass of wine. He liked Sam and had a lot of respect for him as a detective. More importantly, Sam obviously adored Cassie and made her very happy. And he had slipped into their close-knit group with friendly ease. Even Kitten listened to him and that was saying something, given her well-known distrust of the police.

'Rafe Burrows. He's a property search consultant in Truro,' Cassie explained, with a slight curl of her upper lip.

'What's one of those when it's at home?' Sam tucked into his food.

'I'm not entirely sure,' Cassie replied. 'But I think they act for clients who want to buy a house, but are too busy or important, to do it themselves. So the consultants do all the donkey work and then get paid handsomely for their services by the purchaser.'

'As opposed to general estate agents, who act for, and get paid by, the seller?' Sam tucked into his food and then returned to his original question. 'So why is this bloke a knob?'

'Well it turns out that there's some long-running feud between him and Olivia and Rocky that none of us knew anything about.' Kitten's eyes narrowed as her gaze fell on the business partners, sitting side by side on the opposite side of the table. 'What exactly is his beef with you two?'

'Professional differences, that's all.' Olivia drained her wine glass. 'And it's mostly me he has the problem with, not Rocky because we've never got as far as doing any work for him.'

Jago could tell from her tone that she didn't really want to talk about it. Olivia tried her best to keep her business dealings separate from her personal life, but that wasn't always easy in a place like Penbartha. But, as far as he was concerned, Burrows had overstepped the mark by coming to her home and having a go at her, and her friends deserved to know what had happened so they could keep their eyes and ears open on her behalf.

'Apparently, Rafe Burrows has tried to engage Olivia to work on houses he's sourced for several of his wealthier clients in the last year or so and she's always refused…' he began.

Olivia scowled at him. 'I've refused because he's asked me to undertake projects that go against everything we stand for. He assures his clients he'll instruct architects and builders for any work they may need, or want, to carry out and then gets arsey when we decline. Plus he's not a nice man. He's made a lot of money over the last few years selling houses in Cornwall to Londoners at inflated prices.'

'That's not a sin, is it?' Sam asked mildly. 'Surely, it's the property owner's choice to sell and who they sell to? Isn't this Rafe Burrows chap just providing a service?'

Jago winced. Sam was too busy eating to read the room properly. Selling houses to second-home owners from upcountry was an increasingly tricky subject, and Cassie, Rocky and Kitten were all on the same page.

'Let's put selling local houses as second homes and all the social and economic consequences of that to one side for the moment and get this straight.' Olivia spoke firmly and ignored the pained faces around the table. 'My "beef" with Rafe Burrows has more to do with the fact that in many instances he misadvised his clients about needing planning permission, building consent and proper surveys for the work they wanted to do. So they had unauthorised work carried out by upcountry builders who were happy to do the work without the necessary consent. And then, fast forward to now, a few years later, when his original clients are trying to sell their properties because of changes in life circumstances, work patterns or so on, they go back to him to complain because they need to seek retrospective planning permission and so on.'

'And that's where you come in?'

'In theory. Rafe Burrows assures his original clients that they will easily get retrospective planning permission, so they can recoup all the money they've spent. But he needs help with that. Personnel at the planning department has completely changed over the last few years and they've really upped their game.'

'Why won't you help them?' Sam clearly didn't understand how Olivia's professional mind worked yet.

Olivia stared at him. 'It's not my field. I'd rather do the job properly in the first place than try and clear up other people's messes. Obtaining retrospective planning permission is time-consuming and unpredictable. There are reputable planning consultants out there who will do it for a very handsome fee, but even those guys won't guarantee success, despite what Rafe Burrows tells people. No decent architect will ever guarantee obtaining planning permission.'

'And without this permission, you can't sell your property?' Sam persisted in his questions.

Jago turned to watch him more closely. Why on earth was Sam so interested in planning rules and regulations? As far as he was aware, Sam was in the process of buying a small terraced house in Falmouth and spending most of his spare time at the Coach House with Cassie. Jago took a breath. Perhaps he was biased. He'd always hated planning law when he was working his way through the various specialisms as a junior barrister; give him a good old-fashioned criminal punch-up any day.

'No.' He tuned back into Olivia's reply. 'In the last couple of years, most estate agents will tell you they've been asked to sell properties without the required planning permission or building regulation approvals in place. It causes a whole load of problems and basically results in a house becoming un-mortgageable and unsaleable. So people like Rafe Burrows, who have been neither honest or competent in their dealings in the past, presumably have some very angry former clients threatening to sue them.'

'Does this mainly affect second-home owners who are now trying to sell the houses they bought a few years ago?'

Olivia nodded. 'It affects anyone who didn't get the right permissions, first- or second-home owners, but since Rafe's market is the incomers who are prepared to pay inflated prices for second homes it's mainly them. I find it really frustrating, because if you do the job properly in the first place you can avoid a load of hassle.'

'And Burrows's clients either didn't have the correct information or the patience to follow the process in the first place, and now they're paying the price.' Rocky leant forward. 'Tell them about the other stuff he's asked us to do, Olive.'

Her eyes flashed again. 'The man is a total thorn in my side. He's put clients in touch with me who've bought lovely old houses and want to tear them down and replace them with some ugly modern monstrosity.'

'And the para 84 cases,' Rocky put in.

Jago swore he could see smoke starting to come out of Olivia's ears and the amber chips in her dark eyes sparked fire.

'This drives me crazy,' she huffed. 'But there's a provision in the National Planning Framework that allows "exceptional circumstances" for the construction of isolated dwellings within the countryside, including the green belt. The houses have to be, and I paraphrase "of excellent design quality, help raise the standards of design in rural areas and significantly enhance the beauty or character of their immediate setting".'

Sam dug his hole a little deeper. 'What's so wrong with that?'

'It's just not what we're about,' Rocky replied bluntly. 'It would have to be a pretty bloody amazing house to improve the beauty of most places down here. We'd rather work on improving existing buildings for people who want to live here as part of the community, instead of creating even more naff glass and steel palaces for weekenders.'

'And although these particular new houses often incorporate features like green roofs, green technologies and water-harvesting systems, they're usually just paying lip service to sustainability in order to game the system and get their planning permission,' Olivia added.

'And has Rafe Burrows has been involved in cases like that?'

'I think he's been involved in some land purchases at inflated prices for clients on the basis they'll get planning permission. He's approached me on their behalf a couple of times to tender for the projects, but I've always refused.' She paused for a moment. 'I don't think any home, no matter how innovative or superbly designed, justifies its existence in an untouched rural landscape.'

'And we're lucky enough to be in a position that we can turn down work we don't agree with,' Rocky added.

'So why did he take it so personally when you refused to work for him? Don't take this the wrong way, but you're not the only architect in this part of Cornwall.'

'But she is the best,' Kitten declared. Jago smiled at her loyalty.

'And she has the best working relationship with the conservation and planning officers,' Rocky said.

'Because I'm honest. And transparent in my dealings,' Olivia said simply. 'I don't play games. And men like Rafe Burrows can't get their heads round that. As Rocky said, we're in the fortunate position that we can choose not to undertake work that doesn't align with our values.'

'Are you saying Rafe Burrows doesn't like you?'

The atmosphere in the orangery chilled as Sam asked his question. Mylor pricked up his ears, ambled over to Olivia and rested his shaggy head on her knee. She ran her fingers through his fur as tears suddenly filled her eyes. 'I haven't gone out of my way to antagonise him. But he seems to have got it into his head that I'm trying to ruin his business.'

'The way he spoke to her yesterday would be fairly strong evidence of that. The man came to our home, on the basis of a false accusation, and threw vicious, untrue allegations at her. He was on the verge of becoming unhinged. I only got him to leave by threatening to call the police.' Jago frowned at Sam. 'What's all this about?'

Sam shifted in his chair. 'Just trying to assess the lay of the land as far as relations between locals and weekenders, or whatever you call them.'

Jago wasn't fooled. 'Why the sudden interest?'

Sam sighed. 'I was late here because I was called to the Ship. Apparently a number of cars owned by parents whose kids are at Treave School, including Rafe Burrows and Marcus Walker-Smith, were targeted in the car park last night.'

'Targeted in what way?'

'Initially, they thought they'd had their tyres slashed. On closer examination, it turned out they'd just been let down.' A few titters round the table quickly became coughs. Sam looked at them in turn. 'It's treated as criminal damage. If someone was to drive the vehicle without realising their tyres have been deflated, it could have very serious consequences.'

Kitten's face looked a little flushed. 'That will be the Tyre Quenchers.'

'The who?'

'The Tyre Quenchers, ' she repeated. 'They're an environmental action group who are taking action against air pollution and climate change by sending the owners of fuel-guzzling SUVs and fancy cars a pretty clear message that they're not wanted in our towns and villages.'

Jago stared at Kitten. He'd never heard of them.

She held his gaze. 'Those cars are super-polluting, and we don't want them in our villages.' The she turned to Sam. 'I thought they usually left notices on the cars, telling them that the tyres had been deflated and why. Their aim is to inconvenience them, not kill innocent people.'

'No one mentioned any notices.' Sam looked nervous. 'Are you part of this group, Kitten?'

'Of course she's not,' Rocky snapped

'No, I'm not,' Kitten confirmed. 'I've heard about them in some of the other towns and villages with big second-home populations, but I wasn't aware we had any here.'

'So how did they know Walker-Smith and his cronies were going to be at the Ship last night?' Jago wondered out loud.

Kitten's face reddened again. 'He asked if could recommend anywhere local to eat for him and some friends when he came into the Waiting Rooms.'

'And you suggested the Ship Inn?'

She nodded.

'That's not an offence, is it?' Rocky jumped to his girlfriend's defence. 'Kitten was exhausted after yesterday and went home and crashed out. She didn't leave the flat all night.'

'Could anyone else have overheard your conversation? Or did you tell anyone about it?'

'No.' Kitten's reply was instant. 'But anyone driving past the Ship could have noticed the cars and passed the information on. They aren't exactly the sort driven by locals.'

Jago looked at Sam, who was watching Olivia closely.

'Sam?' The older man turned to look at him, and his expression sent Jago's mind into professional overdrive. 'Are you suggesting Olivia had something to do with it?'

'Not exactly. But she was mentioned by name as a possible suspect by Rafe Burrows.'

'What?' Olivia's face was furious. 'Does that ridiculous man really think I've got nothing better to do with my time than go round letting the air of out his and his mates' penis extensions? He really is unhinged!'

'Olivia's right.' Jago placed a hand on her arm. 'It's a ridiculous accusation, Sam.'

'That's what I thought at first. But now I've heard about this history between Olivia and Burrows, I think I'm going to have to look into it.'

5

'What the f—'

Olivia and Rocky stood open-mouthed, staring at their latest restoration project, the Old Foundry, which was built into the side of the steep street that ran up through Penbartha village. They had spent more than eighteen months working with its owners Emily and Silas Hogan, transforming the dirty, neglected and decaying old foundry into a handsome residence with amazing eco credentials, without compromising its history in any way.

Olivia's mood had been cheered by an early run on what was a perfect, crisp autumnal day. When she'd first opened the bedroom shutters that morning, dawn's pinky fingers were streaking across a clear sky, a sprinkling of frost glittered on the Coach House roof and the shrubs in the garden sparkled with intricate spider webs. She'd be lying if she claimed not to be at all bothered by Rafe's bizarre behaviour at Tresillian, and then Sam's tenuous link between their fractious relationship and the damage done to the cars at the Ship. But Jago had reassured her that Sam was overreacting, for some reason, and she knew perfectly well she wasn't involved. And so she and the dogs had set off on the path that hugged the creek, admiring the sea as it sparkled in the distance and breathing in the delicious scent of seaweed mixed with all the leaf litter that carpeted the footpaths and the remnants of woodsmoke from last night's fires. By the time they turned away from the coast and looped back inland towards the village, the strengthening sun, fresh air and hard physical effort the coastal path required had put her in a much more optimistic frame of mind.

Until, that was, she ran down the hill in the village, pausing briefly to admire the glowing beauty of the restored granite walls of the Old Foundry and the newly installed and recently painted sage green sash windows. This is what I love about my job, she reminded herself, suppressing a spurt of resentment towards Rafe Burrows and all his underhand ways: working with like-minded people who wanted to breathe new life into old buildings rather than demolish them and replace them with some modern monstrosity.

It was only when she noticed a trail of white paint snaking down the cobbled parking area to the side of the building and across the road, that she drew to a complete stop, turned to look at the side of the old building and gasped. The large new green double doors set within a granite arch and topped with a stained-glass fanlight were sprawled with huge painted letters, shouting 'ONLY HOMES FOR LOCALS. GET OUT NOW!'

* * *

'The bastards have thrown the rest of the paint pot down the side walls as well.' Rocky was still spluttering and swearing as hopped from foot to foot, angrier than Olivia had ever seen him. He had arrived at the Old Foundry within minutes of her anguished phone call, having already been on his way to start the new week.

'We're supposed to be doing the snagging list this week and the final handover.' He leant back inside his pick-up to usher the dogs in and collect a spare fleece. He handed it to Olivia, who pulled it on gratefully, inhaling the comforting smell of sawdust. The wind coming off the creek had turned cold, and she was starting to shiver.

'How long do you reckon it will set us back?' A familiar feeling of frustration and concern started to uncoil in her stomach. They were due to move full time to a listed building orangery project in a fortnight, and Rocky had requested a rare week's holiday to spend time with Kitten. Suddenly, all their carefully timed plans were falling apart. It was a regular occurrence in their line of work, but Olivia found it stressful and disheartening. She hated letting clients down. Not only were Emily and Silas going to be upset, but they had promised the Woodbridges that their project, which they had been running alongside the Old Foundry for the last few months, would be finished by Christmas. Everything was ready for the final construction of the orangery; all the pieces lovingly created by Rocky and his craftsmen were waiting in the main workshop to be erected on site. Planning and listed building consents had been obtained, the groundworks, plumbing and electricity all in place. Any delay to the start of it was going to put the Woodbridges' extended family celebration in jeopardy. More stress.

'Let's go inside and see if the damage is confined to the external doors and walls.' Rocky pulled the keys out of his pocket. 'I'd like to be able to assess it properly before I speak to Silas and Emily. Silas says he doesn't know how much longer they'll cope living in the caravan.'

'Too late.' Olivia nodded towards a red van that pulled up in a squeal of brakes. 'The Penbartha jungle drums have been jumping.'

They stood side by side as both doors of the van were thrown open and two dishevelled figures appeared. One was in tears, the other silent.

'Who would do a thing like this?' Emily sobbed. 'It's horrible to think that someone hates us so much they would do this.'

'I'm sure they don't—' Olivia began, but Emily was in full flow. 'It's not like we've just swanned in and forced locals out of the place. We've been living in a caravan all this time because we didn't want to rent a house that could have been taken by a local family.'

'We know that, and I'm sure—'

'And we've been working our fingers to the bone building up the flower farm. We've had one baby while living in the caravan, and I really, really wanted to be in the house before this one arrives.' Her voice rose into a crescendo of sobs, and tears ran down her face as she cradled her pregnant belly.

Silas rubbed his wife's back, his own pale face full of concern, but he stayed quiet. Olivia admired his self-control. Presumably, being a hedge fund manager in London, working long hours and dealing with high-risk investment portfolios on behalf of demanding, wealthy clients had equipped him a with a calm constitution, as well as a very healthy bank balance.

'Look, Em, let's just see how bad the damage is before we jump to the worst case scenario.' His voice was low and tender as he pulled out his mobile and took a few quick snaps of the graffiti. 'We might even laugh about it one day.'

He really was the nicest man, Olivia decided. Probably far too nice for his previous career. Perhaps, when this project was completed, she and Jago could get to know them better.

'With a bit of luck, the paint damage is confined to the outside.' Olivia tuned back into Rocky's reassuring tone and forced a smile onto her face. They had to take control here and comfort their clients. It was their job to provide solutions, at all times.

Rocky opened the doors carefully and breathed a sigh of relief. The original furnace area was a large, high space with huge wooden and iron roof trusses that gave it an almost cathedral-like quality. The soot-ingrained granite walls had all been dry-ice blasted, then carefully polished to a warm, silvery glow and as usual, Olivia couldn't resist running her fingers over the warm stones and thinking about the men who had built the foundry and all those who had lived and worked there over the years. Then, the large windows would have been blackened by dust and grime. Now, natural light flooded though the same space that was to be used by Emily to prepare her orders, hold her flower workshops and provide a small showroom. Olivia looked up at the perfectly polished beams and powder-coated roof trusses and turned to Emily and Silas with a smile.

'Everything looks good in here. There's no way they got inside and none of the paint has seeped through.'

'But what about the graffiti on the doors and stone work outside?' Emily insisted. 'How will you get that off without damaging the paint and the doors and the walls?'

'We'll sort it,' Rocky assured her. 'The dry-ice blasting machine will get rid of it all without damaging either the paint or the wood, I promise.'

'That machine has been a godsend.' Olivia winced inside at the thought of how much it had cost. 'It works on almost everything and it's chemical free. What's not to love?'

'I'll get onto it myself, right away,' Rocky confirmed. 'It shouldn't set us back more than a day.'

Olivia intercepted the look between Silas and Emily and her heart went out to them. 'Would you like a quick, unofficial tour before we get on with our day? There's not much left to do now. And the lads finished tiling the rest of this floor, so your cold room is good to go, as well as the kitchenette and cloakroom.'

Emily's face lit up, but then frowned. 'Oh no, Olivia. You're still in your running gear. Is that how you discovered it? I bet you haven't even had breakfast yet.'

Olivia waved her words away with a smile. 'Another half an hour won't make any difference, but any longer than that and the dogs might start eating Rocky's upholstery.'

'Let's get going then.' Silas rubbed his hands together, a smile hovering on his face. 'It looks like I might be able to carry you over the threshold without giving myself a hernia, after all!'

Forty minutes later, Olivia and Rocky waved the happy couple off and then stood leaning against the bonnet of the pick-up.

'They really have been the dream clients, haven't they? Rocky commented. 'I don't really understand how city types like him make their money, but he always seems happy to spend it. I don't think he's ever once asked us for the cheapest option.'

'I've come to the conclusion that most wealthy people remain that way because they like to hold on to their money, rather than spend it,' Olivia suggested with feeling, thinking of all the clients she had worked with. She would never understand human nature.

'Well, Silas isn't like that. He's been on a mission to restore and preserve this place and hasn't compromised once on anything. They've picked the best quality of everything.'

'Because they know it will highlight the original material and show the building off at its best. I can't wait to see it when they've done all the soft furnishings and everything else they've talked about. It's going to be really stunning.' Olivia chewed on a fingernail. 'I just hope they think it's all worth it and that the locals don't hate them.' She waved at the graffiti. 'It's not exactly welcoming, is it?'

Rocky shook his head. 'I reckon it must be kids. No adult would do anything like this.'

'Not even the First Homes Only group?'

'Who the hell are they? Bloody cowards, that's what they are. And stupid with it. This is the Hogans' only home, unless you count their caravan.'

'I don't like the idea that people are actively targeting innocent victims.'

'What about the real second-homers?'

'There aren't that many in Penbartha, are there?' Olivia suddenly realised that she didn't really know the numbers involved.

'Not compared with other villages, perhaps, but there are a few. And more in the last few years since house prices have gone up and locals can't afford them, but Londoners can.'

'Rafe Burrows has never asked me to work on a house here.' She thought for a moment. 'Perhaps Penbartha doesn't have the housing stock that appeals to second-homers?'

Rocky sent her a sidelong glance. 'Well, your lane certainly does. Being on the creek and having fantastic views makes it the place to live. And it's extra special as there are so few houses up your end of it.'

A sudden howl from the backseat of Rocky's pick-up reminded Olivia that her dogs needed feeding.

'You get off and let me get on with removing that graffiti.' Rocky opened the door and released her two hungry dogs who had enjoyed a nice nap after their run and now wanted their breakfast. He dropped a kiss on her cheek. 'Come back when you're ready and we'll see if it's come off cleanly.'

Olivia frowned at him. 'So you're not as confident as you made out to the Hogans?'

Rocky grinned, his teeth white against his swarthy skin and mop of black, curly hair. The twinkle in his eye made him look even more like a pirate than usual. 'What do you reckon?'

Olivia was still smiling as she walked along the lane to Tresillian. She loved working with Rocky and adored her job. Most of the time. The tide was on its way out, and she could hear the distinctive 'peeping' sound of an oystercatcher, one of her favourite sea birds who spent the winter on the creekside, using their long, carrot-like bills to prise open the cockles, mussels and other shellfish they found along the shore line. They had been Mollie's favourite too and she would tell stories of how oystercatchers mated for life and could live for over twenty years, returning to the same breeding and nesting sites year after year, and how their young stayed with them for much longer than most wading birds. Mollie had claimed she could recognise individual oystercatchers that came to the creek. To Olivia's inexperienced eye they all looked alike with their striking black-and-white plumage, reddish-pink legs and long bright orange-red bills, but Mollie always insisted that they had different plumage patterns, beak shapes and behaviours.

Olivia still didn't really know if Mollie had been teasing her all those years ago, but just the thought of her godmother made her smile grow, until her mind automatically wandered to her current troubles and she suddenly ached for the wisdom of her godparents. What would the peace-making couple have made of all this growing rumbling discord between the villagers and second-homers?

Olivia was still contemplating their different answers as she rounded the last bend of the lane before the final approach to Tresillian. For the second time in as many hours, she came to an abrupt halt, her heart once again in her mouth.

There, standing proudly at the slightly overgrown entrance to Gillan Cottage's drive was a very large bright blue and green Prestige Coastal Properties board reading 'For Sale'.

6

News always travelled fast, if not entirely accurately, in Penbartha and was adapted, exaggerated or plain misrepresented, depending on the person responsible for imparting it. The graffiti on the Old Foundry was now yesterday's news as far as the gaggle of village matriarchs clustered round the main counter at the Old Bakehouse were concerned. They had turned their full attention to the For Sale board outside Gillan Cottage.

Kitten sat quietly in her own deliciously yeasty cocoon, at one of the two American-style diner booths Willow and Fraser had installed to enable the elders of the village, who couldn't make it as far as the Waiting Rooms, to rest while they shopped and gossiped. The irony that she was now using one for that very reason while she waited for her GP appointment wasn't lost on her. She tried to make herself invisible, which was easier said than done with her vintage, often loud, clothes and clashing jewellery, but today she had pulled her pink-tipped hair into a simple ponytail and wore one of Rocky's cleaner fleeces over her least-ripped jeans and kept her bright pink Docs under the table. For the first time ever, she was glad that her good friend Willow, the co-owner of the bakery, was still on maternity leave. Her eagle eyes would have immediately noticed something was up. Luckily, these particular matriarchs did not share her compassion and were too busy gossiping to worry about her or anyone else.

'Who's Prestige Coastal Properties when they're at home? Never heard of 'em.'

'Well.' One of the matriarchs was clearly delighted to share her knowledge. 'Caroline Pellow was on it straight away and googled it.' She paused, presumably for dramatic effect. 'Apparently it's that Rafe Burrows chap – calls himself a "buying agent". They're the ones who make money from charging folks from upcountry through the nose for finding their second homes. Now that market's dried up, it looks like he's setting up a regular estate agency so he can make money out of selling them as well, God help us.'

'Why do you think he'd do that, Doreen?'

'Perhaps his buying agency business is grinding to a halt the way things have slowed right down after the boom of the last few years. House prices are falling and people probably don't need buying agents to act on their behalf anymore.'

'How did Caroline react to that discovery?' A louder voice spoke up, and Kitten risked peering over the top of her menu. It didn't look like anyone was prepared to answer that question out loud, but from the heavy silence that fell, they were all pretty sure what Caroline's reaction would have been.

Kitten couldn't put names to any of the faces at the counter. Not many of this group ever made it out to the station site. They didn't like change. In any form. At least now she knew which one Doreen was.

'There's a website, but no properties are actually listed on it yet. Just some tantalising comments about "exclusive properties coming soon". Price on application. And we all know what that means,'

There was a collective murmur of consent, but someone still felt the need to explain. 'If you have to ask, you can't afford it.'

'Thank you, Heather. What I want to know is why Gillan Cottage has gone up for sale now? It must be at least two years since Peggy Swift died, and their son's been coming back on and off ever since.'

'But there's been no sign of him for a few months now. Perhaps he's gone back to Canada for good.'

'Perhaps it's the death duties. He might have to sell the house to pay them.'

'Doreen, it's been called Inheritance Tax for the last forty years and HMRC makes you pay it within six months of the person's death. That will have been sorted out ages ago, and I don't think Rex and Peggy will have left him short of a bob or two. Do you?'

Doreen's face was a picture. She obviously didn't like being outsmarted. 'Unlikely. What I don't understand is why he's instructed Prestige Coastal Properties or whatever they're called, to sell the place, rather than Lanner's like everyone else round here does. At least Jack's local and about as honest as estate agents can get. Although that's not saying much.'

The conversation quickly devolved into a fiery discussion about how much they distrusted most estate agents and the atrocities they had committed against various friends, neighbours and relatives. Kitten found it hard to keep up. The list of grievances seemed endless, including exaggerating the value of properties, fabricating offers, playing down defects to make a sale and being generally dishonest, pushy and deceitful. And according to Doreen, estate agents were regularly rated the most untrustworthy people in the UK, alongside politicians and journalists. 'They're all clueless, tactless and scruple-less,' was her final declaration.

'You're right. But I'm going straight to the horse's mouth and ask Olivia,' Heather stated.

'Since when has Olivia been the horse's mouth?' Doreen sounded put out. 'Just because she lives next door to Gillan?'

'Ah,' said the other woman. 'But Olivia knows all the right people. At the council, in the planning department, all sorts of places. If anyone knows what's going on, Olivia will. Or at least she can find out. And she's good at solving mysteries.'

A sudden slice of cold pain trickled down the right side of Kitten's face, distracting her from eavesdropping. Her heart began to race. *Oh my God, what's happening to me now?* She forced herself to take some deep, calming breaths – a technique she'd learned from an app she'd downloaded to help cope with the mixture of pain, fear and panic that seemed to be permanently threatening to engulf her these days.

Please, no. Is this how I'm going to feel for the rest of my life? What the hell is the matter with me?

'Excuse me, but can I sit here?' Kitten heard a gentle voice – definitely not one of the village matriarchs – and looked up. Through her tears and painful eye, she could just make out a heavily pregnant figure, hovering by her side.

'Of course.' Kitten finished her tea and bent down to pick up her bag. *Big mistake.* Her brain did a somersault inside her skull and she gasped at the sickening sensation.

'Are you okay?' The same kind voice sounded concerned, and a soft hand caught hold of hers. 'Can I get you some water?'

Kitten sat for a moment, unwilling to move her head and set the room moving again. By the time she'd taken a few deep breaths and dared to open her eyes, a glass of water had appeared on the table in front of her. Sitting opposite was a vaguely familiar young woman with fair hair tied back in a long plait, the palest blue eyes she had ever seen and a look of deep concern on her pretty face.

'It's Kitten, isn't it?' she asked quietly. 'I'm Emily. Emily Hogan. From the Old Foundry?'

Kitten's head hurt as she put the words in order and made sense of them. Then she nodded and scrabbled in her bag for painkillers.

'Give me a moment.' She swallowed them with a sip of water, vaguely aware of Emily pouring herself a cup of tea from the pot she'd carried across and then just sitting peacefully, like a protector, blocking Kitten from the view of other customers.

Once Kitten's head had stopped spinning, she attempted a smile. 'Thanks.'

'No worries. How are you feeling now?'

'A bit better, I think.' From the look on Emily's face, Kitten could tell she didn't believe her, but let it go.

'I can't believe we haven't met properly before, but I'm always at the farm, working, or looking after my son, Darragh. And on the few occasions I've made it to the Waiting Rooms, you haven't been there. But Rocky mentions you occasionally, and I've always wanted to meet you.'

Kitten managed a weak smile, pretty sure that Rocky wouldn't have said much about her at all. He was a very private person and much better than she and Olivia were at keeping defined boundaries between his personal and business life. 'Sorry. I'm not feeling too good today. Probably gone down with a bit of a bug, so don't get too close.'

Even Emily's laugh was gentle. 'Don't worry about me. Living in a caravan for nearly two years and working on the farm has given me an iron constitution. Silas says I'm indestructible. I also think that teaching in schools for five years and then working in a freezing cold florist shop and on a street flower stall has supercharged my immune system.'

Kitten warmed to her practical nature instantly. 'I was sorry to hear about the graffiti.'

Emily shrugged. 'I'm ashamed to say I rather overreacted. Silas tells everyone I was wailing like a banshee. But Rocky's cleaned it all off with his amazing dry-ice blasting machine and now you'd never know anything happened.'

'That's good, but please don't ever think everyone in Penbartha feels that way about you and Silas moving into the Old Foundry.' Kitten suddenly felt it was important for the other woman to know that.

'I don't.' Emily smiled. 'Most people have only shown us kindness and support. Caroline Pellow has made her feelings very clear, but we have the formidable Auntie Margaret as our secret weapon. And even Caroline's no match for her!'

Kitten's brain hurt. 'Sorry. Auntie Margaret?'

'Margaret Chynoweth. Ex-postmistress of Penbartha.'

'Ah, I see.' Kitten knew Mrs Chynoweth well. First as the best friend of Olivia's late godmother, Mollie, and secondly as one of the biggest supporters of the various social groups that were held at the Waiting Rooms and Goods Shed, especially those to do with sewing, knitting or crafting. She was a formidable but kind and well-respected woman.

'Her daughter Tressa, who runs the post office now, is Silas's godmother.' Emily explained the connection. 'Tressa and my mother-in-law met at university and Silas remembers the Old Foundry from when he holidayed here as a child. He always had a pipedream about owning it and when we chose this area to look at buying some land for the flower farm, he couldn't believe it was still empty and abandoned.' A huge smile broke out on her face. 'And the rest, as they say, is history.'

Kitten's mind was still trying to decode the various levels of relationship involved in Emily's explanation. They were typical of Penbartha, where everyone seemed to be connected by blood or marriage, divorce or friendship, but the effort was too much and she gave up and asked a simpler question.

'So you moved here to be closer to them?'

'Not at first. We were living in London, but looking for land in Cornwall because the climate here suits flower farming and Tressa told us about a farmer who wanted to sell a few acres near the village. And then Silas saw the Old Foundry and that was that.'

'I presume you weren't flower farming in London?' Kitten was surprised that concentrating on what Emily was saying was helping to distract her, temporarily, from her pain.

'Er, no.' Emily gave another laugh. 'It's a long story...'

'I'm not in a rush.' She didn't tell her that she was recovering after her half-mile walk from the Waiting Rooms. It was a distance she'd always just skipped along without noticing. Now it left her exhausted and in pain.

'Don't worry, I'll give you the shortened version. Basically I taught in a primary school in inner London for five years.' A shadow crossed her face. 'I loved it at first, but after five years of excessive workloads, behaviour plummeting and watching my colleagues leave, I'd had enough. I was already doing floristry courses in the school holidays, so once I was good enough, I left teaching and got a job in a florist's shop.'

'So, did you always want to be a florist?' Kitten leant forward, wanting to know more.

'I always knew I wanted to do something creative, but didn't think it would pay the rent in London.' She brightened. 'I've always gone about things in a roundabout way and managed to get there in the end. I moved to a cheaper house share and learnt to be more frugal, and I managed, just about.'

'It's still a big leap from working in a florist shop to having your own flower farm though.'

'The problem was, as soon as I was working in the shop full time, I became acutely aware of how damaging the floristry industry can be to the environment.' Emily's eyes flashed. 'Did you know that 90 per cent of the UK's flowers are imported from as far away as Kenya and South America? So not only is their carbon footprint huge, they're full of pesticides and chemicals and grown using exploited labour. And there's all the plastic involved as well. It just didn't sit right with me.'

As Emily went into detail about the environmental, ethical

and social implications of buying cut flowers, Kitten's shame that she knew so little about the global flower trade grew. Having said that, flowers had never really played a big part in her life. Rocky was more likely to buy her a fresh Cornish pasty or a pint at the Ship than treat her to a bunch of roses. Now she was glad he did. It was one less thing to worry about. *Why was everything so complicated?*

'So then I had to think of a way round that problem.' Emily was in full flow, and Kitten recognised the fervour of a fellow environmentalist. *Was she that passionate still? Or had all these new, weird sensations she was feeling diminished her dedication to her causes?*

'And I began sourcing sustainably grown, often organic, flowers from farms in England to sell on my stall. Obviously, they're more expensive, so I had to be careful that I chose a pitch where customers had more cash to spend, but that worked out.'

Kitten's head was starting to ache again, but she wanted to get to the end of the story as quickly as possible. She looked at her watch.

'So how have you ended up here?'

Emily cheeks reddened. 'Sorry, Silas always says I ramble when I'm on my bandwagon. Basically, I sold him a bunch of flowers from my stall for his PA's birthday and then for a friend's wife, and eventually he was buying flowers from me several times a week. We got chatting, went for a drink and one thing led to another, you know?'

Kitten nodded, carefully, putting her hand to her right eye and feeling the pressure ease slightly.

'He had a really good job, as a hedge fund manager in the City, but please don't ask me to explain what that is. He worked ridiculously long hours, and he was burning out. We used to fantasise about moving away from London and setting up our own flower farm.' Emily's eyes began to shine. 'And then, after a particularly generous bonus, he proposed to me – not only marriage, but the prospect of selling up in London and following our dream.'

Kitten smiled, suddenly more excited than she'd felt about anything for a long time. 'Can I come and see the farm some time? It sounds wonderful.'

'Of course you can! I'd be delighted to show you round. Come any time. I'm usually there, but I'm having a bit of me-time this morning, and Darragh is with Auntie Margaret and Tressa, which is why I decided to treat myself to a cuppa here on my way back to the farm.' She looked at her watch and gasped. 'Heavens! I must go.' She fumbled in her pocket and pulled out a beautifully hand-drawn business card. 'My number's on there, if you want to call first, but please do come. I've heard so much about the things you do for the environment and it's been great to meet a kindred spirit this morning. I'd love to keep in touch. And I do hope you feel better soon.'

* * *

'Thanks for getting me in today, doctor.' Kitten practically dragged her right leg across the floor behind her and collapsed into a chair.

'That's what I'm here for, Kitten.' Dr Kitson waved away her apologies, but the look of concern on his normally amiable face made her heart race. 'You're hardly a frequent visitor. How are you?'

Kitten froze. *Where did she start? There wasn't an inch of her body that didn't frighten her at the moment.*

She decided to stick to the highlights and opened her good eye.

'Dreadful! My right eye feels like it's going to burst out of my head, my right leg has decided it doesn't want to be part of my body anymore, I'm so dizzy most of the time I feel sick and I have absolutely no energy. I feel like I'm going mad. And now I have this horrible, prickling pain all down the side of my face.' Her voice rose to a wail and then she burst into noisy tears. 'The locum just dismissed everything!'

Dr Kitson passed her a box of tissues and waited for the tears to stop. Kitten blew her nose noisily and eventually met his kind gaze.

'Not so good then, eh?' Another sympathetic smile. 'Do you think you can get up on the bed so I can run a few tests?'

She shredded the soggy tissues between her fingers and gave a slight nod.

The GP helped her onto the examination couch where she sat on the edge. He made her do all sorts of weird and painful movements with her hands and arms, pushing and pulling against his hands, and then closed her eyes while he pricked her arms from fingers to elbow with a very blunt needle on her right arm and then a not-so-blunt one on the left one. She closed her eyes and answered his questions quietly, utterly convinced that she would be told off for burning the candle at both ends and sent on her way. Then he did the same to her legs with the weird needles, and then tapped her knees, ankles and feet with a patella hammer, sending them shooting out in all directions. He finished up by running the handle of the patella hammer along the soles of both feet. Kitten, usually the most ticklish person she knew, didn't react at all. *I really am wasting his time,* she thought guiltily.

Just as she thought he had finished, he asked her to follow his finger, with just her eyes, as he moved it from side to side, in increasingly wide circles. The stabbing pains in her eyes were excruciating, the room spun and her stomach lurched. She swallowed hard, several times, trying to quell the nausea. But it was too late. She threw up on the bed. Then burst into tears.

Waving her apologies aside, Dr Kitson helped her back to her chair, then bundled the vomit-soiled paper sheet up and dropped it in the bin. He sat down at his desk, tapped a few keys on his computer and then turned to look at her.

'I'm going to call the hospital and request an urgent MRI. You're too young to be experiencing all these symptoms without me getting them checked out. What are you, 26 now?'

Hot panic surged through her at the mention of hospitals and scans. 'Twenty-seven. What's the matter with me?'

'Hopefully, nothing. I just want to be extra careful and rule a few things out. Try to stay positive.'

Positive? Positive? It was taking every last ounce of her self-control to stay calm and not dissolve into hysterics.

Another roll of bile was threatening to overwhelm her but she swallowed hard. 'I thought the waiting list for MRI scans was huge. I'll probably feel heaps better by the time the appointment comes through. There are loads of weird viruses about at the moment aren't there? Could it be one of those?' She looked at his face hopefully.

'Let's see, shall we?' His face became sterner. 'Promise me you'll go to the appointment, Kitten. It's important.'

She swallowed some more bile and took some more deep breaths to delay the panic that was threatening to overwhelm her. 'As long as you promise not to breathe a word to my mum, or Olivia. Or Rocky. Or anyone, basically.'

He sighed. 'Well, I am bound by a code of patient confidentiality, but I do recommend that you tell at least one person. You might want someone to go to the hospital with you for support.'

Kitten tried to nod, but the movement caused another wave of dizziness and she clutched the chair for support. 'I'll think about it.'

The rushing in her ears was growing louder and louder and

her chest felt like it was going to explode. She forced herself up from the chair and staggered towards the door, panic engulfing her. *I need to get out NOW!*

7

'I think we should pop in on Kitten on our way to the Goods Shed and see if she's shaken off that bug yet. I'm a bit worried about her, and she's being very elusive.' Olivia handed her cereal bowl and mug to Jago with a smile, for him to load the dishwasher. She'd learnt early on in their relationship that he didn't rate her abilities in that department, and she'd cheerfully relinquished the job to him.

'Good idea. She really wasn't herself on Sunday, and I haven't seen her in the Waiting Rooms for the last couple of days.' He frowned as he slotted the dishes into their perfect homes. 'I just hope this trustees meeting doesn't go on for too long. I've got a telephone call booked in with my senior clerk at 12.'

Olivia's heart sank. It was rarely good news when his senior clerk, Tony, scheduled a call. 'He hasn't booked you in for a trial, has he? You've only just got back.'

Jago pressed the dishwasher button and closed its door, before pulling her to him and kissing the tip of her still slightly pink nose. 'I'm pretty sure he won't. Don't worry.'

'Good, because I need you here. God knows what's going on in Penbartha at the moment.'

Jago whistled to the dogs and picked up his briefcase. 'Nothing's going on,' he said firmly. 'People are just conflating a few isolated incidents and turning them into something they're not. This is Penbartha, remember. Not the wild west.'

Olivia hefted her own work bag onto her shoulder and followed him to the back door. 'And how many times have we said that?'

* * *

The lane was quiet apart from the rustling of fallen leaves underfoot as they walked along, the dogs rushing ahead and checking out any new smells and messages that had been left overnight. She'd deliberately run the opposite way that morning, not wanting to even look at the For Sale board outside Gillan Cottage. She'd left several messages for Jasper Swift, asking him to call her back, but as he hadn't, she was fearing the worst. While she didn't blame him for one moment for wanting to sell the house, like Cassie had said on Sunday, she felt disappointed that he hadn't told her himself. She'd known him all her life, but thought they'd become friends in their own right over the last eighteen months or so that she'd been living full time at Tresillian and he'd been popping to and from Canada to check on Gillan. Then again, people did strange things when it came to buying and selling houses, as she knew only too well.

They were still both deep in their own thoughts as they turned into the Waiting Rooms car park and made their way over to the café, which despite the relatively early hour, was already filling up.

Jasmine greeted them warmly. 'Hey! Can I get you a coffee or anything?'

Olivia looked around with her usual sense of pride; she and Rocky had restored the old and beautiful station building to its former external glory in line with George's vision. Inside was even better. Sunlight poured in from the eight arched windows on either side of the open room which had been transformed from six wood-panelled rooms including the booking hall, ticket office and stationmaster's office. It was now a streamlined, modern café with a vintage twist, and the whole building was retrofitted to the highest energy efficiency levels. Its success had exceeded all their expectations.

She tuned back to Jasmine's question with a smile.

'Not now, thanks. We were just wondering if Kitten was working today?'

'I think she may be in later, but I've told her to take it easy,' Jasmine admitted. 'She's still not feeling very well, so I said I'd cover her shifts as I'm off school this week and next.' She suddenly looked awkward. 'I hope that's okay?'

'Of course it is,' Olivia rushed to reassure her. Although most members and employees of the various elements of the Penbartha station site saw her in overall control, she trusted the people she had chosen to work for her and was always delighted when they took the initiative. 'You've done exactly the right thing. Are you managing on your own?'

'Harry's in the kitchen, and Alfie's due in any minute.' Jasmine looked at her watch and frowned. 'Actually he's late, which isn't like him.' An agitated expression crossed her face. 'I hope he hasn't gone down with Kitten's bug. We're expecting things to really pick up at the weekend. Treave's already finished, but the state schools are on half-term break next week—'

'Sorry I'm late, Jas!' The back door to the café flew open and Alfie rushed in, tying an apron around his waist, his hair standing in tufts. He took one look at Olivia and Jago and his face reddened to match his hair. 'I overslept, sorry. Hi Olivia, Jago.'

'These things happen.' Jago nodded to the teenager, then nudged Olivia. 'Come on, we've a meeting to get to, and Alice won't be happy if we're late.'

'I'm really sorry, Jasmine,' Alfie repeated. 'I had a bad night. It won't happen again.' A sudden gust of wind and a scattering of leaves blew through the building as a group of walkers came though the platform doors and headed over to the settees around low tables at the far end. Alfie pulled his order pad from the front pocket of his apron. 'I'll see to these.'

'At least Kitten's being sensible with this bug. Let's hope she shakes it off,' Olivia commented as they walked across to the Goods Shed; it was the heart and soul of the whole station site and where George's vision for a coworking enterprise had started. It combined his ambition to restore the disused station site he had bought from British Rail for a ridiculously low price following a major series of route closures and cuts made as part of the restructuring of the railway system in the 1960s, with his commitment to sustainability and the environment. He'd discovered the concept of coworking on his many visits to Olivia in New York, and decided to use the station site to help local creative and eco-conscious people to break from traditional ways of working, giving them more freedom by providing them with an affordable shared workplace. They'd renovated the other site buildings, including the Signal Box, Weighbridge Hut and Engine Shed, one by one, and their success equalled that of the Waiting Rooms.

'She must be really feeling bad to take time off. I can't remember her ever calling in sick before.' Olivia paused at the double glass doors that now gave the Goods Shed the grand entrance it deserved.

'Perhaps she needs some over the counter modern medicine,' Jago observed drily. 'It seems to have done the trick with you.'

'Sshh! Don't say that. It might get back to Cassie and I'll never hear the end of it.'

'Oh no! You've already heard?' Alice, the Goods Shed manager, pounced on the last words of Olivia's sentence before they'd even reached the reception area. She stood at the door to her office, hopping from foot to foot, her face pink with worry.

Olivia's heart sank. She knew that look well. She glanced at Jago and he nodded.

'I'm not sure we know what you're talking about, Alice, but why don't we come in and you can tell us all about it over a cup of tea.'

That did the trick. Jago was an expert at dealing with Alice. As soon as she had something to occupy her hands she calmed down. She rushed off to make the tea and Jago and Olivia sat in silence, wondering what the hell had got Alice so worked up, but knowing from experience it was always better not to speculate.

Alice had barely sat down to stir the tea in the pot when she started. 'I'm sure it will be all over Penbartha by now, but Dave the postie just popped by to show me this.'

Good old Dave, thought Olivia. Dave the postie was one of the most prolific and reliable sources of news in all the local area.

'C'mon, Alice,' Jago teased her gently. 'Put us out of our misery.'

Alice lifted the leather blotter pad that protected her desk and whipped out a plastic pocket file like she was presenting an evidence bag in court. 'Just look at this! He peeled it off a gate post.'

Olivia and Jago both stared at the object within it, stuck to a used A4 envelope. It was a sticker the size of a dinner plate that looked just like an Historic England blue plaque, complete with a white rim, declaring in large white capital letters: 'A LOCAL FAMILY ONCE LIVED HERE'.

Jago let out a low whistle. 'Wow – that's quite hard hitting.' Olivia took the bag from her and turned it round in her hands, peered at its contents.

'It's very professionally done. They've got the font and the colour exactly right,' she observed, admiration mingling with concern. 'Where've they been put?'

Alice's face grew pinker. 'Some on windows, some on front doors, some on gate posts if there's a drive.'

'How many has Dave seen on his rounds?'

'About twenty so far.'

More than they would have ever guessed. Jago and Olivia exchanged a look. 'Someone has obviously done their homework. If they're accurate,' Jago commented.

'I'd be surprised if it's that many,' Olivia added.

'I don't think it is accurate, actually,' Alice declared. 'I've already had a few of the members come in to say their houses have been targeted, even though they live in the village permanently and don't have a home anywhere else.'

'George used to say that the locals don't trust anyone who crosses the Tamar to live here for at least the first fifteen years,' Olivia commented. 'I always thought he was joking, but this suggests there are still people who think like that.' She pointed at the offending sticker. 'It's not very friendly, is it?'

'No, and unfortunately, a few members are now saying they don't feel welcome anymore.' She turned an anxious face to Olivia. 'We need to manage this situation, before it gets out of hand and we start losing members. We've worked so hard to build a solid community here and include people from all sorts of places. It would be awful if this makes anyone feel so unwanted that they leave. It reminds me of last time this happened, and I don't want to go through it again.'

Olivia felt her stomach lurch as memories of all the problems that had beset the Goods Shed when she'd first arrived from New York flooded her mind. It had been a horrible time, and not one she wanted to repeat.

'Let's not jump to worst case scenarios, Alice. I'm sure it won't come to that.' Jago covered Olivia's hand with his and nodded towards the teapot. Alice took the hint, pouring them each a mug of strong Cornish tea and adding milk. They sat in silence for a few moments, sipping their tea. Olivia's mind raced.

'So, have the majority of the stickers been put on houses that are known to be second homes?' Jago, being the lawyer he was, sought clarification of the facts.

Alice nodded. 'Yes, from what I've heard. It seems that only a few incomers were targeted, so I wonder if they just had a few stickers left over and weren't bothered who they upset.'

'But they still managed to locate the houses of recent incomers?'

A sudden thought struck Olivia. 'What about the Old Foundry?'

Alice stirred her tea vigorously. 'I haven't heard, but I hope not. I think the graffiti incident made some people's feelings quite clear about Silas and Emily, don't you?'

'Some people?' Olivia latched onto Alice's words. 'Like who?'

Her face reddened again, and she took a large mouthful of tea.

Nice try Alice, but you're not getting away with this one.

The older woman eventually capitulated under Olivia's intense stare.

'I don't want to gossip.'

Olivia bit back her reply. Alice could give Dave the postie a run for his money in the gossip stakes, but her loyalty to the Goods Shed and Olivia was unshakeable. She exchanged a look with Jago who nodded.

'Please?'

'Well, Caroline Pellow's really got it in for Emily and Silas, as you know. She's getting more and more extreme in her opposition to second-homers and just lumps them in with what she sees as "the enemy within".'

'But Emily and Silas have invested everything they've got in the Old Foundry and the flower farm. They're providing employment and contributing massively to the village. They're not our enemy.'

Alice looked away. 'Caroline's a very persuasive woman. Her family have lived in this village for generations. People listen to her.'

'It sounds like she's making unnecessary trouble,' Jago observed.

'Do you think we should have a word with her?' Olivia couldn't believe she was actually saying the words that were coming out of her mouth.

Neither could Jago, judging by the surprised look on his face.

'Why don't we see if we have time to include a brief mention of recent events in AOB, at the end of the meeting?' he suggested. 'And take it from there?'

* * *

'Now we come to Any Other Business.' Pippa Roscoe had settled well into her new role as Chair of Trustees and she ran the meetings with a calm and efficient demeanour. She tucked her sleek bobbed hair behind one ear and looked round the table, a worried expression on her usually smiling face. 'Alice has brought something to my attention which might be upsetting some of our members.'

Olivia perched on the edge of her seat as the offending sticker in its wallet was carefully passed round the table to a varied reception of gasps, snorts and suppressed laughs.

'I think this anti-second home business is getting out of hand,' Callum, the Goods Shed treasurer, declared crossly. 'Especially if these idiots can't differentiate between genuine incomers who've moved to Penbartha or nearby permanently, and those who own a holiday home here and only visit for a few weeks a year.'

'Even if those who move here are outbidding locals for local homes?' Pippa asked.

'It's a free market! You can't legislate against people moving between areas,' Callum retorted, ever the accountant.

'No, but you have to admit that people buying second homes at inflated prices has caused significant problems for locals who can't possibly afford them on the wages that are paid here.' Pippa stood her ground.

'I don't think anyone would argue with that, Pippa.' Jago spoke calmly.

'And they shouldn't. This whole second homes business is destroying communities and families!' Louisa Nankivell burst out.

Olivia turned to look at her closely. Louisa was a longstanding member of the Goods Shed who had recently gone into partnership with a couple Olivia knew who ran an ethical holiday lettings company and always acted with the utmost integrity. Short, round and usually jolly, Louisa reminded Olivia of the farmers' wives she'd read about in adventure books as a child. But today, her face had lost every last trace of its jolliness.

'Forgive me for playing devil's advocate here, Louisa, but how do you square criticising second-homers with the fact that you're letting out people's second homes and making money from them?'

An audible gasp rippled round the room and everyone turned to look at Tim Gray, the members' voted representative and green financial advisor, but the expression on his face and in his voice were ones of concern.

'You might not be aware of this, Tim, as you're fairly new here, but many of the properties in our portfolio were old, abandoned estate cottages and farm buildings that no locals at the time wanted to buy or do up. And now we always refuse to take any new cottages on that could sell at a price that would be affordable to locals.'

Louisa spoke calmly, but Olivia could tell she was upset at having to defend her business. 'Explain to Tim what else your company requires, Louisa, so he understands why we're happy to have you as tenant here.'

Louisa sent her a grateful look. 'We have very strict ethical guidelines; not least that we require every homeowner to reduce their rates in the quieter months to ensure occupancy and constant work for the housekeepers and regular business for shops in the community, and they all have to donate at least one week's rental in high season to a local charity that supports affordable housing for locals.' By the time she finished speaking, Louisa's face was scarlet and her eyes bright with unshed tears. 'Is that what you're thinking? That I'm a hypocrite?'

'Not at all!' Olivia rushed to calm her down. 'You employ locals, pay above the living wage, champion local businesses and charities and have created a really eco-conscious business model that you should be proud of. Like it or not, tourism is vital to our economy here, and you're being responsible and ethical by minimising the impact it has on our housing market and the planet.'

'Which is what we're all about here at the Goods Shed,' Pippa added, sending a stern look in Tim's direction. 'And we should be supporting each other, not falling out.'

There was a general murmuring of consent, but Louisa was keen to be heard.

'Second-homers have made things harder for locals in another way too. My mother moved here from Dorset ten years ago, because she wanted to be nearer to me and my family. And all was great for eight years, until she broke her hip. So Finn built an extension on our house and she moved in, so we turned her house into a holiday rental. Then she had a stroke last year and we just couldn't meet her needs, and she had to go into a care home.' Louisa started crying quietly and a silence fell round the table.

Somehow, she'd kept all this to herself and it was now bursting out. 'And do you have any idea how expensive care homes are these days? There's no way we can consistently clear enough money from renting out her house to cover the fees so we have no choice but to sell it to pay them.' She gulped. 'But we can't. Because of the changes in legislation – the increase in stamp duty, the doubling of council tax – that sector of the market is swamped with second homes that people don't want, or need, anymore. So folks from upcountry aren't interested at the moment, and they're still way too expensive for most locals. We've dropped the price to the bare minimum we need to cover her fees for the foreseeable future. But still nothing. And we're getting desperate!'

Alice magicked up a box of tissues from thin air and poured Louisa another glass of water.

'I'm so sorry, Louisa.' Olivia recovered herself first. 'I had no idea you were going through all this.'

'I'm sorry too. I hadn't looked at it from that point of view.' Tim pulled an awkward face. 'I have little sympathy for second-homers who can't sell up, but hadn't thought of the impact the new rules would have on locals trying to sell. It's a much more complicated issue than I realised.'

Louisa blew her nose. 'Yes. And we're caught between a rock and a hard place. And I can usually cope with it all, better than Finn does, anyway. But all this second homes talk gets me mad. Mum's house was her only home, and now we can't sell it to pay for the care she needs.'

'You're right, Louisa.' Jago's voice was calm and reassuring. 'I'm afraid to say that it looks like you're the victim of an unintended and unforeseen consequence here.'

'Well, we certainly didn't see it coming. Who knew that companies would want their staff to go back into the office? Even people who moved here permanently, thinking they would always be able to work remotely, are now having to sell up. The market's awash with houses that no one wants to buy.' She sniffed into her tissue again. 'Mum put loads of thought into buying her house here. She even employed a buying agent to make sure she was doing the right thing, and he persuaded to her put as much of her money into it as possible. He told her it was a solid investment and she would be able to sell it quickly and easily if she needed to.'

Familiar prickles of concern began marching up Olivia's spine. 'A buying agent?'

Louisa sniffed. 'Yes.'

Olivia and Jago exchanged a look. 'May I ask who you used?'

'Burrows Prime Property Search. And we had the personal service of the owner himself, Rafe Burrows. I just hope he keeps a low profile round here, because if Finn sets eyes on him, I don't think he'll be able to control himself.'

WHATSAPP GROUP #PenbarHomeGuard

@KernowCurrent: This is a special group right? By invite only.

@BanSecondHomes: Gr8 job last nite m8.Thnx. Good reaction in village

@VividInkVibes: I heard

@BanSecondHomes Need ur help again.

@VividInkVibes: Why

@BanSecondHomes: Needs to be on QT. Meet me at WRs at midnight. Masks on. We'll walk.

@KernowCurrent: Do we need help?

@VividInkVibes: Prob

@BanSecondHomes: What about homes4locals? Did a gd job with the stickers

@VividInkVibes: Deffo not. Too risky.

@BanSecondHomes: Ok. Know just the guys **@NoSecond, @ CoastalCrusader** Leave it with me

@VividInkVibes: 👍

8

'Why does that wretched man's name seem to crop up in every conversation we have these days?' Olivia sighed crossly as she sank onto the chesterfield sofa which took pride of place beneath the wall of windows in the Signal Box, the dogs at her feet. The Signal Box stood on the opposite side of what would have once been the railway line from Penbartha to Falmouth and Truro, with a clear view of the station building opposite and in each direction along what was now a well-used network of paths for walkers and cyclists. It had been the second building to be exquisitely renovated by Olivia and Rocky and home of the railway memorabilia business that Jago had run alongside George Stevenson before his death, when he took over. Jago was now in sole charge and loved his workplace.

Jago sat behind his oak stationmaster's desk, which was placed so it also had a view of the walkway, and thought carefully about what he was going to say. He usually looked forward to the hour they spent over a mug of tea, talking about their respective days before they left their work lives behind and walked home together. But today he knew that Olivia was not going to react well to what he had to tell her. He caught her looking at him, her head to one side, almost like she was reading his mind and then felt his lips twitch into a smile, before he quickly sobered again. *Of course she could read his mind.*

'What's up? What aren't you telling me?' Olivia pounced immediately, her dark eyes flashing. 'How did it go with Tony? Does he want you back in London?'

'Not at all!' Jago rushed to placate her. 'It was about a heavy trial due to start in the new year that he wants me to take a look at. Nothing else. Although he does send his regards.'

'Hmmph.' Olivia snorted, softened and asked after Tony's family, which Jago was unable to answer as, being a man, he rarely bothered with pleasantries when there was business to discuss. But she wasn't letting him off the hook that easily. 'Okay. So, what's up?'

Jago sighed. There was no way he was going to wriggle out of this one. He thought he'd perfected his poker face in court. He was described as 'one of the leading criminal silks in crime, a charming and persuasive advocate and one of the best cross-examiners in the business' in the Legal 500. And yes, he was fearless of the mightiest opponent and grouchiest judge in court, but when it came to the woman he loved, he was a lost cause and no longer able to even attempt to pull the wool over her eyes.

'I've been doing a bit of research into Rafe Burrows and his businesses.' He ignored Olivia's snort and carried on, keen to get it over with. 'It looks like he and Marcus Walker-Smith started their careers together at some high-end London estate agents. And whereas Marcus eventually set up his own agency in London, Rafe decided to specialise as a property buying agent in coastal areas, presumably meeting the need for second homes for Londoners and personally chosen contacts of Walker-Smith. First of all, he went to Sussex but then moved down here about ten years ago, which fits with what Louisa told us.' He paused, wondering whether to share the next snippet of information. 'It looks like he built a real name for himself as a buying agent in Cornwall and made an absolute fortune at the beginning of the decade helping people to buy second homes in all the Cornish property hot spots. And as soon as they all got saturated, he moved further afield.'

Olivia's face was a picture of contempt. 'Like Penbartha? Which, much as I personally prefer it, doesn't have the ostentatious appeal of places like Rock, Padstow and Polzeath, does it?'

Jago shook his head. 'Perhaps it was Louisa and her mother who first introduced him to Penbartha when they engaged him as a buying agent all those years ago? It sounds like she was determined to buy here, doesn't it? And then he decided to revisit when he started to run out of houses in other areas.'

Olivia groaned. 'Please don't say that in front of anyone else. Ever. I don't think Louisa would ever show her face again.'

'Well, however he found out about it, he's certainly been involved in property deals round here in recent years, as you know.' He pointed at the screen of his laptop. 'I'm quoting from his website now: "Penbartha is a peaceful alternative to nearby Falmouth, a hidden creekside gem with significant investment being injected into the area's unique railway heritage. The original station, goods shed, engine shed and signal box have all been beautifully renovated and are now a hub for local creative entrepreneurs and champions of sustainability. As a result the village – which has more palm trees than anywhere else in this part of Cornwall – now boasts the best independent food shops, a bakery, a quaint pub and an amazing community spirit, where everyone is made welcome."'

Olivia snorted again. 'Oh, spot on! If you ignore the deflated tyres, graffiti and unwelcoming stickers.'

Jago decided to remain silent.

'I can't believe that he's using us as a magnet for his business. The cheek of the bloody man! He's the opposite of everything we stand for here and yet he's already dividing us.' She closed her eyes for a moment and when she opened them, they were swimming with tears. 'What are we going to do?'

'We'll sort it.' Jago spoke with more conviction than he felt. 'I promise. Let's go home.'

They'd only just left the Signal Box and were crossing the walkway in the direction of the Waiting Rooms when a tall, rake-like figure with long grey hair tied back in a ponytail came stomping towards them, a sour expression on her face.

'Uh-oh.' Jago felt Olivia tense beside him and grip his hand harder, but it was too late to change direction.

The woman stopped in front of them, folded her arms across her stringy body and cast a critical gaze over them, coming to rest on their joined hands. She tutted loudly, her narrow lips in a line of disapproval.

'Good afternoon, Caroline,' Olivia said politely and turned to Jago with a slightly desperate expression in her eyes. 'Jago, have you met Caroline Pellow?'

He was slightly distracted by all three dogs' uncharacteristic response to the woman. Far from greeting her with their usual exuberance, their tails went down as one, and they stood stock still. *Interesting.*

'Oh sorry.' He shook himself slightly and held out his hand. 'Good afternoon. I'm Jago Trevithick.'

Caroline Pellow kept her arms firmly crossed and sniffed loudly. 'Oh, I know exactly who you are.'

Wow! That wasn't the customary warm Cornish welcome Jago had come to expect in Penbartha. Taken aback, he cast an anguished look towards Olivia, hoping she was made of sterner stuff. She didn't let him down.

'Are you on your way to see Alfie?' she asked, in a falsely bright voice which matched the smile on her face.

'Not sure what business that is of yours,' Caroline retorted. 'Can't honest local folks go about their business in their own village without being questioned by upcountry folks like you?'

'Now come on, Caroline.' Olivia spoke patiently. 'You know

that both Jago and I are Cornish born and bred. We might have gone upcountry for our careers, but that's not against the law, is it? And besides which, we're back now, with no plans to leave.'

'And don't we know it! Lording it over us locals and helping incomers buy houses in the village that should, by rights, be lived in by villagers.'

'We do not lord it over the locals!' Olivia had obviously reached the end of her already short fuse where Caroline Pellow was concerned. Her shoulders went back and her chin was out, and Jago feared that the older woman might just have met her match.

'That's unfair, Caroline,' Jago interjected quickly. 'I'm not entirely sure what you're talking about, but if it's the Old Foundry, the Hogans bought that after it had been on the market for a long while and no one local had made an offer for it.'

'That's because no local could afford to buy it at the price being asked, not with everything that needed doing to it.'

'And I'm sorry about that,' Jago sympathised. 'But at least it's no longer decaying slowly and becoming more and more of an eyesore. Now it looks fantastic, will provide a few jobs for locals and will bring more people into the village to spend their money. That's got to be a good thing for Penbartha, hasn't it?'

'We don't need more people coming into the village!' Caroline retorted, and then pointed an accusing finger at Olivia. 'You've got a lot to answer for young lady. With all your fancy American and upcountry ideas. Not everyone wants Penbartha to become some sort of tourist attraction and bring in all kinds of incomers who push our house prices up. It's because of people like you my daughter had to move away.'

'That's not true!' Olivia's voice was full of indignation. 'I'm sorry your daughter had to move away, but that was before I moved back here, before the Goods Shed had even been started. The fact that house prices were going up had nothing to do with me then. Or now.'

'A daughter ought to be able to afford to live in the place she was born.'

'I'm really sorry too, but it's happening all over the country,' Jago said. 'All over the world. You hear it all the time. It's not peculiar to Penbartha.'

'Perhaps not. But in those places, houses are lived in by new families full time, not left with empty cottages for most of the year, constantly reminding us of what we've lost.'

'That may be true,' Jago agreed. 'But you can't blame Olivia for that. Or George before her. The Goods Shed was his idea, remember.'

Caroline glowered. 'I'd never blame George, but there will be repercussions. Locals won't take all this lying down.'

Jago seized on her words. 'Do you know anything about the graffiti, the flat tyres or the stickers, Caroline?'

A mask came down over her angular face and hollow cheeks, and she turned away. 'No.'

'They were all acts of criminal damage. Crimes that are being taken seriously by the police. And if you do know anything about them or who is behind them, I advise you to suggest that they stop right now.'

'Don't you come the high-and-mighty lawyer with me, Mr Trevithick. You might impress some folks round here with your posh words and fancy ways, but not me. I don't know anything about the things you're talking about, but if I did, I'd buy those who did it a pint in the Ship.' Her face hardened even more. 'And I doubt they've finished yet. So if I were you, I'd watch your backs. You don't know who you're dealing with.' She pointed down at the dogs before she stomped off. 'And if I were you, I'd watch these, too.'

'What a delightful woman!' Jago decided to make light of the older woman's comments as they walked up the lane to Tresillian. But Olivia wasn't listening. Since turning into the lane she'd spent the entire time peering into front gardens and beyond, looking for signs of occupancy. The end of the lane furthest away from Tresillian and nearest the village had more cottages, but only a few lights twinkled in cottage windows, curtains remained open and plumes of woodsmoke rising into the slowly darkening skies were few and far between.

'Look at this!' her voice rose. 'I knew a few of these cottages were holiday homes now, but not that many. It doesn't look as though any are lived in at the moment.'

'It's only four o'clock,' Jago pointed out, trying to placate her. 'Perhaps people are just not home from work yet. And besides, these aren't the type of houses that Rafe Burrows sells.'

'No, but they're the sort of second home that's more affordable to many people.' Olivia declared. 'And look, only a few have pumpkins outside.'

'You've lost me completely now.' Jago carried on walking.

'Kitten's organised a big charity pumpkin-carving competition, and practically the whole village is joining in.'

'And what happens to all the carved pumpkins afterwards? Not to mention all the innards?' He mimed being sick. 'Please don't tell me Harry has flooded the Waiting Rooms menu with pumpkin-flavoured food!'

'Not at all!' Olivia thought back to all the pumpkin pie she had been made to eat in New York and grimaced. 'As usual, Kitten's thought of everything. Some of them are going to Falmouth restaurants, others are being donated to local farmers to feed their pigs, goats and chickens. Fraser's roasting a lot of the seeds to use in his baking, and the rest are being composted by the Hogans at their flower farm. Apparently, pumpkins make wonderful compost if you do it properly.'

'Who knew?' Jago was pleased that Olivia had been distracted from her forensic examination of cottage windows and chimneys until they reached the part of the lane where it thinned out into larger homes, more spread out and with sprawling gardens. The fallen leaves lay in crunchy russet and golden piles, which the dogs took great pleasure in running though, chasing each other and tossing the leaves up into the air, barking happily. He let out a sigh as they rounded the final bend before the gradual incline to Tresillian. But his relief was short lived. The dogs quietened down as they neared the bend where Gillan Cottage stood at the end of a long drive, and despite the noise of the wind whipping through the trees, they could hear voices raised in what sounded like anger. Outside the gate, beside the Prestige Coastal Properties sign, stood Rafe Burrows and Marcus Walker-Smith. And to the casual observer, it definitely looked like they were in the middle of a very heated argument.

'Good afternoon.' Jago decided to take control of the situation. There was no way he was slinking past like a naughty schoolboy.

'Afternoon.' Rafe composed himself more quickly than his friend, an unconvincing smile replacing the glare. 'Just showing Marcus here the delights of Gillan Cottage.'

Jago intercepted a warning look between the two men and turned to watch Marcus's reaction. He did quite well, and managed his own unconvincing smile. *Bloody estate agents!*

'And very nice it is too, just what I'm looking for. Rafe has surpassed himself. Again!'

'Have you looked round?' Olivia didn't bother to hide her suspicion. Mylor growled, picking up on his mistress's unease, and she quickly bent to clip on his lead and told him to sit.

'It's perfect,' Walker-Smith declared, glowering at the dogs. 'Just needs bringing into the twenty-first century. The old couple who owned it had lived there for sixty years apparently and haven't done a thing to upgrade it.'

'It's an Arts and Crafts listed building!' Olivia spoke through clenched teeth. 'What did you expect?'

Walker-Smith ignored her. 'It would be much better without all those inglenook fireplaces and wooden beams. And the wood panelling and stained glass windows make it really dark. I reckon we could get a massive swimming pool and a pool house in the garden if we get rid of all those stone terraces and untidy flowerbeds, don't you Rafe?'

'You can't do that!' Jago could see the steam coming out of Olivia's ears. 'The garden's full of history and specimen plants!'

'People pay more for views than for gardens,' Rafe stated with a sly smile. 'Buyers want low maintenance these days, so they don't have to spend a fortune on gardeners, particularly when they're not here very often. And this location has fantastic views!'

'Absolutely!' Marcus moved closer to Olivia. 'You should be grateful I don't want to knock the whole place down. Although, thinking about it…' A cunning look spread across his face. 'I always say it's easier to seek forgiveness than permission.' The two men shared a snigger.

'I'd like to see you try.' Jago spoke firmly. 'The planning authorities down here are very strict on things like this. And if I could offer you a word of advice, I think you need to understand that not everything can be bought in Penbartha. Locals have a lot of respect for their little corner of the world and don't like people trashing their houses and their history.'

'Oh get real, Trevithick. Money talks. Anything can be bought for the right price. I know how the planning system works. How do you think I'm so successful?'

Jago took a deep breath and mentally rearranged the list of people he despised, putting estate agents just above criminals and traffic wardens. 'I only have your word that you are successful, Mr Walker-Smith. And I have no idea what you base that statement on. You might want to remember that Penbarthans don't value money and possessions above everything else. We're not in London now.'

'So, I wouldn't share your plans for Gillan Cottage with locals, if I were you,' Olivia suggested. 'Unless you want a mutiny on your hands.'

'Is that a threat, Olivia?' Rafe took a step towards them.

'Of course it's not,' Jago said smoothly. 'Just a neighbourly word of advice.' He caught hold of Olivia's arm. 'Good evening, gentlemen.'

* * *

The harsh sound of sirens slicing through the air pierced Jago's uneasy sleep. He and Olivia had been unsettled all evening and decided on an early night. Leaping out of bed, his heart in his mouth, Jago ran to the window that looked up the creek towards the village and could make out a procession of blue-and-white lights flashing up the lane. He threw open the window and leant out. Thick, acrid smoke curled upwards into the cold and clear night sky, and then he saw the flames. Cursing loudly, Jago slammed the window shut and began pulling on his clothes.

'What's going on?' Olivia's sleepy voice was muffled by the duvet. She'd obviously been sleeping better than he had.

'I need to wake Cassie and warn her. Gillan Cottage is on fire!'

9

'Right on time. That must be a first for me!'

Kitten managed a smile and climbed, awkwardly, into Emily's car. 'Thanks for the lift.'

'No problem. It's hardly out of my way.' She flashed a smile as she indicated to pull back out onto the main road. 'After all, I'm going to bore you silly for the next two hours, so it's the least I can do.' She drove towards the village. 'How are you feeling today?'

'Much better, thanks,' Kitten lied, with the usual stab of guilt at how easily it came these days. She peered out of the car window as they drove past the Bakehouse, which looked full to bursting with the usual crowd of suspects that made up Penbartha's very own instant messaging service.

'Uh oh. It looks like the coven is in full swing.' She stopped herself. 'Sorry, that's what Rocky and I call them.'

Emily laughed. 'Don't apologise to me! Some of them haven't always been the nicest to us. But I suppose they've got something really meaty to gossip about now, haven't they?' She slid Kitten a sideways glance. 'The fire at Gillan Cottage? Auntie Margaret was telling me about it.'

'Oh yes.' Kitten closed her eyes for a moment; the movement of the car was making her feel slightly sick. 'Mum's in a real state about it. You do know she lives between Gillan and Tresillian?

Although there wasn't any chance of it spreading as far as them, by all accounts.'

'Was there much damage?'

'Hard to say yet. The Fire and Rescue Service is still there. Thankfully, they arrived before the fire took hold in the house, which is quite a bit larger than its name suggests, I can tell you. Unfortunately, I think the gardens took more of a hit.'

Emily shuddered. 'How awful. A lifetime's work gone up in smoke! Auntie Margaret was telling me how fabulous the gardens were, I'd love to have seen them.' She slowed down as they drove past the Old Foundry, warm and glowing in the gentle late autumn sunshine, and let out a little squeal of excitement. 'Oh Kitten, I know I'm being selfish, but I can't wait to get our stuff out of storage and move in.'

Kitten slid down in her seat a little, in case Rocky was on site and spotted her. That would lead to a whole load of questions she wasn't ready to answer yet, the first of which was bound to be why she wasn't at work. Emily didn't notice and just drove onto the edge of the village, where cottages soon gave way to farmland and then indicated right. They turned onto a track and bumped along for a while.

'Sorry.' She must have noticed Kitten wincing. 'We're hoping to get the track laid properly as soon as we move out. Otherwise, driving up and down here a few times will be a surefire way of making sure this baby comes out when she's supposed to.'

Kitten smiled, realising she was liking Emily's down-to-earth approach to life more and more.

'Here we are.' They drew up outside a slightly battered and worn-looking green-and-white static caravan.

'Welcome to HortusFlorum HQ, our delightful 38 by 12 foot modern and inviting two-bedroom temporary home that offers the perfect blend of space, comfort and functionality.' She mimicked the pitch of a salesman as she got out of the car.

'HortusFlorum? Cool name. Sounds a bit like a spell.'

'It's Latin for flower farm. Silas came up with it as the most ridiculous name for something that is definitely not cool. Apart from in winter when it's bloody freezing. She pulled her face. 'If I have to spend more than another week in this caravan in the middle of a Cornish field, with no amenities, one toddler and a baby on the way, I will scream!'

'But what a beautiful Cornish field it is!' A tall slim man with longish dark hair scraped back into a top knot and heavy-rimmed black spectacles appeared from behind the caravan and dropped a kiss on Emily's head. He held out his hand.

'Hi, I'm Silas. You must be Kitten. Pleased to meet you at long last.' He had a lovely warm smile. 'I've heard a lot about you from Rocky.'

She nodded and smiled back, hoping it wasn't too much of a grimace. 'You too.'

She felt Emily scrutinising her face and then shoo her husband away gently.

'I'm showing Kitten round the farm and she hasn't got much time.'

Silas bowed gracefully. 'Well don't let me get in the way of the grand tour, ladies. I have flower beds to mulch!' He pulled a pair of gardening gloves out of his jeans pocket and brandished them in the air as he sauntered off.

'Silas can get very enthusiastic about the farm. But it's lovely to see him so much happier and more relaxed than he was in London. You should have seen him going off to work every day in his three-piece suits. And now look at him – jeans, sweaters and no more haircuts.' Emily chuckled. 'But he forgets that everyone isn't as passionate about the science of organic flower farming as he is.'

'It's great that he's as enthusiastic about it as you.'

'Yes it is.' She pulled her gaze back to Kitten. 'Are you sure you're up to a quick tour? You've gone very pale again.'

'I'm fine,' Kitten lied, keen for some distraction. 'After you...'

* * *

Emily kindly kept her tour of the flower farm to the highlights, pointing out the different areas from the highest point of their land. They stood overlooking the flower farm fields stretching out ahead of them, the various cut flower beds, poly tunnels, glass houses, wildflower meadows and a series of rustic-looking sheds. In the distance, Penbartha creek glistened under the golden autumn sun.

'When visitors come into the Waiting Rooms and see all the stuff we do for the environment, they often ask me why the Cornish care so much about it all.' Kitten began slowly, not taking her eyes off the view in front of her.

'And what do you say?' She could feel Emily's eyes on her.

'I say that when you have this much beauty and history and the land and the sea around you every day it becomes part of your soul and your identity, and you want to do everything you can to protect it.' Kitten's voice took on a harsher tone. 'When I lived in Manchester, I was surrounded by buildings and concrete and I was totally unaware of everything that was going on in the world. But when you live somewhere as beautiful as this and see the damage and changes taking place right in front of your eyes, it really makes you want to do something to help. That's why we have so many action groups down here. When you talk to the fishermen in the pub and they tell you that they don't catch cod and haddock around here anymore because the sea temperature has risen and those fish have all migrated north to Norway and Russia and Iceland, it makes you realise we've been experiencing the effects of global warming for years, but a lot of people don't seem to notice. Or care.' Tears filled Kitten's eyes. 'Olivia says we shouldn't preach or judge, or shame people into action, but that's easier said than done, sometimes.'

'I know exactly what you mean.' Emily patted her on the arm. 'And that's why I know we fit in here, with all the people who are doing their bit. It's like we've found our tribe.' Her pretty face clouded. 'Even if not everyone accepts us yet.'

'You're a great fit!' Kitten declared. 'And I remember Willow, at the Old Bakehouse, going through the same thing in their early days. And now look at her. A real pillar of Penbartha! You just have to grit your teeth and power on through.'

'I get that, but we spend so much time here on the farm we don't get into the village that much.' Her face brightened. 'Perhaps when we move into the Old Foundry, we'll be able to launch a charm offensive.'

'And make sure you tell everyone exactly what you're doing here. They'll love it!'

'Hmm.' Emily went back to her tour. 'So in a nutshell. My job is to choose which flowers to grow, source the best seeds and plants and then oversee the planting and harvesting to make sure we get the right combinations of colour and textures for our bouquets and workshops. Silas is in charge of the grunt work and making sure we farm by strictest organic and eco-friendly standards. Which is what we're all about. Going back to the old days, before pesticides and chemicals that harm the flowers, water systems and, even more importantly, the farm workers.'

She pointed to several colourful raised flower beds, lined with railway sleepers, nearest to the largest shed which Kitten assumed was their office. 'We're lucky that here in Cornwall our growing season is longer than most of the country, and because of the tunnels ours can start as early as March and go on to the end of October.' She took a breath. 'We still have heaps of dahlias coming from these beds, and they should keep us going until the first frosts. And the good old chrysanthemums of course.'

'Oh my God – aren't the colours heavenly?' Kitten marvelled at the warm golds, rich browns, berry reds and purples of the large showy blooms beneath her. Even from where she was standing, she could see there were so many different varieties, some small like daisies and others like pom-poms the size of dinner plates.

'I think they're my favourites as they keep their blooms until last. Just when most of the colour is going out of the farm, they arrive in all their splendour and remind you that the best is yet to come.' Emily grinned happily. 'Did you know that there are forty-two species of dahlia? And we're still working out which ones work best for us. Their colours and textures are just perfect for arrangements. And if you add in some of the seasonal foliage, seed heads and berries, they can be fabulous.' She turned back to Kitten, her eyes shining. 'Actually I think autumn may be my favourite season. All these beautiful colours, the misty mornings and watching the sun rise slowly over the flower beds. It always feels like there's something magical in the air!'

Emily's enthusiasm was infectious. 'I love it too. The cosy evenings, open fires, crunchy walks and the smell of fallen leaves mixing with the sea,' Kitten agreed. 'Olivia always says she prefers spring, as it's a new beginning, but I'm definitely an autumn girl.' She turned back. 'Did Olivia say you were going to run workshops in the Old Foundry?'

Emily rubbed her stomach. 'If this one plays ball and doesn't make an early appearance, yes. The idea was to have a shop of sorts on the ground floor, alongside a design studio. I love teaching people how to create arrangements that reflect the natural beauty of the flowers, not the old-fashioned, formal bouquets and bunches of the past. And I'm hoping to train someone up to help run Christmas wreath workshops too.' She waved at two women wheeling barrows between the flower beds. 'In the meantime, we're busy planning, ordering seeds and getting the beds cleared and mulched in order to start sowing and planting, ready for next spring.'

Her gaze wandered across the neat fields, with a look of contentment. 'Cornwall's got a really long history of flower farming. At the beginning of the 1900s, whole wagon-loads of seasonal flowers were loaded onto the flower train which ran from Penzance to the Covent Garden flower market. Just think, some might even have gone from Penbartha station!'

'What a lovely thought!' Kitten made a mental note to ask Jago about the flower train.

'Until about thirty years ago, most cut flowers bought in this country were grown in England, but then the flower industry in Holland took over and soon dominated the world flower trade. We're now trying to go back to those old days and sustainable techniques, and we know that our flowers aren't only beautiful to the eye, they don't harm the planet or its population. More and more people are coming round to our way of thinking.' She paused. 'Time for tea, I think.'

Kitten turned to follow Emily, but the sudden movement made her head spin and she lost her balance, ending up in a crumpled heap on the path.

* * *

'Now are you going to tell me what's really going on?' Emily handed her a glass of water, sat down opposite her at the tiny table and fixed Kitten with a surprisingly stern look.

Kitten's heart began to race. 'I don't know what you mean.'

'I'm going to be blunt with you, so please forgive me. I've heard so much about you from Olivia and Rocky. How passionate and driven you are, what good fun it is to hang out with you, what a powerhouse you are! And yet, the girl I see in front of me isn't any of those things. She looks exhausted and ill. And above all, scared.'

Kitten didn't have the energy to even feel offended. She just sat there, shoulders slumped, eyes squeezed shut and felt a tear trickle slowly down her cheek.

'Please talk to me, Kitten. I promise it won't go any further. I just know that you're not well and you're not happy, and I want to help you.'

She felt gentle hands take hold of hers, and when she slowly opened her eyes, Emily was on her knees in front of her, and there were tears in her own eyes. 'Please?'

It was that last plea that made Kitten finally give in to the emotions she had kept bottled up inside for the last few months. She opened her mouth, gave a primeval howl and dissolved into shuddering sobs as she told Emily everything that was happening to her, all the weird symptoms – the eye pain, the numbness, the pins and needles – and how she had almost convinced herself that she had a really bad virus and that the blurred vision was caused by the tears that she so often found in her eyes, rather than anything else. She told her all about her visit to the GP, the horrendous MRI she'd had the next day when the hospital called her with a last-minute cancellation, and how she thought she was going to die, strapped into that tunnel with a cage over her face, the subsequent wait for the results. It all just came tumbling out.

'I feel like I'm going mad! My body is doing such horrible things to me. And I'm so frightened that I'm not going to ever feel like me again.' Kitten's sobs eventually lessened, and when they stopped, Emily heaved herself back onto a chair and held onto her hand.

'And you haven't told anyone else about all this?'

Kitten sniffed. 'No. Everyone's got enough going on in their lives already. And they'd all probably think I'm being a drama queen.' She gave Emily a sideways, embarrassed look. 'I have got a bit of a reputation.'

Emily burst out laughing. 'I'm sorry, Kitten, and I'm not laughing at you. But that is such an absurd thing to say. I'm sorry you don't feel you can talk to Rocky or Olivia about all this. But I'm sure they would understand.'

'I'm not telling them yet. Not until I know what I'm dealing with.'

'When do you get the MRI results?'

A feeling of dread crept through her. 'I'm seeing Dr Kitson at two o'clock.'

Emily checked her watch. 'Right, I'm coming with you. No, you're not going alone. No way. Let me have a quick word with Silas – and no, I won't say anything to him – and I'm all yours for the rest of the day.'

* * *

'I'm very glad to see you've brought someone with you today, Kitten.' Dr Kitson's kind but tired face looked relieved. 'Mrs Hogan, isn't it?'

'Yes, Emily.'

He looked at his computer screen, clicked his mouse and then turned and gave Kitten his full attention.

'I'm just going to tell you what the MRI showed and then we can talk about our options.'

Emily caught hold of her hand and squeezed it.

'The scan shows a significant number of lesions on your brain.'

That didn't sound too bad. 'Is that what's causing my headaches and eye problems?' She couldn't keep the hopeful note out of her voice.

Dr Kitson nodded. 'Yes. Unfortunately, the MRI shows you have multiple sclerosis.' He must have noticed her dazed expression. 'That's when your immune system mistakenly attacks the protective covering around your nerves – which is called the myelin sheath – and stops the messages travelling along your nerves to your brain, resulting in the symptoms you're experiencing.'

Kitten's entire world started spinning, and she zoned out for the rest of his explanation. She racked her brain for what she knew about multiple sclerosis and eventually dragged a distant memory of a friend's great aunt.

'Will I end up in a wheelchair?' A tear ran down her cheek and splashed onto the desk. Dr Kitson passed her a tissue.

'That's probably unlikely, but it's too soon to tell.'

'Can they do anything?' Emily spoke up, her voice quavering.

'There's lots they can do these days,' the GP reassured them both. 'The management of MS has come on massively over the last ten years. My friend's a neurologist in Truro, and I've got you an urgent appointment to see her. She'll explain everything much better than I can. And these should help you in the meantime.' He handed her a prescription. 'They're steroids that will calm down the inflammation of the myelin sheath and reduce your symptoms. Get this filled as soon as possible and start them today.'

Kitten sat there, numb with shock. The movie reel of her life that she often played in her mind had just turned into a horror film. Knowing she had to escape the doctor's room before she lost it completely, she shot a desperate look at Emily and staggered to her feet.

'I understand this is a lot to take in, Kitten.' Dr Kitson stood up too. 'Read these leaflets, and come back to see me in a couple of days.' He held them out to her, and she snatched them from his hand as she stumbled to the door, desperate to get outside. She needed to be alone.

10

'Well, thanks for that, Jasper. And I'm sorry I had to be the one to break the news, but at least you've got the chief firefighter's number now so you can talk to them directly.' Olivia sat at the refectory table in Tresillian's orangery and watched the late-afternoon sky turning a dark grey and the creek reflecting the same colour back. In true Cornish style, the morning's sunshine had soon given way to a steady drizzle.

A disembodied sigh came down the line. 'And I'm sorry I've been off grid all this time and caused you so much worry. Please believe me when I say I've never even heard of Rafe Burrows. But I'll be back in Toronto in less than an hour, and will speak to the Fire Service then. I'll also be having a stern word with Mr Burrows, if I can track him down.'

'Sounds good. And keep in touch, okay?'

'Will do. And just bill me for any work Rocky needs to do at Gillan. Bye.'

Olivia ended the call and turned to face Jago who had just come back in from delivering another round of tea and coffee to the firefighters still on-site next door, bringing a cloud of bonfire smoke in with him.

'The rain's helping to dampen the garden down.' Jago sniffed at his jumper. 'And fortunately the fire didn't take hold in the house, but there's some smoke damage. Rocky's on standby to make everything secure when the Fire Service is finished. Who were you talking to?'

Olivia slumped in her chair. 'That was Jasper Swift. He's been away at his cabin at Lake Joseph, writing his latest sailing book, and he deliberately doesn't have any mobile signal or Wi-Fi there. He's now on his way back home to Toronto, and when he hit a signal he was swamped with about twenty-six missed calls from me.'

Jago pulled up a chair. 'And?'

'And he was very upset to hear about the fire. I've passed on the number for the firefighter in charge so he can speak to them directly.'

Jago ran a hand over his face. 'I don't envy him trying to sort all that out from four thousand miles away.'

'I said we'd help out, and he's prepared to come back if necessary.' She shot him a worried look, and he leant towards her.

'Did you ask him about Prestige Coastal Properties?'

'Of course I did. He said he knew nothing about them and had never heard of Rafe Burrows.'

'Do you believe him?'

Olivia stared at him, the frustration she'd been feeling all day mounting. 'Of course I do. Why wouldn't I?'

'I'm just asking.'

Olivia felt a spark of irritation with Jago that she hadn't since their early days together. 'Just because you don't take anyone's word for anything without them swearing an oath first, doesn't mean I can't trust someone I've known my entire life.'

The surprised look on his face told her that she'd gone too far, too quickly, but he recovered himself.

'Okay. I apologise. But if Jasper is telling the truth, you know what that means, don't you?'

'Of course I do. I'm not stupid.' The reality of what they were both thinking was sinking in, and she could feel a tight knot of dread coiling in her stomach.

'I didn't say you were.' The patient tone in Jago's voice sounded forced to her, which infuriated her even more, but she took a deep breath.

'Okay. If Jasper is telling the truth, it means that Rafe Burrows is playing silly buggers by putting that sign up without authorisation. Why do you think that might be?'

Jago just shrugged, obviously deciding that keeping silence was a better option when she was in this mood.

'And is Marcus Walker-Smith in on that charade? What would be the point? What are they trying to achieve?' Olivia began pacing round the kitchen and then stopped suddenly and turned to Jago. 'Do you reckon Rafe and Marcus are connected with the fire?'

'Would they stoop that low?' Jago eventually asked.

'I wouldn't put anything past them. Could they be trying to force Jasper's hand to sell at a reduced price? As you just said, it's not going to be easy trying to sort everything out from Toronto. And the value of a fire-damaged house will be significantly reduced, won't it?' She refilled the dogs' water bowls and sat back down at the table. 'Or as a way of getting around planning permission and listed building consent?'

'That's a bit extreme, isn't it?' The fact he hadn't dismissed her suggestion as nonsense unsettled her even more. 'Not to mention foolish, seeing as Burrows's company board has been seen by all and sundry outside the house. I'm pretty sure he's the first person the fire investigation people will be talking to.'

'What about the anti-second home brigade? Could they be stepping up their action and targeting any house that could become a second home? I vaguely remember George telling me about that Welsh group that set fire to English-owned homes in Wales some years ago.'

'You mean Meibion Glyndŵr?' *Of course Jago would know about it. And how to pronounce it perfectly, at least to her untrained ears!* 'That was a paramilitary Welsh nationalist group who fire-bombed hundreds of English-owned holiday homes, estate agents and MPs in the 1980s.' He frowned. 'I hardly think a bit of graffiti, deflated tyres and a few unfriendly stickers put what's happening here in the same ballpark as that.' He frowned again. 'Although, now I come to think about it, there was a group here in the eighties called An Gof, who were of the same ilk.'

'What did they do?'

'As far as I recall, they bombed the court building in St Austell and set fire to a few other places.' Jago recounted what he knew about it in such a matter-of-fact way that Olivia was left open mouthed. 'And there have been a few groups since who claim to be the resurrected An Gof, and spray anti-English graffiti on buildings and slash English flags. There's always someone prepared to cause trouble. But it usually fades away.'

Olivia pushed her chair back and stomped across to the Aga, where she yanked the hot plate cover up and banged the kettle down so hard that water flew out if its spout and bubbled and hissed across the surface.

'Are you okay?'

Olivia kept her back to him. 'I can't believe you're sitting here, smelling of smoke and talking about all this in such a carefree manner.' When she turned round, she couldn't keep the wobble out of her voice. 'What if Penbartha is the centre of the resurgence of one of these groups?' She shushed him. And the tears began to fall. 'This is our home, Jago. The place I've always felt safe and part of, but just lately that's begun to change.'

He was across the kitchen in a few strides, slid his arms

around her waist, turned her gently and held her close. The smell of smoke on his jumper gave her the clarity to admit to herself and to him what was wrong. She'd been on edge for a while, but it had built up since the beach clean, when the tension between the villagers and visitors had boiled over in public for the first time. Of course, she'd been vaguely aware of it before. You only had to read the local papers to know that there was some animosity between the two sides. And in recent weeks she'd started to overhear the occasional snide remark in the Goods Shed or in the Waiting Rooms, but she'd put it down to the long, hot summer and perhaps too many tourists for some locals. But with all the incidents that had taken place over the last few days she could no longer ignore it. Individually, perhaps, they didn't amount to much, but collectively, they were adding up in a most unpleasant way. Olivia's sense of justice was being tested on an almost daily basis, and she despised bullies and cowards who hid behind their anonymous actions.

Jago held her and let her rant. Then he told her to sit on a sofa while he made a pot of tea. Only when she'd nearly finished her mug and the dogs were curled up beside her, did she speak again.

'I think we need to talk to Rafe Burrows,' she declared.

'I agree.'

'You do?'

'Well, we have no idea who's in the group targeting second homes. Or even if it is a co-ordinated movement, rather than just a bunch of disgruntled locals who are acting individually and randomly. Until we find out who these people are, it makes sense to speak to the other obvious suspects.'

'Do you really think Rafe and Marcus were trying to damage Gillan Cottage to the extent that it could be sold off cheaply, or to get round planning restrictions?' Olivia held her breath, not really wanting to hear Jago's reply.

'It's a pretty stupid thing to do, or perhaps the actions of someone who's desperate,' he observed. 'And the only way we can find out is to talk to Rafe.'

'Do you think he will talk to us?'

A determined look set across Jago's face. 'If we can persuade him it's in his best interests, he might.'

Olivia looked at him. He was back in court mode. 'And you're happy to do this?'

He nodded. 'I think we have to.'

'You didn't want to get involved in the summer, when it was all kicking off at Peneglos Hall, remember?'

'That was different.' Jago looked away for a moment and then met her eyes. 'I was wrong, and you were right. All this is obviously getting to you, so we need to take control and get to the bottom of it before anything else happens.'

A thought darted through her mind. 'Do you think we should involve the police? Or at least talk to Sam about it? Get his copper's take on it?'

'Not yet.' Jago's voice was determined. 'Let's see what we can discover first.' His rare smile slowly spread over his face and melted her heart. 'With your gut instinct and intuition and my reason and logic, we're the dream team, remember?' He pulled her closer and she let herself lean into him.

The jangling of the heavy front doorbell interrupted anything that may have been about to happen. With the dogs rushing to the door, barking excitedly, the moment was broken, and Olivia heaved herself up to see who was partaking of the very non-Cornish practice of using the front door, the knot of concern in her stomach tightening.

A firefighter, in full uniform and holding a white helmet under his left arm, stood there. His face looked vaguely familiar.

'Hi Olivia. Remember me? Max Gordon. I was the Watch

Manager of the crew who came out to the fire at the station last year.'

A rush of unwanted memories ran through Olivia's mind. That was a time she'd rather forget. She pulled herself together and waved her hand vaguely in the air. 'Of course, sorry. I think you kept the helmet on last time.'

He smiled. 'And it was a stressful time.'

'Yes.' She recovered her manners. 'Do you want to come in? Has Jasper Swift spoken to you?'

'Yes, he has. And no, I won't come in. But could you come next door with me? It will be easier to explain what I'm talking about. Jasper has asked me to talk you through it.'

'Of course. I'd like Jago to come too, if that's okay? He's just inside.' At Max's nod, she called out and Jago appeared, his arm outstretched. The two men shook hands, and then they set off down the drive, leaving three disgruntled dogs behind.

'Look, I'll get straight to the point. Jasper has asked me to speak to you directly about what we know so far,' Max began as they walked up the lane. 'I've been brought in because I'm a Group Manager now.' He pointed to two black stripes on his helmet. 'And I specialise in getting involved in fires that we think may be suspicious.'

Olivia's heart sank, and she exchanged a look with Jago.

'So what are your thoughts so far?'

'I can't commit to anything at the moment.' Max nodded at the firefighter standing at the gateway to the drive of Gillan Cottage, who held up the red-and-white Fire Service barrier tape for them to duck beneath. Olivia stopped and nudged Jago. 'Where's the board gone?'

Max frowned. 'What board?'

'A For Sale board. A bright blue-and-green Prestige Coastal Properties board,' Jago explained.

'I haven't heard anything about one. I'll check with the lads later. They're searching the garden now.' They passed two fire engines on the drive and arrived at the front of the large house sitting low and squat in its grounds. In the gloom of the late afternoon, they could make out several firefighters in their brown uniforms with high-viz stripes around their jackets and trousers moving portable flood lights from one area of the garden to another so they could undertake detailed searches.

'What I can say is that the fire didn't have time to take hold in the house.'

'That's probably because they built houses like this to stand the test of time,' Olivia observed. 'The builders were proper, traditional craftsmen who used locally sourced materials – in this case, granite – so the houses would blend in with the natural surroundings. Many Arts and Crafts houses have a lot more timber in their structure, but its use is fairly minimal here externally, probably due to the house's proximity to the creek. And wood and water aren't a good combination. They put a lot more thought into things like that in those days.' She spoke with feeling.

'Well, I think that might have just have saved it,' Max commented. 'There is some smoke damage inside, but it's minimal from what we can tell so far. A structural engineer should be here tomorrow to confirm it's safe, but I don't foresee any problems with that.'

'What about the gardens?' Olivia asked. 'Can we see?'

Max paused for a moment. 'Okay, if you just walk in my footsteps. We haven't completed all our searches yet.'

They followed him around the side of the house to where the gardens stretched along the bank of the creek. The smell of acrid smoke was strongest here. Olivia gasped in horror.

What had once been a large and wide lovingly tended garden with magnificent planting cascading over iron rose arches, brick walls and pergolas, was now one big muddy, burnt mess.

'It looks like the fire spread quickly through the parts of the garden that had piles of dead foliage still on the wooden structures,' Max explained. 'It would have gone up like a tinderbox. Luckily the brick pathways and water features acted as natural firebreaks in some places, further away from the house.'

'Rex and Peggy Swift developed and nurtured this garden for over sixty years.' Tears filled Olivia's eyes. 'It was often featured in magazines as the perfect Arts and Crafts garden.' Her breath caught in her throat at the happy memories of having picnic teas in the garden with Peggy and Mollie when she was a child. 'It was the most wonderful, magical place.'

'Any idea where the fire started?' Jago asked, squeezing Olivia's hand at the same time.

'There seem to be several points of origin, at various spots around the garden. And so far, it looks like they were created simultaneously.'

'So we're talking more than one person being responsible?' Jago seized on his words. Max nodded his head. 'That's likely, but it's too soon to tell how many as the grass is all churned up so we can't distinguish footprints at the moment. We should know more tomorrow.' A sudden commotion on the terrace nearest the house caught his attention. 'There's a lot of stuff to go through. I think that potting shed is the last big structure though.'

'Boss!'

There was no mistaking the sense of urgency in the call. Max rushed up the garden, closely followed by Jago and Olivia. By the time they reached the terrace, a floodlight had been positioned in the entrance to the potting shed, highlighting all the half-burnt, wooden-handled garden tools, flower pots, seed trays and other gardening paraphernalia that had been stored in there over the years.

And there at the back lay a charred body, with a badly scorched Coastal Prestige Properties board impaled through its chest.

11

The Waiting Rooms were just opening when Jago, Olivia and the dogs approached the next morning. They'd both had a pretty sleepless night, and as the police had cordoned off their end of the lane with blue-and-white tape in order to carry out detailed searches as soon as it was light, they'd turned left out of the top of Tresillian's drive and walked the long way round the headland before looping back towards the station and the creek.

The white Old Bakehouse van drove quickly into the car park, pulled up sharply by the side of the building and a harassed-looking Fraser jumped out and ran round to the back doors and started unlading crates of baked goods.

'Hey, Jago, you couldn't just open the kitchen door for me could you, mate?' He called. Jago obliged, and within minutes a very relieved-looking Jasmine had taken them from him.

'You had me worried there for a minute, Fraser,' she confessed. 'I thought I'd forgotten to put our order in, and as it's the first day of the proper half-term break, we're expecting a bit of a rush this weekend.'

'I'm so sorry, lass.' Fraser looked mortified. 'It's no excuse, but wee Dougie had us up for most of the night, and I overslept.'

Jago took a look at his friend's face. His sandy hair was standing on end and his pale, freckled face was almost white with exhaustion.

'I thought you'd got cover in for the bakery at weekends?'

Fraser sighed. 'We had. A guy called Ricky Parsons. And he's been grand. But he had an accident at work on Thursday and couldn't come in last night. And, of course, young Dougie decided that would be the night he'd start teething big time.'

'That's hard, for all of you.' Olivia sympathised. 'And how is my gorgeous godson today?'

Jago couldn't help smiling. Having always said she wasn't keen on babies, Olivia had fallen in love with young Dougie on the day he was born. Even Jago had to admit that the chubby-cheeked, blue-eyed cherub who had inherited his mother's white-blonde hair was very cute. And if talking about him put Olivia in a better mood, he was happy.

Fraser managed a chuckle, despite his tiredness. 'He'd finally settled when my alarm went off. The wonders of liquid paracetamol!' He slammed the doors of the van shut. 'Oh! Willow asked me to remind you about the gleaning session later this morning.'

'I'd completely forgotten!'

Jago glanced sideways at Olivia, whose face was a picture of remorse. He had no idea what gleaning was, but it was no wonder she'd forgotten about it, with everything that was going on. If he knew her at all, he was pretty sure she wouldn't want to be the object of village scrutiny once the news of last night's grisly discovery was common knowledge. He could imagine what would be said.

'I'll do my best to be there, but please tell Willow I might not make it today,' Olivia apologised. 'Next time?'

'I'll tell her, and she won't let you forget. She says that getting involved with the Gleaning Network since Dougie was born has saved her mental health.'

Olivia brightened. 'That's really good to hear. And I must say that the idea of picking cauliflowers in a muddy field is quite attractive at the moment.'

Jago glanced at Fraser, but he jumped into his van and roared off. He turned back to Olivia. 'What's gl—'

'Hi guys!' Jasmine bounced back out. 'You coming in for coffee? Those pastries Fraser's just dropped off look and smell amazing!'

Olivia peered over her shoulder. 'How busy are you?'

'We're quiet at the moment, but it will pick up soon.' A conspiratorial smile spread across her face. 'Who are you avoiding? Or is the list too long?'

'Not at all!' Jago ushered Olivia and the dogs through the door and led the way past their usual table in the window to one at the back. Jasmine said nothing. She gave the dogs treats and took the humans' order.

'Is Kitten due in today?' Olivia looked round the almost-empty café.

'Not until later. But she says she's feeling a bit better.'

'This bug has really taken it out of her,' Olivia commented. 'I've never known her be so quiet. Even Rocky says he hasn't seen much of her.'

'Well, the doc's given her some magic medicine, and she says she feels better already!'

'And are you managing all right without her?'

'Yes, thanks. Alfie's been a godsend, and Ned Roscoe's done a few shifts too, so we've coped okay. It will be good to have Kitten back this week though – things could get hectic with all the half-term activities we've got planned.'

'Well, thanks for all you've done for Kitten this past week, I really appreciate it.'

'It's the least I can do. Kitten's been a good friend to me.'

Jasmine wandered off with a big smile, and Jago turned to Olivia. 'Do you think Kitten's okay?'

She frowned. 'I'm not sure. There's definitely something up, I just don't know what.'

'Have you seen much of her while I've been away?'

Olivia thought hard. And when she looked up at Jago her dark eyes were troubled. 'Not much, no. I've been really busy with the Old Foundry and she's been tied up with her plastic-free status campaign. We've messaged each other fairly regularly, but it's easy to hide behind those.'

'Has Cassie said anything?'

'No, but she's still a bit loved up with Sam.'

'Rocky?'

Olivia threw him a pointed look. 'Rocky wouldn't notice if she was on fire.' She winced. 'Bad analogy, sorry.'

'Coffee and pastries, fresh from the Bakehouse.' Alfie arrived at their table with a tray and very carefully placed their order in front of them.

Jago looked more closely. Alfie's right hand was heavily bandaged, looking almost comical against his skinny arm and hindering his usual nimbleness.

'What've you done to your hand?'

He immediately hid it behind his back. 'Me and my mates were messing around at the cove the other night, and I burnt myself on a sparkler.'

'That's a very professional-looking bandage.'

Alfie blushed to the roots of his red hair. 'Isn't it? Way over the top really, but Gran got carried away.' He looked over to the counter, where Jasmine was gesticulating at him. 'Right, must go. Enjoy your drinks.'

Jago watched him go. 'Interesting.'

'He's a kid. Kids do all sorts of stupid things with fireworks.' She glared. 'You're not suggesting Alfie was involved in the fire at Gillan, are you?'

Jago stirred his coffee and refused to react to her accusation.

'I don't think we can rule anyone or anything out at this stage.'

Olivia paled. 'So we're back to looking at everyone with suspicion, are we? I hate being like that with people I know. I remember what it's like to be wrongly accused of murder!'

Jago sat back, the old infuriating mix of frustration and admiration he'd felt towards her at that time making an unwelcome return. They were incompatible on so many levels, and their differences were highlighted on occasions like this, when she allowed her emotions and loyalties get in the way of approaching things logically. But they'd managed to work together before, and he was sure they could do it again.

'C'mon Olivia, this isn't the same thing at all.' He caught hold of her hand across the table and squeezed it gently. 'We may well be conflating two entirely separate issues, so let's leave any potential murder investigations to the police.'

'I agree.'

'There's a big part of me that thinks the fire, or fires, may be completely unconnected to the dead body, but they've got mixed up somehow.'

Olivia was thoughtful. 'Really? Do you think the smaller fires may have been set by locals as a warning to second-homers, and then just used as a smokescreen by the murderer to cover up the dead body? No pun intended.'

Perhaps she had changed after all. Her train of thought was exactly the same as his.

'That's what I'm thinking, at the moment,' he confessed. 'I can get my head around the locals doing small, spiteful things to annoy second-homers, but trying to set fire to Gillan is a massive jump from that. And impaling someone on a For Sale board is entirely different territory. Nothing escalates that quickly. Not in a place like Penbartha anyway.'

'I do wish you'd stop saying that. It's a jinx.' She buried her face in her hands, dark curls tumbling forwards and narrowly missing her coffee cup.

'But because this is Penbartha, we can use your superpower.'

She raised her head, eyes narrowed. 'What superpower?'

'The fact that you know practically every person who lives and works here and they all talk to you. I've seen the way all sorts of people open up to you and tell you stuff. Stuff they certainly wouldn't tell the police in a million years. Look how much local knowledge has helped us in the past.'

'Not everyone opens up to me,' she said with feeling. 'I think Caroline's struck me off her Christmas card list this year.'

'Okay. Almost everyone.'

'So we need to start talking to locals about the FHO campaign?'

'I think so. And I'll think of a way to find out what Rafe Burrows was up to with Gillan Cottage.'

Olivia pulled a face. 'Well, it had better be a roundabout way. I don't think either of those two will speak to you willingly.'

'And of course, what we really need to know is the identity of the person in the potting shed.'

'Well, I don't think it was either Marcus or Rafe.'

Jago did a double take. 'How do you know that?'

A triumphant look crossed Olivia's face. 'Well, as well as being totally emotional and irrational and good at talking to people, I notice things.'

'And?'

'When we saw Marcus and Rafe outside Gillan on the day of the fire, they were both wearing brown leather shoes. Oxfords.'

Jago felt his upper lip curl. He hated brown shoes.

'And the person who was found in the potting shed was wearing an ancient pair of wellies.'

* * *

'You're not talking about our dead body by any chance, are you?' A shadow fell across their table and the familiar face of Detective Inspector Ross Trenow appeared.

The three dogs jumped to their feet, happy to greet their old friend. Mylor and Steren were content with thumping their tails against his legs, but Zennor had to throw herself onto her back so he could scratch her tummy. Part of Jago believed it was Zennor's uncharacteristic fondness for the detective that made Olivia so willing to trust him.

'I couldn't possibly comment.' Jago and Trenow shook hands, and then the policeman waved in Olivia's direction.

'I'm not here in an official capacity. Yet,' he explained quickly as he drew up a chair and waved at Jasmine to order a drink. 'I've just seen Sam at Gillan Cottage and he suggested you might be here. Do you mind?'

Jago and Olivia exchanged a look. 'Not at all.'

They made small talk until Jasmine delivered Trenow's coffee and pastry. He swallowed a huge mouthful, ate his pastry and then turned into detective mode.

'Bit of bad luck you two being there when another body was found.'

Jago decided that was an observation, so didn't require an answer. Olivia was more forthcoming.

'We were there at the request of Max Gordon, on behalf of Jasper Swift, the owner of Gillan Cottage. Nothing else.'

Jago placed his hand on her knee beneath the table and gave it a warning squeeze.

'It was unfortunate timing,' he conceded.

'And it was you who called the rescue services to the fire?'

'No, it was the sound of the sirens that woke me. I've told your officers that already.'

Trenow looked down at his notebook and scribbled something. 'Do you know who called 999?'

'No idea, sorry.'

'Have you been aware of any unusual activities at Gillan Cottage recently?'

'I know we're officially next door, but we're still quite a long way further up the lane, and the Coach House is between us, so no.'

'Until the For Sale board appeared last week,' Olivia added.

'Ah yes. The Prestige Coastal Properties board.'

'Which Jasper Swift knew nothing about.'

Jago squeezed her leg again and she glared at him.

Trenow nodded. 'I've spoken to Jasper Swift.'

'What about Rafe Burrows?'

'I haven't been able to get hold of him yet.'

'Have you tried Marcus Walker-Smith?' Jago asked.

'It would appear they're away together for a few days. Golfing or something.'

Jago and Olivia exchanged a look.

Trenow closed his notebook. 'Look, I'm going to be honest with you. We haven't been able to establish the identity of the deceased yet. We might have to rely on dental records.'

Olivia winced. *She knew what that meant.*

'But the reason I'm talking to you now is that Sam's told me about some incidents in the village between locals and second-home owners.'

'Is that sort of thing within the remit of CID these days?' Jago didn't even try to keep the disbelief out of his voice.

Trenow sighed. 'Not exactly. Sam spoke to Walker-Smith and Burrows about their tyres, decided there was nothing to it, so passed it back to Uniform. Any accusations they may have been trying to make against Olivia were found to be baseless.'

'Good of him to tell us.'

Trenow ignored him. 'But it's got us thinking. Especially as there have been other incidents that haven't been reported to the police.' He reopened his notebook and turned a few pages. 'Namely the graffiti on the Old Foundry and some stickers attached to certain houses.'

'What are you getting at, Inspector? Criminal damage is one thing, but arson with intent to endanger life requires a different personality altogether.' Jago slipped back into barrister mode without realising it.

'I'm not getting at anything,' Trenow snapped and then subsided. 'I'm sorry. It's just this bloody village drives me crazy. Everyone obviously walks round with their eyes and ears firmly closed.'

'It's a shame they don't keep their mouths closed more often and do the job properly,' Olivia observed with feeling.

'Oh they do where I'm concerned, believe me.' Trenow managed a wry grin.

'I remember Rocky telling me that Penbarthans have a long history of sticking together. In the old days, apparently, it was hiding smugglers and wreckers from the excisemen. And today it's not answering detective's questions.' Jago thought back to their first case, when he was despairing of the close-knit community. Now, hopefully, he was part of it, but he knew he'd never be accepted to the extent Olivia was.

'And I can confirm that nothing's changed. People seem more concerned about the damage that's been done to the wonderful garden that was owned by much-loved locals for so many years than they do about any potential anti-second home sentiment,' Trenow said harshly. 'Or even a murder.'

Jago and Olivia stayed silent.

Trenow gave a heavy sigh. 'I need to establish that these incidents aren't all connected somehow. Local knowledge can be extremely useful in cases like this. So I was hoping that if you've already heard anything, you might share it with me.'

'We haven't.'

'And if you do?'

Jago ignored his question. 'I definitely think you need to establish the victim's identity first. Otherwise you could find yourself going down all sorts of rabbit holes.'

A buzzing sound came from the depths of Trenow's jacket pocket. He fumbled around for it and then looked at the screen with a sigh.

'It's Sam. I must be off.' He drained his cup and pushed his chair back. 'Keep me in the loop, won't you?'

* * *

'Fancy another drink?'

'Not really.' She looked at her watch. 'I've changed my mind. If we go home now, I'll have time to get changed and back into the village to go gleaning with Willow.'

She'd lost him again. 'What on earth is gleaning? I've seen the posters about it all over the village, but I still have no idea what it is.'

'You need to get with it, Jago.' She shook her head in mock despair. 'It's something Willow's got involved in organising. You know how the Bakehouse and the Waiting Rooms always give their leftover food to food banks? Well, it turns out that quite a few of the local farmers end up with crops that they can't sell to supermarkets for various, usually ridiculous reasons, just sitting in their fields, waiting to rot.'

'I quite like wonky veg.'

'But not everyone does, so the farmers allow volunteers to pick what's left, then it's collected and sent to food banks, hubs and community kitchens all over Cornwall.' Olivia brightened. 'It stops methane being introduced into the air by letting crops rot, limits food wastage and helps people living in food poverty.'

Jago looked serious. 'No wonder there's such growing resentment against those people who have second homes and treat Cornwall as a rich boys' playground, while thousands of locals are struggling to make ends meet.'

'Exactly. But there's stuff we can all do to help, and Willow has found her niche in organising the gleaning events and co-ordinating the collection of the crates. She's really cementing her role in the village and the wider community.'

'So who gets involved?' He grimaced. 'It's not just the great and the good of Penbartha, is it? Although, I can't imagine many of the ones I know being prepared to stand in a muddy field, picking cauliflowers in all weathers.'

She shook her head. 'You'd be surprised who gets involved, according to Willow. All sorts. And if we don't get a wriggle on, I'll be late.'

Realisation dawned, and Jago cursed himself for being so slow. 'Unwanted veggies aren't the only things you're hoping to glean today, are they?'

WHATSAPP PERSONAL MESSAGE

@VividInkVibes: U around m8?

@ScrumAndSoul: Got a match l@ter. Around b4 & after

@VividInkVibes: Can we meet?

@ScrumAndSoul: Sure. Wassup?

@VividInkVibes: Can't say here

@ScrumAndSoul: More trouble?

@VividInkVibes: Maybe. Big time. NGL

@ScrumAndSoul: FFS! Wot u done now?

@VividInkVibes: Not here

@ScrumAnd Soul: U at work?

@VividInkVibes: 👍

@ScrumAndSoul: Gimme 10

@VividInkVibes: 👍

12

Upstairs in her flat above the Waiting Rooms, Kitten was feeling slightly better. After just three days of mega dose steroids, she could already feel an improvement in her eyes and balance. It was a huge relief to know she wasn't going mad after all. She'd even treated herself to a bath for the first time in ages, having been scared she wouldn't be able to get out on her own. But now she was washed, dressed, had clean hair and was determined to make it down to the Waiting Rooms to see everyone and try and do a bit of work.

She walked carefully towards her bedroom, glimpsing herself in the mirror. Even her appearance had improved, the steroids lending a rosy flush to her previously grey face. Those little white pills really were like magic bullets. She decided to tidy her living area, as bending over now made her feel only slightly nauseous. Thankfully she tried to live by the motto she'd had framed in her first term at university, and now hung on her wall: CLUTTER SMOTHERS, SIMPLICITY BREATHES. Kitten may have been happy to wear outrageous outfits and wild combinations of jewellery, but in her home she craved order and peace.

After ten minutes of gentle tidying, everything was back in its place and she was exhausted. She contemplated going back to bed for a little rest and then decided to make herself some toast first. Her sense of taste was still a bit weird, but she had discovered a sudden liking for marmite. She was just forcing slices of bread into the toaster when her intercom buzzer went. Another of Rocky's suggestions months ago, to save unnecessary journeys up and down the steep stairs. It was one for which she was eternally grateful now she had become the queen of avoiding people she loved who might notice something was wrong and ask questions she didn't want to answer.

Kitten pressed the intercom button, praying it wouldn't be Rocky. She still couldn't face him and all his questions, and she was constantly pushing away thoughts of his arms around her, the way he kissed her and the fact that he was the only man who'd ever understood her. To her relief, a voice that was recognisable, and definitely not Rocky's, crackled through the speaker.

'Kitten! Can I just have a quick word? It's me, Ned. Ned Roscoe.'

'Of course, push the door. And come up.'

It sounded like a herd of elephants were running up the stairs, but just one rugby-playing 17-year-old appeared in the kitchen.

'Is everything okay, Ned?' She looked at him, clothed in his tracksuit, a heavy-looking rucksack slung over one shoulder, clearly on his way to a rugby match.

'Yeah, yeah, well no. Not really.' His already-handsome face crumpled. Despite his muscles, deep voice and designer stubble, he was still a kid. 'I need your advice. Please.'

Kitten's stomach turned. It wasn't very often she was asked for advice. By anyone. But Ned looked like he'd got the worries of the world on his shoulders, and she only knew of one surefire way to get teenage boys to relax. 'Toast?' she offered brightly.

His face lit up. 'Now you're talking. I'm starving.'

As far as Kitten could remember, Ned was always starving. 'Marmite? Peanut butter? Marmalade?'

'Ooh! Could I have peanut butter AND marmalade? Mum only lets me have one or the other.'

Kitten smiled. 'Of course you can. Just don't tell your mum.' She nodded towards the wooden island unit that divided the kitchen and living areas. 'Take a seat.'

Ned grabbed his water bottle from his rucksack, dropped the bag in the middle of the floor and sat at one of the stools, gazing round in admiration.

'Kitten, this place is SO cool! I've never been up here before.'

'Thank you. It's been a lot of hard work, mostly by Rocky, but I've done my bit too. Practically everything in here is reused, restored or upcycled.' She felt the spurt of pride she always did when someone complimented her home.

He shook his head in amazement. 'It's sick – I mean amazing! And you're so convenient for work – literally above the shop!'

'Yes, it comes with the job. And it was the only way I could afford to get my own place. You know what it's like round here.'

She followed his gaze as it moved round the room, seeing it through his eyes. What had once been the upstairs accommodation in the stationmaster's house, attached to the original station building, had been transformed from three cramped bedrooms and a tiny bathroom into a warm and inviting open-plan space with one bedroom and a quirky bathroom. Rocky had removed all the ceilings, leaving open wooden rafters to create height, and refitted the wooden floorboards with extra sound insulation to limit noise from the Waiting Rooms below. Kitten had chosen the earthy paint colours and the vintage mid-century furniture that they had rescued, repaired and restored together. The entire project had been done on a tiny budget, with Kitten matching Rocky in his Wombling abilities, and every piece of furniture told a story.

'What d'you call this style?' Ned fumbled for his words, interior design obviously not being his forté.

Kitten laughed, handed him a plate of thick slices of toast and then led the way to the living area and waved him towards the large squashy corner sofa with oak legs that she had rescued from a house clearance and then reupholstered in butterscotch velvet fabric with the help of one of the designer-makers who rented space in the Engine Shed. On the wall behind it was an eclectic mix of old silver frames containing photographs of the railway station staff over the years and several vintage rugs were scattered on the floorboards. She wasn't going to admit this to Ned, but she regarded them as family now and often spoke to them.

'I call it boho mid-century chic, but I don't know how anyone else would describe it.'

Ned's eyes widened, but he concentrated on eating his toast. 'I've no idea,' he admitted. 'But I really, really like it. Especially all the houseplants. I've never seen so many in one place.'

'They fill the gaps nicely and I prefer them to just stuff.' She smiled at his blatant attempts to avoid what he was really there for. 'And I discovered that cheese plants are really, really hard to kill. And very easy to propagate. So are spider plants, umbrella plants and those ferns.' She waved at the houseplants, hanging from the rafters, sitting in pots of all sorts on the floor, on stools and on the sides and then out of the two large arched windows overlooking the tree-lined walkway. 'They make me feel like I'm bringing the outside in and living in the treetops.'

'Cool.' He finished his toast and then licked his fingers. 'It's very, very… homely.'

Kitten smiled at the clumsy compliment and sat back in a leather armchair, worn by years of use and polished to a warm sheen. 'Thanks. And as much as I'd like to sit here with you all day, discussing the finer points of interior design, Ned, I don't think that's what you came round for.'

The part-boy, part-man reddened and then held his hands up in surrender. 'You're right.'

'So, spit it out.'

His mouth opened and closed a few times before he eventually managed to form the words. 'It's Alfie.'

Kitten blinked. She wasn't expecting that. Then again, Ned and Alfie had been mates since preschool, and she knew that this all-round talented, good-looking boy looked out for his skinny, arty friend. Her heart went out to him. 'What's the problem?'

'I'm worried he's got himself caught up in something.'

'What sort of something? At school? In the village?' Her mind spooled back to talking to Alfie at the Waiting Rooms the day Marcus Walker-Smith showed up. That same night several large cars had their tyres let down. She watched Ned fidget for a few seconds and then decided to put him out of his misery.

'Is Alfie involved in any of this anti-second homes stuff? The Tyre Extinguishers, perhaps?'

Relief flooded his open face. 'You know about that?'

'I put two and two together. And while I don't agree with what he did, and it could have had very dangerous consequences' – she recalled Sam's lecture at the time – 'I don't suppose it was Alfie's idea, was it?'

'No. But that's Alfie's problem. He's always been easily led, and he gets carried away. I think he may have gone too far this time.'

'What do you mean? There's more?' She leant forward.

He nodded. 'He's got a bandage on his hand. He said at first that he'd cut it, but when I asked some more, he finally admitted it was a burn.'

Kitten's stomached turned again, faster this time. 'He could have got that in the kitchen downstairs.' It sounded like a feeble explanation, even to Kitten.

Ned shook his head. 'He admitted he was at Gillan Cottage. The night it was set on fire.'

She drew in a deep breath. 'Okay. What else did he say?'

'Not much. He's scared what will happen if anyone finds out.'

'Who was he with?'

'He won't say.' Ned held her gaze. 'He said "snitches get stitches". Do you think I should go to the police?'

'No!' Kitten had inherited her Cornish grandmother's and mother's instinctive distrust of the police. *Although her mother seemed to be coming to terms with them since her relationship with Sam had blossomed.* She caught her breath. 'Not yet, anyway. Let me think.' She gazed out of the window for a moment and then turned back to him. 'Have you told anyone else? Your mum?'

'Shit no!' He subsided. 'Sorry, no. She wouldn't understand.'

'Do you think Alfie's told anyone else? His gran perhaps?'

He shook his head quickly. 'Don't think so. Things can be a bit...' He cast around for the right word. 'Tricky between him and his gran.'

Kitten buried her face in her hands, her mind whirring so fast she couldn't keep up with it. Pain was shooting through her head again.

'Kitten? Sorry, I need to get to my match.'

She pulled herself together and opened her eyes. Ned was heaving his bag onto his shoulder and just standing in front of her waiting for a response. 'Sure, sure. Can you leave it with me? I'll talk to Alfie.'

'Thanks so much, Kitten. I didn't like to ask, but I was hoping you'd say that.'

Kitten felt a familiar wave of exhaustion surge through her body. 'He's a good kid, and I like him. I want to help.'

'So, you'll catch up with him before he finishes his shift?'

She nodded.

'Kitten, are you okay? You've gone really pale. I forgot that Alfie said you had a bug. Sorry.'

'I'll be fine.' She shooed him out. 'And I promise I'll talk to Alfie. Now go and have a good game.'

And she locked the door behind him, set an alarm, swallowed some painkillers and crawled into bed.

* * *

Three hours later, Kitten made her way down to the Waiting Rooms. She'd slept well and woke feeling more human.

So much for getting any work done today. At this rate she'd just about make it for closing up. She walked round the side of the building to the platform which was full of families making the most of the late-afternoon sun. She waved at the faces she recognised as she headed inside. Thankfully, no one asked her how she was feeling. She wasn't sure how much longer she would get away with the 'bug' excuse, yet she wasn't prepared to tell anyone the truth until she had seen the neurologist and understood what lay ahead.

'Hi, Kitten!' Jasmine hailed her from behind the counter and then rushed across to greet her. 'Don't worry about coming into work now.' She pointed across the café to where Alfie was helping a skinny teenage girl, with cropped dark hair and the most amazing pair of spectacles Kitten had ever seen on a teenager, clear a table. 'Remember Mya Pascoe from the beach clean? She's on half-term break from sixth form college in Truro and is more than happy to pick up shifts here whenever we have any going.'

Kitten could have kissed her. 'Yes, I remember her. Is she good?'

Jasmine beamed. 'She's worked in coffee shops before, and she's great. And she's hit it off really well with Alfie. Two geeks together!'

'Well, if you're happy, I'm happy. I was worried we might be short-handed as Clemmie's away this week, but it looks as though you've got it sorted.'

'I wanted you not to feel as though you had to rush back before you're completely ready.'

Hot tears filled Kitten's eyes, and she blinked them away

rapidly. Jasmine was so kind and calm, and she never asked questions. *I'm so lucky to live here.*

Jasmine hugged her again. 'You go and grab a seat and let me get you a drink.'

Kitten glanced round the still-busy room. 'I'll go in the annex if that's okay? And can you do without Alfie for ten minutes?' She noticed the cocked eyebrow. 'Nothing to do with work. Peppermint tea, please.'

'Of course. I'll send him through with it.'

Kitten escaped into the annex and sat in the bay window of what would originally have been the downstairs front room of the stationmaster's house. After the success of the café when it opened, and the demand for an area in which village groups could meet in private had grown, it had been agreed they should knock through to extend the space. They were now cleverly divided by double sliding-pocket doors made of frosted glass, etched with a detailed outline of the old Victorian station. When the café was particularly busy, or hired for a big event, the doors could be opened to provide a large light-filled space, but today they were closed and the annex empty.

Since when had she, the rabble-rousing Kitten Polmere, defender of every cause known to the planet, become the person teenage boys came to for advice?

She didn't have long to go over what she needed to say to Alfie. He appeared with a tray holding a glass infuser teapot and a mug.

He placed it on the table and hovered in front of her for a moment, and she waved at him to sit down. He fiddled with the bandage on his right hand.

'That looks sore.'

Alfie immediately hid both hands beneath the table. 'It's fine.'

'Did you do it at work? Did you put it in the accident book?'

He wouldn't look at her. 'Er, no. It wasn't at work.'

She nodded. 'Can I ask how you did it then?'

'I'd rather not talk about it. It didn't happen here, so does it really matter?' His voice rose and his face reddened.

'Alfie.' Kitten put her hand on his arm. 'I'm trying to help.'

He snatched it away. 'I don't need help.'

'Don't you?'

He squeezed his eyes shut. 'No.' His voice was a whisper.

'Shall I tell you why I think you do?' She carried on. 'I think you've got yourself mixed up in something in the village, something to do with all this anti-second homes stuff, and it's got out of hand. Am I close?'

Silence.

'Alfie, am I close? Please talk to me. You can trust me.'

He didn't look up. 'Can I?'

'Of course you can. I want to help. I'm in no position to judge you after some of the things I've done in my time, in the name of worthy causes. You're a good lad, Alfie, and I hate to think of you being mixed up with something that's causing you harm.'

Still silence, and then Kitten realised tears were running down his face.

'It was just a laugh to begin with, nothing serious.'

'So what changed?'

Alfie sniffed loudly, wiping at his face. 'I was made to do stuff I didn't want to.'

'What sort of stuff?' Kitten grabbed his arm, in instant mother-tiger mode.

'Nothing weird.' He looked up at her with swollen eyes.

'Like what?'

'The fire at Gillan. Stuff before that, but that was the worst, I didn't want to do that.'

'So why did you?'

'This person saw Gran doing something and said if I didn't do as he said, they'd tell the cops, so I did what they wanted. Then when I said I'd had enough and wanted out, they said they'd grass us both up to the cops if I didn't carry on.'

Kitten could feel her concern growing. 'Who was this person?'

'I'm not sure. It was all done by messaging.' He looked up at her, his expression a mix of fear and shame.

'Have you really no idea?'

He shook his head, but Kitten wasn't sure she believed him. 'Who dressed your hand?'

'Gran.'

'Didn't she ask you about it?'

Another emotion crossed Alfie's face; one she couldn't identify. 'I told her I was messing about with fireworks.'

'And she believed you?'

'She's got a lot on her plate at the moment. I don't want her dragged into this.'

Kitten tried again. 'Were there other people involved in the fire at Gillan?'

He nodded. 'Yes, but I don't know who. We all wore masks and didn't talk.'

Kitten didn't believe him. 'Alfie, you do realise how serious this is, don't you?'

He leapt to his feet, his voice rising in fear. 'Of course I do, I'm not stupid! I've heard the gossip about the cops being at Gillan and that a private ambulance was there earlier. I do know what that means.' The mention of a private ambulance was news to Kitten. She hadn't been keeping up with the village grapevine properly since she'd felt so ill. 'Don't you think that I've worked out that there may have been more than just a few buildings in the garden that whoever it was wanted burned? If someone died in that fire, the cops are gonna be crawling all over the village, and being seen with a bandaged hand is going to land me straight in it.' He collapsed back onto his chair and buried his face in his hands. 'What am I going to do? Gran's gonna kill me.' His voice rose. 'Oh, Kitten, I'm gonna be in such deep shit!'

13

'I really needed this today.' Louisa stretched her back and arms as she unbent from stooping to slice a head of cauliflower from its stem and tossed it into the hessian sack at her feet.

'Really?' Olivia groaned as she uncurled her own spine and stood, ankle-deep in mud, in a mizzle-drenched field near Hayle. In the forty minutes it had taken to get there by minibus the weather had worsened steadily, and there was no sign of improvement. She looked around at the rows and rows of cauliflowers behind her that had now been harvested of their crops by the twenty or so waterproof-clad volunteers surrounding them, armed with sharp knives, sacks and wooden crates. 'Even in this weather?'

'Absolutely!' Louisa declared. 'I needed to get outside and do something practical. The fact that we're doing something good for the planet and people at the same time makes it even better.'

'It certainly does! I've met so many people since I joined the gleaning group.' Another woman with her hair in rat's tails and a huge smile on her face spoke up. 'It's very sociable.'

'And you really do meet all sorts.' An elderly man wiped the mizzle from his spectacles with a cotton handkerchief, sighed at the misty mess he'd created on the lenses and put them back on. 'We were gleaning on the Roseland last weekend, weren't we, Lou? And there were some very interesting volunteers there.'

Louisa sighed. 'That's one word for them. I usually find gleaning good for my mental health. But not last week.'

Olivia's ears pricked up.

'It all turned a bit political,' Ron explained. 'This new guy turned up and kept spouting about how it's all the government's fault that folks are having to take matters into their own hands over so many issues.'

The smiley woman with the wet hair groaned. 'He really wanted us to recognise that he knew his facts and figures about the exact number of tonnes of food wasted at farm level and how damaging that is for the environment, not to mention how appalling the levels of food poverty are in Cornwall. He gave off really bad vibes, and I don't think he was a good fit for our group all. Do you?'

'You're right, Ellen. And who knew that methane, the gas produced by rotting food, is so much more damaging than carbon dioxide?' Ron asked with a definite glint in his eye. 'I'm afraid I find people like that very hard work. Just because we may have one or two causes in common doesn't mean we're going to agree on everything, or that one cause is more important than any other. Life isn't that black and white, so why can't we just all do our bit and try to live in harmony?'

Olivia decided she liked him.

'It was when he started on about second homes that he rubbed me up the wrong way,' Louisa confessed. 'Did he really think we don't get the irony of driving past all those fancy holiday homes while we're collecting volunteers to glean food for locals who can't afford to put food on their tables now the seasonal work is at an end and the fuel bills are going up? I get enough of that at home. Did he really need to mansplain it all to us?' She stopped herself. 'Sorry, Ron. No offence.'

'Oh, none taken, my dear. I found him quite abrasive, too. Some people just see things in black and white, with no shades of grey in between. Sadly, life's not like that.' Ron smiled kindly. 'Oh look, here comes Willow. Time for refreshments. We'll be back to put everything into crates '

He and Ellen wandered off towards the Bakehouse van while Olivia and Louisa stayed behind to cut the last few vegetables. The Cornish mizzle, which had got heavier and heavier over the last two hours, had now been joined by a thickening mist making it hard to see, but the sound of chatter and laughter of the other gleaners carried through the air as they gathered round the van.

Olivia wiped the water from her face. 'This weather drives me crazy.'

'That's what waterproofs are for.' Louisa laughed. 'Those years in New York made you soft.'

Olivia felt a stab of guilt. There was no way she was as committed to some of these local causes as other people were. Would she really be standing in a muddy field in this weather if she wasn't after information? *Does that make me a bad person? Or is it okay that I do my bit in other ways, ways I'm more comfortable with? Wasn't there room for all kinds?*

'I think you may be right,' she admitted. 'This mizzle was the one thing I didn't miss when I was living there.'

Louisa shrugged. 'I'm used to it.' She waved her scarily sharp gleaning knife in the direction of unharvested crops. 'Anything that gets me away from Finn and all his moaning is fine by me at the moment.'

Olivia seized her moment. She'd wanted to get Louisa on her own, and now was her chance. 'That doesn't sound good.'

Louisa sliced through another stem of cauliflower with a vicious stab. 'Don't get me started. He's becoming impossible to live with. All he does is go on and on about how the second-homers have ruined our lives and how he's having to work so many extra hours to help pay for my mum's care home fees until we can sell her house. And when he's not at work, he's out at his meetings.'

Olivia searched her memory, wondering if she'd ever heard that Finn was an addict of some kind. All she could summon up was a vision of a handsome, cheerful electrician who played rugby with Rocky and was always happy to help out if he needed to on site. 'Meetings?'

'Your guess is as good as mine.' Louisa sliced at a cauliflower plant. 'He's always rushing off to something or another. I reckon they meet under the guise of one cause, which is probably worthy, but end up discussing other ones which may not be so good. That's probably where he is now.'

'Do you ever go to them?'

'No. I'm the enemy as far as a lot of them are concerned.' She hacked at the leaves. 'Even though they know what our credentials are for taking on holiday lets. They're blind to the very fact that these owners are letting the houses out and bringing in more people to our shops, giving year-round work to local housekeepers and so on, is helping the local economy.'

Olivia frowned. 'We can't pretend that Cornwall's economy doesn't depend heavily on the tourist industry. Doesn't it support something like one in five jobs?'

'At least. And yes, it's not perfect, but we're doing our best.' Louisa emptied her hessian sack full of cauliflowers into a wicker crate and packed them carefully. 'The FHO lot are living in some sort of rose-tinted past, and we need to be more realistic. Life changes, and we need to look for a way forward, not backwards.'

Olivia nodded. 'Look, Louisa, I'm not going to the police with what you might say, but was Finn involved in any of the anti-second homes stuff that's been going on in Penbartha? The deflated tyres or the stickers?'

Louisa busied herself with another sack of cauliflowers. 'I

didn't realise it at the time, but yes, I think he might have been. After that last trustees' meeting I went home upset, because of what had been said to me, and do you know what he did? He laughed at me and said that I was as bad as Rafe Burrows.'

Olivia winced. She'd known Finn all her life, and this was a side of him she wasn't aware of. *Why couldn't people just be straightforward?* 'That wasn't very nice. And it's certainly not true.'

Louisa sniffed. 'Thank you. But Finn has got it into his head that people who own second homes in Cornwall have caused all our personal financial problems. And don't even mention the estate agents. Not being able to sell my mum's home in order to pay her care fees is crippling us. Finn needs to blame someone, and unfortunately he's found a group of people who are happy to fan the flames of hate.'

'So, what makes you think he might have been involved with the village incidents?'

Louisa gave her a look. 'When you've been married for as long as I have, you get feelings about the things your partner does. I think kids were responsible for the tyres and probably took it on themselves to do that. I reckon the stickers were a more organised campaign. They needed access to graphic design software, materials and printers and so on.'

'What about the fires at Gillan Cottage?'

She shook her head. 'Finn's very good at avoiding trouble. He was late home that night because he'd been helping a mate with an electrical fault. And then was messaging on his phone for a while after that. But he definitely didn't come home with any burns, or smelling of smoke.'

'Did you ask him who he was messaging?'

'He said it was the mate with the tricky electrics problem. They were still running checks, or something.'

'Did you believe him?'

She hunched back over the crate. 'I didn't pay him much attention. I was still angry with him for saying what he did after the trustees' meeting, and I was trying to get on top of my accounts.'

Olivia emptied another sack of cauliflowers into a new crate and stacked them neatly. 'So, do you think he was involved in the organisation of the fires, even if not actually setting them?'

Louisa started to cry. 'What does that say about me? That I think my husband is capable of arson?' She scrubbed at her face with a very soggy tissue. 'I don't want to say anything else.'

Olivia rubbed her back, sympathetically. 'I understand. You end up second-guessing everything, and it's not nice. Can I ask you just one more question?'

Louisa gave a teary smile. 'Just one.'

'Have you any idea who else is in the group?'

She shrugged. 'Your guess is as good as mine. I have my suspicions.'

'Care to share?'

'I'd put money on Caroline Pellow being involved. She's always had a problem with my business, and it's got worse recently. She just glares at me and cuts me dead. And some of her old cronies are just as bad. Perhaps some of the youngsters? But most people in the village aren't interested, from what I can make out, and want to get on with their own lives.' Her face hardened and Olivia could see the cogs turning in her brain, processing her thoughts. 'But I'm going to find out exactly what Finn's been up to. This has got to stop. We need to pull together, like we used to.' Her face crumpled, and the tears began to fall again. 'All I know is that Penbartha isn't a very nice place to live or work at the moment.'

***

'The cauliflowers in the field we were harvesting were too small for the supermarkets to sell, but the perfect size for single people or couples. I've just dropped a basket in the church porch so people can help themselves in the morning and have cauliflower cheese for Sunday lunch.' Olivia gave Jago a brief run down on her gleaning activities.

'I didn't know that Cornwall is the cauliflower capital of the UK.'

'Well, now you do.' Olivia wrinkled her nose. 'I don't think I want to see, or smell, another one for a while though.'

'Well you certainly smell better after your bath,' Jago commented as she snuggled up to him on the sofa, dressed in her pyjamas and dressing gown. They had closed the shutters against the wet night and were relishing the warmth from the wood burner. All three dogs were competing for top spot in front of the fire. 'Do you feel better?'

'I'm not sure. There's something seriously wrong if a so-called civilised society can't make sure that all the food it produces is actually used to feed the people who live there, rather than being left to rot in the ground while people go hungry. And that's before we start on the environmental impact.' She gave Jago a sideways glance. 'Don't look at me like that, Jago Trevithick. I'm sure most people would be horrified if they knew.'

'I'm sure they would. And I'm also sure that Willow and Louisa and all the other people you met today, and no doubt exchanged numbers with and will meet again, are doing everything they can to spread the word and get more support.' He dropped a kiss on her damp hair. 'I think we should concentrate on what we're best at, don't you?'

'Well, there weren't that many Penbarthans gleaning today, so my resources were limited. Willow thought it was because we had to go over to Hayle even though transport's always provided, but Louisa reckons there was some sort of unofficial anti-second homes meeting taking place in the village this afternoon.'

'Did she have any evidence to support that?'

Olivia frowned at him and then recounted their conversation, describing how Louisa's distrust of her husband grew as she talked about him. 'I wasn't cross-examining her, Jago. It was almost like she was seeing her marriage slowly crumble in front of her eyes as she put two and two together.' She nibbled at a nail on her right hand. 'It was horrible.'

'That must have been hard for her.' Jago patted her leg gently. 'Perhaps she's been ignoring the signs that all's not good for a while and this has just brought it into focus.'

'But what's he playing at? Louisa's got enough on her plate as it is, without this to worry about.'

'Who knows? But it looks like we've learnt at least one thing.'

'It does?' Olivia peered up at him. 'What's that?'

'From what Louisa told you, it sounds as though the majority of villagers *aren't* in league with the FHO lot and are busy working and getting on with their lives, leaving the older ones who view the past with rose-tinted spectacles and the youngsters, who have to be angry about something, to make up most of this group. Does that make you feel a little better?'

Olivia thought for a moment and then couldn't keep the hope out of her voice. 'Yes, it does. Because I hate to think of Penbartha being so full of hate and resentment.'

'Which takes us back to Caroline and her coven.' Jago sighed. 'But I still can't believe she's the main force behind everything that's going on. It just doesn't feel right.' He reached out a foot to stroke Steren's tummy. 'I really need to talk to Rafe Burrows about whatever game he was playing with the For Sale board at Gillan. I can't put it off any longer.'

Olivia shuddered. 'Rather you than me. I can't even look at that man without my blood pressure going off the scale.' She went back to nibbling her nail. 'And I'm really dreading the can of worms Louisa may be opening when she starts asking Finn questions.'

14

Jago waited for the Monday morning rush-hour traffic on the A39 to subside before he drove to Truro, still debating with himself the best way to go about his morning's self-imposed task. He parked near the quay and walked up the hill to a wide street lined with handsome Georgian residential townhouses built of luxurious Bath stone and designed to reflect the status of families who had gown rich from tin mining. His mind briefly returned to Tresillian, which had been built by a mine captain as a symbol of his wealth and success. These much grander residences had been built for the mine owners themselves, and the street was still regarded as one of the finest in Britain. The fact that they were still standing was testament to their solid construction, but unfortunately most of them were no longer family homes and had been converted into offices.

Two minutes later he stood in front of Elite Aesthetics, an attractive double-fronted building with a solidly built stone portico above the glossy black front door. He and Olivia had studied the website together the night before, her eyes growing rounder and rounder as she read out the descriptions of every non-surgical beauty procedure, each one sounding more barbaric than the last. In the end she had declared that he would achieve far more on his own, suggesting that if he dressed appropriately and stuck to their script, he would soon have Amanda Burrows, co-owner of Elite Aesthetics and wife of Rafe, eating out of his hand. Jago wasn't sure he liked the idea of that. He was used to being valued for his abilities rather than his looks, but Olivia had dismissed his concerns, muttering darkly about being welcome to her world, so he'd reluctantly agreed.

Trenow had been in touch to say that Rafe was still not answering his calls, and his wife had confirmed that he was away on business. The fact that Trenow had not been to see Amanda to ask, in his opinion, some vital questions, riled Jago, so he and Olivia had decided to take the matter into their own hands. And now, here he was, on her clinic doorstep, by himself.

Taking a deep breath, he pressed the bell. And waited. No reply. He pressed it again. Then again.

Eventually, he heard high heels clicking down a stone floor, and the front door was thrown open by a tall, glamorous woman, wearing very tight-fitting clothes of various shades of white and cream, and looking like she was off the cover of one of the lifestyle magazines he saw at the dentists.

'We're not open,' she snapped and pointed at her clothes to prove her point. Then glanced backwards to the door at the end of the hallway.

'I'm terribly sorry.' Jago used his most formal court voice, and it did the trick. Her head snapped back round. She looked him up and down, and he was suddenly was very glad that he'd taken Olivia's advice and was wearing smart navy blue chinos, a striped shirt, his best waxed jacket and Chelsea boots. Not his usual jeans and quarter-zip. 'Are you Amanda Burrows? I wanted to chat to you about something.'

Her eyes lit up, and she opened the door so he could join her in the vestibule, which was tastefully decorated in a way that was obviously meant to impress potential clients. It smelled like a mixture of the dentist and the beauty halls of the London department stores he only ever walked through to get to his preferred destination. Usually the book department.

'I am, yes. What can I help you with? Would you like to know more about the services we offer? Jawline contouring, wrinkle removal and hair restoration are the most popular treatments among our gentlemen clients at the moment.'

Jago swallowed and silently cursed Olivia for abandoning him on such unfamiliar territory.

'Although, there's nothing wrong with your hair or your jawline. Quite the silver fox, aren't you?' She flashed him a smile and continued to study his face. 'You could probably do with some Botox here, here and here.' She ran cool, manicured fingers over his forehead, round his eyes and between his eyebrows, and then declared. 'You'd look so much more youthful with fewer frown lines.'

He froze at her touch, remembering a throwaway remark Olivia had made to him about frowning when they first met. Then he pulled himself together and decided to play Amanda at her own game. 'I've never thought about it.' He appeared to give the idea serious consideration. 'Is it painful?'

Amanda laughed lightly. 'Didn't anyone ever tell you that you have to suffer to be beautiful?' She flicked her hair from her bony shoulders. 'Look at me. Isn't it worth it?'

Jago shot her a quick glance. For all her tweakments and non-surgical treatments, she looked harsh and artificial. A vision of Olivia, with her glowing skin, natural dark ringlets and incredible eyes, make-up free and clad in her running gear or usual outfit of black skinny jeans and a vintage Liberty shirt, floated into his mind. There was no comparison. Then he tried to imagine Amanda gleaning for leftover vegetables in a wet and muddy Cornish field and coming home aching but happy. And failed.

Amanda mistakenly took the smile that lifted the corner of his mouth as confirmation of her question and moved closer. 'See.

But if you don't fancy it, do you have a girlfriend?' She corrected herself quickly. 'A partner? What about treating them?'

Jago took a step backwards. 'I don't think my partner would be that impressed if I suggested she might need it.'

Amanda smiled knowingly. 'Oh, she's one of those, is she? When we moved here from West Sussex eight years ago, women in this part of Cornwall didn't make any effort with their appearance at all; probably because there was no one to impress. So I opened this clinic and worked on empowering them to do it for themselves, and it took off like a rocket. You partner should try it.'

'I'm afraid she spends most of her days either on building sites or running the coastal path. She's quite empowered enough, thank you.'

Amanda's lip curled in a dainty fashion, and she moved closer. 'Oh dear. And I suppose she reckons that having bagged one of the best-looking men in Cornwall, she doesn't need to make an effort?' She shook her head. 'That never ends well in my experience.'

Jago took another step backwards, desperately trying to think of a way to change the subject, but keep her talking. He needn't have worried. It looked like Amanda was happy to chat.

'Are you local?' She fixed him with what she obviously thought was her best smile, even though most of her face didn't move, and twirled a piece of blonde hair round her finger.

'Penbartha. About six miles from here, on the way to Falmouth.' He was met with a blank look, so decided to jog her memory. 'There's a nice little pub there, the Ship Inn?'

Amanda looked like she was attempting a frown, but her face didn't move much in that direction either. 'Is that the place where we had our cars vandalised?'

'Surely not?' He pretended to look shocked.

'It was. And very inconvenient.'

'Did you ever find out who was responsible?'

She shrugged. 'It was some local hooligans probably. People who are jealous of our success and want to spoil what we've worked hard for. We were only there because we couldn't get into any of the Falmouth restaurants we like, and my husband's friend Marcus had been told about the village pub.'

'How many cars were damaged?'

'Four. There were four couples, and we agreed to make our own ways. It was only the tyres that were deflated, but that's not the point. Have you any idea how hard it is to get a cab to pick you up from a backwater like that? And they did leave very helpful notices on the windscreen telling us what they'd done.' She gave Jago a sly look. 'We forgot to tell the police that bit. Oops.'

Oops indeed! 'Were the police helpful?'

'Of course not.' Amanda attempted another frown. 'We haven't heard anything. I suppose they have bigger fish to fry, but my husband does like that village for some reason. He's always trying to get people in the better houses there to talk to him. He's a very successful property-buying agent.'

Jago decided to take a risk. 'I live on the creek in that village.'

She perked up again. 'My husband says there are some fabulous houses there. You should speak to him.'

'I wouldn't mind a quick word with him.' He flashed a smile back at her. *Two could play at that game.* 'Business, you know.'

'He'd love that. It's a highly sought after location. He'd find a buyer for you, no problem. Probably someone from London who's prepared to pay enough that you could afford to move to Rock or Padstow. That's the dream, isn't it?'

More like Olivia's worst nightmare. 'Is he around?'

'Afraid not.' She moved closer again. 'He's away on a working holiday at St Wenna's golf resort, near Plymouth. Do you know it?'

Jago shook his head. 'I don't play.' There was no way he was going to apologise for that.

'Never mind. You could always take it up. It's a fabulous networking tool. Anyway, Rafe – that's my husband – is away with a load of industry professionals from London. You'd be amazed at how much business is done on the golf course. He'll probably come back with a list of purchasers who'd be interested in your place.'

'Is there any way of getting in touch with him?'

'Not while he's away. There's a kind of embargo on making calls. None of us wives have heard from any of the men. Juliet, the friend who's married to the guy who told us about the pub, went back to London after staying with us for a week, and when I spoke to her last night she hadn't heard anything from her hubs either.'

'Is that usual?'

'Yes.' There was a definite glint in her eye. 'Rafe left Thursday, the boys went off to a CCF camp with school on Friday and Juliet went back to London. So I'm having a few days of me-time.'

'When's Rafe due back?'

'Tomorrow, I think. Maybe tonight?' She glanced backwards. 'Give me your business card and I'll get him to call you.'

Jago patted at his jacket. 'I haven't got any with me, sorry.' He didn't explain that he had never owned a business card in his life.

She tutted at him and reached for a card and pen from the slim console table in the vestibule. She scribbled on the back of it and then handed it over.

'That's my card, with my direct line so you've got my number if you change your mind about booking a treatment for either you or your partner. And I've written Rafe's on the back. But like I say, don't even bother to call him until tomorrow at the earliest.'

Jago pocketed the card and turned to go, keen to leave before she asked any more questions. 'Thanks for your help.'

'Any time.' She held out her hand. 'You didn't tell me your name. I'm Amanda.'

'James.' He automatically reverted to the anglicised version of his name; the one he always used in court.

A door suddenly banged and a man, dressed in work gear and carrying a huge tool box, stormed down the hallway from the back of the building towards them, his face red with fury and glaring at Amanda.

'I haven't got time to hang around waiting for you, while you flirt with half of Cornwall. Some of us have jobs to get to.'

She caught hold of his fleece with a tinkling laugh. 'Don't be like that. It was business.'

'Yeah. Sounded like it.' The man didn't even bother looking at Jago. 'I have to go, Amanda.'

'Please!' But he was not to be placated. He wrenched his arm away from her, shrugging out of his fleece, which fell to the floor as he strode off.

Jago reached down to pick it up and handed it to Amanda. 'Will he come back for it, or do you want me to follow him?'

She shook her head. 'He'll be back. He just needs time to cool down.' She took the fleece and smoothed it out as she held it, so the logo on the back was visible. And while Jago couldn't make out the design itself, the name of the company was clear: Nankivell Electrical Contractors.

* * *

'How did you not recognise him?' Olivia was alternating between laughing at Jago's obvious embarrassment over his encounter with Amanda Burrows and frustration at his observational skills.

Jago had driven straight from Elite Aesthetics to Olivia's studio on the mezzanine floor of the Goods Shed, where he had recounted the entire exchange. Olivia was sitting at her desk surrounded by the usual piles of paperwork, a detailed drawing of what looked to Jago like a huge orangery spread out on her 1920s Bauhaus architect's wooden drawing table. It had been a twenty-first birthday gift from her godparents, and it now took pride of place in her studio. Jago perched on the matching swivel chair and let her laugh.

'In my defence, I wasn't expecting anyone else to be there, and I'm not sure I've ever seen Finn Nankivell at anything but a distance.'

'And does my learned friend think he was there in his professional capacity, or do you reckon it was overtime of a more leisurely sort?'

He laughed. And not for the first time thought that Olivia was wasted in her chosen profession and could have enjoyed a stellar career at the bar. 'Well, let's just say I don't think you or I have ever spoken to a tradesman in that tone. It suggested a certain level of intimacy.'

'What a cheating bastard! Poor Louisa. It looks like her suspicions about Finn were spot on, but not in the right way. Do you think he could be using all the FHO stuff as a cover for his relationship with Amanda?'

'Possibly, but how on earth do Amanda Burrows and Finn Nankivell know each other? Didn't Louisa tell us that Finn hated Rafe Burrows? Perhaps Finn's getting his revenge on Rafe in a more personal way.' Jago groaned. 'Talk about making things complicated!'

He and Olivia exchanged a rueful look, then he pulled himself together. 'I guess that's what we have to find out next. I'm not at all comfortable with interfering in Louisa's marriage, but if we're able to rule Finn out of the serious FHO stuff, we can concentrate our efforts elsewhere. Can I leave Finn Nankivell to you, if you don't mind?'

Olivia sighed. 'Okay. I'll check Rocky's schedule and find out when he's next working on one of our projects.' Her gaze rested on her beloved drawing board, and her dark eyes lit up. 'In fact, I think I might know exactly where he'll be this week.'

They moved to the sofa and discussed ways to approach Finn, throwing ideas backwards and forwards like a game of mental ping-pong. Jago realised he was thoroughly enjoying himself, even though they were discussing serious issues. It reminded him of the hours he'd spent with his oldest and greatest friend and colleague, Maeve Kelly, in their early days as Treasury Juniors, with the added bonus of being with the woman he loved and wanted to spend the rest of his life with. His thoughts jumped to the enormous elephant that seemed to follow him from room to room these days. Their impending wedding.

He cleared his throat and Olivia threw him a look. 'Are you about to make a speech?'

'No.' He spoke more harshly than he'd intended to. 'I just wanted to talk to you about something.'

'Sounds ominous.' Her faced creased with worry. 'Is everything okay?'

He caught hold of her hand. 'Everything's fine. I was just thinking how much I love you.'

'What?' The look of surprise on her lovely face made him curse himself. Despite his best intentions, he still didn't tell her enough. 'What's brought that on? What haven't you told me?'

'Nothing. Can't a man tell his fiancée that he loves her once in a while?'

'You told me back in June. It's the end of October now. You don't want to start repeating yourself too often. It might get boring.' She started to laugh, a deep musical sound that made him laugh too.

'We need to talk about—'

The studio door burst open and a tall, skinny whirlwind

practically fell into the room, sobbing loudly, closely followed by an equally distressed-looking Alice. While Jago was pretty sure Alice's distress was caused by the other woman's flagrant breach of her rules about non-members making appointments to see any of trustees, he failed to even recognise the offender.

Olivia jumped to her feet. 'Caroline, whatever's the matter?'

She stood in front of them, her hair wild and her bony shoulders heaving as she tried to control her breathing. Then just as she'd calmed down another wave of emotion overtook her, and she burst into noisy tears.

'I need your help,' she wailed. 'My Alfie's been arrested. For murder.'

15

'No I don't want a cup of bloody tea. I want you to help my grandson!'

Any hope that Olivia had that Caroline's shock would soften her harsh tongue had been very short lived.

'The two aren't mutually exclusive, Caroline. I think Alice is offering us all a hot drink to give us time to calm down and collect our thoughts.' Jago spoke firmly.

Thank God he's here. Olivia's head was in such a spin, she couldn't even form her words, never mind say them. *There was no way that lovely, gentle Alfie could be guilty of such a horrendous crime. What the hell was Trenow thinking?*

Alice recovered herself quickly and trotted off to make the tea. Caroline sank onto the sofa, buried her head in her hands and continued to veer between sobs and rage as she poured out the sorry tale of Alfie's arrest. Olivia sat beside her, patting her back every now and then. To her amazement, Caroline didn't pull away, just carried on sniffing into her tissue.

'Is it even possible to arrest someone for murder if the victim's identity hasn't been established?' Olivia whispered to Jago.

'Yes. Unfortunately, the legal definition of murder doesn't require the victim to be identified,' he whispered back. 'But the lack of an identity can make it harder to secure a jury conviction for various reasons. So my bet is, the police will be pulling out all the stops to find out who he is.'

'Rather than looking for the actual killer.' Olivia let out a strangled cry. 'Alfie didn't do this, Jago. Trust me. My gut's telling me it wasn't him.'

'Your gut's usually right. I saw the victim too.' He reminded her. 'I agree with you.'

'We have to help him.'

Caroline lifted her head. 'Thank you.' Her voice was small and sounded broken. 'You're a kind girl, Olivia. Mollie and George would be proud of you.'

Tears rushed to Olivia's eyes. Any mention of her godparents sparked an emotional reaction, but this was praise indeed from someone like Caroline. Mollie and George had always spoken up for her, for reasons they never explained. *Perhaps there was more to Caroline Pellow than met the eye? And now there was more pressure on them than ever to help Alfie.*

Alice reappeared, bearing a tray with a teapot, milk jug and cups. Silence fell as she poured the tea and then retreated, clutching her own cup.

'Is Alfie entitled to an appropriate adult at the police station?' Olivia asked.

'Is he 18?'

Caroline nodded. 'Last month.'

'Then probably not. Unless he's classed as legally vulnerable. Is he?'

'No.'

'Could you represent him in his interview, Jago?' Olivia tried again. 'At least you'd be a familiar face. He must be so scared.' She spoke without thinking, and Caroline let out another wail.

'I could. In theory. I made sure I was qualified to do so after your brief run-in with DS Burridge two years ago.'

Olivia gaped at him. 'I thought you told him that you were qualified back then?'

His face reddened. 'I might have been a bit economical with the truth as far as the overenthusiastic DS Burridge was concerned, but it worked, didn't it? Believe it or not, as a King's Counsel, I'm not often called on for police station interviews, especially as I mainly prosecute. But in order to address that particular gap in my credentials, I made sure to obtain that qualification as soon as I returned to London.'

Why did he always lapse into lawyer speak when discussing the… law? Olivia bit back her sarcastic retort. 'So can you represent him, or not?'

'Caroline can instruct me informally and then I can take formal instructions from Alfie after I've chatted to him.'

Olivia turned to Caroline who now seemed to be in a complete daze. 'That's okay with you, isn't it?'

The older woman pulled herself together and turned anxious eyes on them. 'You'd do that. For Alfie? For us?'

'Of course we would.'

'We'll pay. Whatever it costs.'

Jago waved her offer away. 'Let's worry about that later, shall we? Shall I ring Detective Inspector Trenow and talk to him?'

Caroline's face soured. 'Is he that dark, lanky one who looks like his shirt could do with a good iron?'

'That's the one.' Olivia and Jago answered in unison. For a brief moment, all three of them smiled, united in their opinion of the policeman and in their belief in Alfie's innocence.

'Right, let me ring Trenow. If I know how the police operate, they won't be rushing to interview him yet. He'll be cooling his heels in a cell.' He intercepted Olivia's glare. 'Sorry, Caroline. I'll just find out what time they need me, and we can take things from there.'

***

An hour later, Jago and Caroline set off to the police station in Truro, and Olivia, in need of distraction, wandered out of her studio on the mezzanine floor of the Goods Shed. This level now housed five self-contained workspaces with glass partitions separating them from the landing, carefully designed to enable their occupants to soak up the creative atmosphere from the open space downstairs, while retaining privacy. There had previously been six workspaces, but no one had wanted to take on a murderer's office while the memories of his horrendous crimes were still fresh in people's minds. So Rocky had removed the dividing wall between two offices to create a large studio/office space which Olivia had stripped of every memory and made her own. The pale wood, glass and chrome furniture had been replaced with antique solid oak pieces and an old architect's plan chest took the place of his low glass coffee table. Rocky had even taken the walls back to the brick so, combined with the high ceilings, wooden trusses and Olivia's favourite upcycled GWR red fire bucket pendant lights, the space now had an authentic industrial vibe to it. She loved it.

Standing on the landing outside her studio, Olivia listened to the soft hum of background noise of people at work on the floor beneath her. The ground floor of the Goods Shed was where the creative, passionate and driven members who produced the dynamic and collaborative environment that she and her godfather had wanted to attract mostly worked.

Several more dedicated members were sat at their desks scattered throughout the workspace, and a dozen or so other members, who were taking their lunchbreak, were congregated on the sofas and armchairs grouped in clusters at the far end breakout area, separated by reclaimed galvanised metal water tanks planted with exotic ferns which acted as both physical and sound barriers from the more formal section of the workspace.

This area was where the inspiration and sharing of ideas among like-minded people flourished. She allowed herself a small smile at the thought of how happy and proud George would be if he were here today.

As usual, thinking about George brought tears to her eyes, and Olivia went back to her studio to occupy herself with work. That had always been her godparents' universal cure-all for emotional upsets, along with a cup of strong Cornish tea. She called Angus Webster, the planning department's conservation officer, for a final update on the Woodbridges' orangery and to confirm that Rocky and his men were now on site and rang off with a churning feeling in her stomach. Then she checked her mobile. Nothing from Jago or Caroline. *Did Caroline even have her number?* She chucked her reading glasses onto her desk and lay her head on her arms for a moment.

As if on cue, her mobile rang, and she snatched it up, squinting at the screen.

'Olive?' There were only two people in the world allowed to call her that, and only one had a female voice.

'Kitten?'

'Are you free?'

'Are you crying?'

There was a big sniff. 'Just a bit. I heard about Alfie. Can I come up?'

'Of course.'

Olivia met her at the door, gave her friend a big hug and then held her at arm's length. Kitten looked distraught, with red eyes and an even redder nose.

'Oh, Olive, I've let Alfie down so badly. I meant to talk to you about him, but I just…' She trailed off and went to perch on her swivel stool, swayed a bit and then changed her mind and practically fell onto the sofa.

'How are you feeling?' Olivia shut the door carefully and tried to distract her. 'That was a nasty bug you had. Are you sure you're over it now?'

Kitten avoided her gaze and fiddled with the pink tips of her braids. They were so pale now, the pink was hardly noticeable. She'd obviously not dyed them for a while, and she hadn't bothered with any eyeshadow, which usually was a perfect match for her hair. *She really must have been feeling bad.*

'I'm getting there, thanks. It's been a stinker.'

'Rocky told me you'd been keeping him at arm's length in case he caught it. And Cassie.'

'Well, there's no point in us all going down with it, when we're all so busy, is there?' She sat up straight. 'Anyway, I'm not here to talk about me. I can't believe they've arrested Alfie.' She turned anxious, amber eyes to Olivia. 'He didn't do it, Olive. You have to believe me.'

'I don't think he did it, either.'

Kitten grabbed hold of her hand. 'And you're usually pretty intuitive, aren't you?'

'Not always.' Olivia's stomach flooded with anxiety. 'I just hope I am this time.'

'He told me he was worried, you know.'

'Alfie?'

'Yes, Alfie. Who else would I be talking about? Well, actually, it was Ned who came to see me because he was worried Alfie was in trouble. So I spoke to Alfie and he told me what happened.' Kitten launched into her usual way of talking, diverting off at tangents, not mentioning specific names or details but repeating others, until Olivia's head was spinning.

'Slow down, please!' She finally begged. 'Stop!'

Kitten turned impatient eyes on her. 'What?'

'Start again, at the beginning, and go through it chronologically. And slowly.'

Kitten repeated the conversation she'd had with Alfie, in a loud and careful voice, as if she was talking to a child. Olivia sat and listened without interruption, her mind whirring as more and more pieces of the puzzle were thrown at her, adding to the pile that she still didn't know what to do with.

'So, Alfie admitted he'd been involved on the FHO stuff?'

'Yes.'

'And someone saw Caroline doing things she shouldn't and then blackmailed him into doing more?'

'Yes.'

'But he wouldn't tell you what?'

'Not exactly.'

Olivia gave her a look. 'And then they blackmailed him again into setting fires at Gillan?'

'Only in the garden.'

'But he wasn't alone.'

'No.'

'And he didn't know who any of them were? Or recognise any voices?'

'Not that he's saying.'

'And he has no idea who was blackmailing him?'

'No, but he did say that they knew quite a lot about him and his family, so he reckoned it could be someone local.' Kitten's face fell. 'It's not looking good, is it?'

'He's not exactly helping himself at the moment. He needs to be more open.'

'He also said that there was talk in the village about a private ambulance driving away from Gillan. Apparently the village grapevine is saying someone died.'

'But he definitely doesn't know anything about that?' Olivia winced.

Kitten exploded. 'Absolutely not! He's a kid, Olive. A sweet kid. Who wouldn't hurt a mouse. He only set the fires in the garden at Gillan because he was made to. He wouldn't have set fire to a house. You've seen how skinny he is, there's no way he'd have the strength to hurt anyone.' She peered at Olivia's face. 'Did someone die?'

Olivia tried, but failed, to keep her face expressionless. The vision of the dead body was still firmly imprinted on her mind, and she gulped.

'Shit.'

Olivia waited for a tsunami of emotion and anger to burst out of Kitten, but she just sat there, blinking and looking like she was searching for the right words.

'So what happens now?'

'Alfie's at the police station, being interviewed by Trenow. Jago's with him as his legal representative.'

Kitten relaxed a little. 'Thank God for that.'

She tried to manage her friend's expectations. 'Jago can't wave a magic wand. Alfie needs to be more forthcoming with him. And the police.'

'Do you think the police really would go for the easy option to secure a conviction and improve their statistics?' Her suspicion was back.

Olivia's mind went spiralling back to when she'd asked Jago that very question. And he'd told her about cases he'd been involved in where the police only investigated what suited them to build a case against a suspect that would stick; how sometimes the facts which pointed away from a suspect's guilt would be ignored or not properly examined; and how he'd come across plenty of occasions in his legal career where evidence that exonerated a suspect had gone undisclosed. Jago had gone on to assure her that he didn't think Trenow would charge a person with murder just to help his own statistics, but – and this was now Kitten's worry – he wasn't foolish enough to believe that his superiors wouldn't be putting him under pressure to get the case sorted.

But she didn't tell Kitten any of that. The girl who sat in front of her looked like she was about to topple off the sofa with worry and exhaustion. And she already had a fairly low opinion of the police, so it wouldn't help anything. Olivia decided to not really answer her question.

'I suppose a lot depends on the identity of the victim.'

Kitten's eyes widened. 'Don't they know who it is?'

'I'm not sure.' Olivia leaned forward. 'You mustn't repeat any of this.'

'Sure. Do you reckon the victim could be the person blackmailing Alfie? Because that wouldn't look good for Alfie, would it? It would make him the obvious culprit.'

Olivia closed her eyes. 'It could be just a coincidence.'

'Come off it, Olive. What are the chances of that?'

'Slim.'

'So we don't know the identity of the blackmailer or the victim. What we do know is that Alfie isn't the killer.'

Olivia stayed silent.

'Alfie isn't the killer, Olive. I swear he isn't. But we could have a blackmailer and a killer out there. Penbartha's turning into a place of intrigue and death again. And you know what that means, don't you?'

Olivia lifted her weary eyes.

'You need to find them, Olive. You and Jago. Because not only Alfie's future depends on it, the whole village's does.'

16

'How is being released under investigation different from being released on bail?' Olivia had barely got through the door from her early morning run the next day before her questions started.

Jago chewed on his toast, reliving the relief he'd felt when Trenow had reluctantly, but eventually, come to his decision and it had been agreed by his superior. He had got home at midnight and fallen into bed, thankful that once Olivia knew that Alfie was safely home with his grandmother, she had been prepared to leave the details until the morning.

'It's a less formal option. Basically, it means they haven't got sufficient evidence to charge him yet, and they require more time to investigate.'

'So, he's not in the clear yet?' Dark, anxious eyes watched him from the kitchen island as she prepared the dogs' breakfast.

'He could still be arrested and charged at a later date if sufficient evidence emerges. But until, or if, that happens, he's free to try and live his life as normal. And my job is to monitor the police investigation.'

'Poor Alfie.' Olivia put the dogs' bowls on the floor and gave then the signal to eat. 'How was he?'

'Terrified.' Jago gave her a brief run-through of everything that had been said at the police station, by both Alfie and Trenow.

'Well, it certainly sounds as though he told Trenow pretty much the same version of events as he gave Kitten. Isn't that a good sign?'

'Perhaps. I'm not sure that I entirely believe him when he says he doesn't know who the blackmailer is.' Jago munched on another piece of toast.

'Kitten says that Alfie reckoned he must be local in some way to know so much about him and his family. Rafe or Marcus could have been told all the family details by their sons, couldn't they? And then used it to frighten them?'

'Or Finn Nankivell could know it anyway, through Louisa and the village grapevine.'

They looked at each other. Olivia eventually broke the silence. 'What's the latest on the victim's identity?'

'Trenow's hoping they might hear more today. It's taken longer than they expected as they've had to go down the dental record route.'

Olivia winced and decided not to pursue that particular query. 'D'you reckon the killer and the blackmailer are the same person?'

Jago shrugged. 'Unlikely. But as soon as Trenow has an ID for the victim, he'll pull all the stops out. And Alfie is still his number one suspect for the murder.'

'So the clock's ticking?'

'Loudly.' Jago loaded his plate into the dishwasher, giving Olivia a pointed look as he did so, but she ignored him. 'I'm just amazed the village isn't abuzz with the news of Alfie's arrest.'

'Perhaps that tells you more about Caroline's usual role in village gossip. She's not going to want Alfie being the subject of the Penbartha grapevine, is she?'

Jago shook his head. 'Obviously not.' He closed the dishwasher. 'But who knows how long it will be before it gets out?'

'What can we do?'

'I'm going to try and track down Rafe Burrows. According to Amanda, he should be back from his golfing jolly today, so I'm going to see him before Trenow does and see what I find out from him.'

Olivia's eyes flashed. 'Well, good luck with that. While you're dealing with the delightful Rafe, I'm due on site at the Woodbridge's to check on their orangery. And I just happen to know that Finn Nankivell will be there to discuss first-fix with Rocky. So I might have a little chat with him.'

Jago swallowed. 'I know I don't need to say this, but tread carefully, won't you?'

'Always.' She dropped a kiss on his cheek as she walked past. 'Right, I'm going to jump in the shower and then go sleuthing.'

***

For the second time in two days, which was something of a record, Jago drove into Truro. This time he parked at the top end of Quay Street, so he wouldn't have to walk past Elite Aesthetics and risk being spotted by Amanda Burrows. The buildings here were as grand as those further down the hill; smart offices of solicitors, surveyors and upmarket estate agents. Burrows Prime Property Search fitted in perfectly; designed to appeal to the London-based house-hunter. There were no rows and rows of property details sandwiched between layers of plastic and hung on pieces of wire filling the windows. Instead, there was a large screen in the centre of the window with smaller digital picture frames each side showcasing the finest properties they had sourced for clients with beautiful photographic images and prosaic words about what these wonderful homes meant to the people who'd bought them.

Jago paused to look at the houses on show. There were no prices here, but he only had to look at the size and location of them to know that they were all at least seven figures. Okay, so they weren't exactly prices locals could afford, but he wondered how many, if any, were lived in year round. Only that would stop the slow hollowing out of the souls of many villages. He memorised a few of the details, took a deep breath and pushed open the chrome-framed glass door.

Once inside, he was surprised to see that only one of the three large glass desks, no doubt used for schmoozing their finest prospective clients, was occupied. A tall, almost ethereal-looking young woman, dressed in tailored trousers and a white shirt, with long red hair and wide-set green eyes, rose gracefully and wafted across the wooden floor to him. She reminded Jago of the women in the pre-Raphaelite paintings that Olivia was so fond of.

'Good morning.' She spoke so softly Jago had to lean forwards to hear her. 'How can I help you?'

Jago hesitated and took a step backwards. The insinuation was plain, even to him. He cleared his throat and gazed around the empty space until he'd regained his composure.

'You've got some fine properties in the window,' he replied, remembering to slip into the vocabulary all house hunters seemed to adopt as soon as they put their home on the market.

'Well, we do specialise in high-end properties. Homes that often appeal to the more discerning eye, often people who live in London or the home counties.' Once again, he found his appearance being appraised by a businesswoman in this street, and he didn't like the way it made him feel. 'I take it you're not local?'

Jago dodged the question. 'I've lived in London for years, but am looking to spend more time here, if I can find the right property.'

The green eyes brightened. 'Well you've come to the very best place for that. We're totally committed to finding the right property for the right person here at BPPS.' She held out a pale hand with long, delicate fingers. 'I'm Grace Evans, Senior Associate.'

He shook it, not daring to think how old the junior associates might be, if such a role existed. 'I'm James. I particularly like the look of that property on Restronguet Creek.'

Grace's whole face brightened. 'A very good choice, if I may say so. Obviously that's a property we sourced for another client, but if you come over to my desk, we can have a chat.'

Thirty seconds later Jago was sitting with Grace, a super-sized tablet in her hands, being asked all the requirements he might have for his future home. It seemed endless.

'You sound like you really enjoy your job.' He decided to get back to the purpose of his visit.

'Oh yes,' she gushed. 'I love meeting new people and helping them move to the home of their dreams. It's just so wonderful to help people feel confident and supported throughout their property journey. So, what else is on your list of must-haves? I need to hear what's really important to you so I can get as close to your perfect property as possible.'

Jago thought quickly. 'A large garden is fairly near the top of my list.'

Grace looked disappointed. 'Really? In our experience, most second-home owners prefer a garden that's low maintenance and easier to maintain.'

He sucked his teeth. 'I'm afraid a garden is non-negotiable. I can't be asking too much, can I? Lots of properties round here must have large gardens.'

Grace tapped her fingers on her iPad. 'That might not be possible in that price bracket. Are you prepared to go any higher? Two million plus, perhaps?'

Jago frowned. 'Only for the right property.'

Grace smiled brightly. 'That's what I'm here for. Particularly as many of the houses we eventually secure for our clients don't ever reach the open market.'

'Oh?'

Grace leant forward. 'Don't tell anyone, but many estate agents contact us for any ultra-keen buyers before they would ever think of listing a property online. Most high-end properties are shared only with a select inner circle of private brokers, industry contacts, or buying agents like Rafe.'

'So while the rest of the country's busy refreshing well-known property search engines, most deals are happening behind closed doors?' Jago was astonished. This was a whole new world.

'Exactly!' Grace beamed. 'When you come to a company like BPPS you're paying for access to Rafe's little black book of contacts and his vast network. He has excellent relationships with all the leading estate agents in the south west.'

'And you assist at all stages of the buying process?'

'Oh yes. Rafe provides strategic counsel throughout so we can ensure all our clients make informed and advantageous decisions.'

Like hell he does.

'And of course, discretion is paramount.'

'Of course.'

'But between you and me, some homes are taking longer to sell than they have for ten or fifteen years. You could be in a great bargaining position, if you're savvy.'

Very discreet.

'That sounds promising. Are you saying I could look at properties that are slightly out of my price bracket and you would put in a cheeky offer on my behalf?'

'You're always welcome to try. In fact, Rafe has been known to do that quite a lot recently, on behalf of his clients. And any saving we make is reflected in our fee, of course.'

Of course.

Jago peered over Grace's shoulder to a closed office door. 'Is Rafe in this morning?'

'Not yet.' The green eyes surveyed the empty desks. 'There was a big industry golf do over near Plymouth that went on for four days, can you believe? The boys should be back any time today.'

'That's a bit sexist and elitist, isn't it? Unless you play golf, Grace?'

'No, I don't, thank you. I'm nowhere near forty yet.' She laughed lightly. 'I was there for the weekend so I could get some networking done.' She shot him a secretive look. 'If you know what I mean?'

Jago didn't have a clue, but he nodded. 'So when did they all go?'

'Rafe, the boss, went straight from work on Thursday. The other two boys went on Friday evening. I held the fort here on Saturday and then went over to Plymouth in the evening, for the gala dinner. I left early yesterday morning to be back in time to open up. The rest will be in later today. When they've recovered, probably.'

'That's a lot to expect you to do, on your own, isn't it?'

'Rafe says I'm his right-hand woman. And the market's quiet at the moment, so I managed perfectly well.'

'Not many employees would be happy to stay behind while the boys go off on a golf jolly,' Jago observed. 'I hope Rafe realises how lucky he is to have you.'

A dreamy look crossed her face that even Jago recognised. 'Oh, he does. He's very good to me.'

'That's nice.' Jago winced. 'So, who was this event for?'

'Mainly estate agents, and buying agents, private brokers, surveyors. Like I said, networking is vital in this business. A lot of London agents attend as they're the ones who have clients who are looking for second homes and want to make contacts down here. It used to be a really lavish affair, but this time felt like a bit of a last hurrah, given all the changes to taxes on second homes that have been brought in.' Her face clouded over. 'It's a bit worrying, actually.'

'Do you work closely with any particular London agents?' Jago jumped on her words.

'We work with all the high-end London agents who are dedicated to helping clients fulfil their aspirations of living the Cornish lifestyle. They put them in touch with us and we do the rest.'

Jago smiled encouragingly. 'That sounds great. Just as a matter of interest, I bought my last London place through a guy called Marcus Walker… something or other. I know this is a complete shot in the dark, but do you know him by any chance?'

Grace beamed. 'It's a very small world! Marcus happens to be one of the agents who refers many clients to us.'

'So, are he and Rafe friends?'

'Oh, absolutely! In fact, they're such good friends that Marcus and his wife stayed with Rafe last week. Their boys are all at boarding school here.'

'Was Marcus at the golfing event?'

A frown creased Grace's pale face, and Jago decided she hadn't availed herself of any treatments offered by her boss's wife. *She probably gave Amanda as wide a berth as possible, for reasons that were becoming clearer by the minute.*

'I don't think I saw him, come to think of it. Although I was a bit pre-occupied with Rafe.' Her cheeks flushed.

'When did you last see Marcus? I have a friend who is looking for a property in Clapham and I thought I could connect them.'

Grace put her chin in her hand and tilted her head to one side while she thought. 'That's a great idea. Let's see. I definitely saw him last Wednesday, when they had a meeting in Rafe's office before they went off to view a property somewhere.'

Was that Gillan? 'But not since then?'

She shook her head. 'I guess he might have been called back to London. That can happen with these high-end property deals, if the boss is needed to smooth things over at the last minute. The customer is king, and all that…' She looked at Jago and then seemed to realise their conversation had gone off at a complete tangent. 'Right, do you want me to see if we have any more exclusive properties with larger gardens on our books?'

Jago looked at his watch. 'Please, if it won't take too long. I have a meeting in half an hour. I didn't expect to be here for so long, but it's been so interesting to meet you.' He gave his most charming smile.

She smiled back warmly as her fingers tapped away at the keyboard. 'Of course.'

'Ooh— wait a minute! Someone was telling me that a village called Penbartha is a good place to live. It's on a creek, isn't it?'

'There is, but unfortunately, the properties directly on the creek are rarely listed on the market, and although our local contacts usually grant us early access to properties in all stages of the listing process, I'm afraid there's nothing available there at the moment.' She smiled brightly. 'But there's a few here with the most wonderful waterside views. If you give me your email address, I can send them to you.'

Jago pulled his mobile out of his jacket pocket and waved it at her. 'Just airdrop them across to this number, would you please?'

She did as he asked and he got to his feet. 'Well thank you very much for all your help, Grace. It's been nice meeting you.'

'And you.' She handed him her business card. 'And now I've got your number, I'll be sure to send you any other properties with large gardens that I hear about. Of course you'll have to come in and sign a contract with us before we can take anything forward.' She gave him another smile. 'I really do hope we are the agents to help you find your new home here in Cornwall.'

'Thank you very much.' As Jago got to the door, Grace called him back. 'Actually you're not the first person to come in here asking about Marcus.'

'Really?' Jago didn't turn round. 'He's obviously a popular guy.'

'I don't think the other gentleman was after his property-selling skills. He was a bit rude, actually.'

'Oh?' As much as Jago wanted to beat a hasty retreat, he got the feeling that Grace had an enticing titbit for him. He turned back to her with a smile.

'He said he was from the police. Plain clothes, but he could have been anyone. And his shirt needed a good iron.'

'Didn't you ask to see his warrant card?' Jago couldn't help himself.

Grace pulled a face. 'Do you know how it easy to fake those things?"

'Not really. So what did he want?'

She shrugged. 'He wanted to know where Rafe was and I told him he was at an event and couldn't be disturbed. That's what he always tells us to say. I took his number and sent it on to Rafe.'

Jago nodded. 'What else did he want?'

'He was asking about Marcus. So I told him he was with Rafe. Which I thought he was.' She turned her green eyes on him. 'I hope I won't be in trouble for that, will I? If he really is the police?'

'I wouldn't worry about it. It's probably something and nothing. A traffic offence perhaps?'

'Thanks. That's what I thought. Remember, if there's anything at all I can do to help you, do get in touch.'

* * *

'I'm sure I saw Rafe's Range Rover coming down the hill as I walked back up to my car.' Jago waited for his heartrate to settle as he spoke to Olivia on his mobile. 'It was a closer call than I'd like.'

'And you didn't fancy sticking around and speaking to the bossman himself?' He could hear the teasing tone in her voice, even though the line wasn't great.

'I reckoned I'd got all the information I needed out of Grace. She hasn't seen Marcus since Wednesday, and he wasn't at the event in Plymouth, apparently. And as a bonus, I didn't get the impression Grace had any clue about Gillan Cottage being on the market.'

'But if she only works as a buying agent, why would she? Prestige Coastal Properties is a separate business, and perhaps Rafe kept it quiet.'

Jago checked in the rear-view mirror before he indicated to pull out. 'It didn't sound like Grace thought Rafe kept much from her.'

'Perhaps she's more discreet than you think,' Olivia teased. 'So do you reckon Rafe's having a bit of a thing with Grace?'

'I wouldn't be at all surprised.'

'Flippin' hell. Talk about living complicated lives. Rafe and Amanda Burrows really don't spoil a pair, do they?'

17

Olivia was so busy thinking about how best to approach talking to Finn Nankivell that she arrived at the drive to the Woodbridges' farmhouse without noticing anything about her journey. As she slowed down to cross the cattle grid, she opened the car window and breathed in deep lungfuls of fresh air, tinged with the woodsmoke she could just about make out drifting lazily from the house's stone chimneys. She drove slowly up the winding drive and parked next to Rocky's pick-up at the rear of the outbuildings. Climbing out of the car she could feel the cold nip of autumn in the air, despite the best efforts of the low sun, and she grabbed her fleece, plan tube and hard hat from the back seat before setting off in search of her business partner.

The Woodbridges' Grade II listed farmhouse stood at the top of the downs outside Penbartha and enjoyed the most amazing views over the surrounding rolling countryside and across to the creek and the Carrick Roads estuary beyond. The farm had been in the family for generations, and they'd all worked the land, but Keith and Theresa had handed over the farming reins to their eldest son and his wife. Unlike many farming families, it was the older generation who opted to stay in the main house while the younger ones built themselves a modern bungalow with all mod-cons on the site of an ugly grain store in a neighbouring field. With Olivia and Rocky's help, the senior Woodbridges were now completing a lifetime restoration of their once higgledy-piggledy house with the addition of a stunning green-oak orangery which, like the one at Tresillian, both honoured the past and embraced the future as well as giving them a much-needed open plan living space.

She spotted Rocky poring over a set of plans balanced on a pallet of reclaimed bricks alongside what was definitely the skeleton of an impressive orangery.

'Wow! It's coming on really quickly now, Rocky,' she enthused. With a bit of luck we'll be finished ahead of schedule.' She walked round the outside. 'Siting it here has squared the back of the house off perfectly and opened it up to be a really useable space.' She did a happy little jig. 'I'm so relieved the planning department was able to see how it was going to enhance the old building rather than detract from it. It's going to be amazing!'

He grunted. 'Keith was just saying he reckons we'll be doing more and more of this type of work, the way the property market's going. And it's true. People are staying in their houses and extending and improving rather than moving, with all the uncertainty in the property market and tax rises everywhere.'

Olivia stared at him. *This wasn't Rocky. He was always such positive, glass-half-full kind of guy.* 'But look on the bright side!' She tried to jolly him along. 'With a bit of luck that means more people will start retrofitting the homes they've got to make them more energy efficient and future proof.' She nudged him. 'That's what we want, isn't it?'

'Yeah, but I prefer working for people who are doing it for the right reasons, not just to save money on their fuel bills.'

'So do I, but with summers getting hotter, storms getting harsher and winters getting colder, if we're enabling people to live more sustainably and their houses to be more climate resilient, we're doing our bit, aren't we?'

'I suppose so. And I do like doing this kind of work for a change.' He pointed a dirty finger at the plans. 'It's like a giant Jenga game.'

'You were always far better than me at Jenga when we were kids. D'you remember?' She punched his arm gently, but he didn't smile. 'C'mon Rocky. This isn't like you. What's up?'

'Nothing.'

Olivia positioned herself between Rocky and the pallet of bricks and peered into his face. The sparkle she was used to seeing in the jet-black eyes had gone and his dark, piratical looks were definitely grumpy.

'Rocky.' She put her hand on his shoulder and spoke gently. 'I'm your best friend. Talk to me.' She spooled through all the reasons he might be upset and grabbed the most obvious one. 'Is it Kitten?'

He looked away and when he turned back, his expression was stricken. 'Who knows? I'm not even sure she's talking to me at the moment.'

Olivia thought quickly and checked her watch. 'Are the lads at lunch?'

He nodded. 'They've gone down into the village.'

'Right.' She caught hold of his arm, moved him out of sight of the farmhouse and pulled him down onto a low wall. They tossed their hard hats to one side and sat in silence, legs stretched out in front of them, gazing at the view below them.

She nudged him gently. 'So, what's going on with you and Kitten?'

He shrugged again. 'I haven't seen her at all since the beach clean, and not much before then. She said she wanted me to keep out of the way in case this bug she's had was infectious. She said she didn't want to be responsible for me catching man-flu.'

Olivia chuckled. 'I can just imagine her saying that.'

'But you had the bug too, and you're over it. Why isn't she?'

'I don't think it was the same bug. Mine was more of a heavy cold. Kitten's sounded much more like the proper flu.'

'So why is she struggling to shake it off?'

'Perhaps she's more run down than any of us realised? You know how Kitten always lives life at a hundred miles an hour.' Olivia felt a pang of guilt. 'And in her defence, she's probably stuck to Cassie's herbal cures. I felt so rough at one point I may have resorted to more conventional medicines.'

'What! You, a traitor to the old ways?' Rocky started to laugh. 'What would Cassie say, or Mollie?'

Olivia grimaced. 'I'm not sure Cassie's remedies are as potent as Mollie's. I don't think she's got her magic touch.'

He laughed again. 'You're probably right. Mollie's potions always did the trick, didn't they? Particularly the hangover ones. And we had our fair share of those.' They reminisced about some of their wilder exploits as teenagers, and then Olivia came clean.

'Jago was fed up of my snoring. So I took the road of least resistance, for the sake of domestic harmony.'

Rocky puffed out his cheeks, making his black curls dance against his cheeks. 'Why didn't I think of that?'

'Perhaps you're more polite than Jago?' She looked at him sideways.

'Or perhaps we're not honest enough with each other. Being polite hasn't got me very far, has it?'

He looked so crestfallen, Olivia put her arm round his shoulders. 'You need to talk to her, Rocky.'

'She's made it pretty clear she doesn't want to talk to me.'

'You two are as stubborn as each other! Do you want to be with Kitten, or not?'

His black eyes held hers. 'Of course I do.'

'And have you told her recently?'

'Like I said, she's not talking to me.'

'Okay. So when was the last time you told her you want to be with her?'

He scrunched up his face like a little boy. 'Er, not sure.'

Olivia sighed. 'Do you ever talk about the future? Make plans?'

He narrowed his eyes at her. 'Do you and Jago?'

She felt a stab of guilt, and then pushed it away. 'Don't change the subject. We're not talking about me and Jago. Do you and Kitten ever make plans about the future?'

'Er, no. We're usually both knackered by the time to see each other.'

'I know we all hang out together quite a bit, but do you ever go anywhere special, just the two of you?'

'Do you?' He was getting touchy now.

'When we're in London we go to the theatre and events like that. Sometimes we go to art galleries, but Jago's not too keen. But when we're here, not so much special stuff, no.' She groaned. 'God, we're as bad as each other!'

'You still do more than us,' Rocky admitted. 'We go to the rugby and down the pub. But that's about it. We're busy people.'

They lapsed into a thoughtful silence and then Rocky shifted position on the bricks.

'D'you reckon I should make more of an effort with Kitten? Make a grand gesture or something?'

'Good grief, no! She'd hate that. Why don't you just try talking to her? Tell her how you feel and that you want to spend the rest of your life with her. Do you?'

He went quiet. After a few minutes, Olivia elbowed him in the ribs. 'Rocky?'

He turned anguished eyes to her. 'Of course I do! But I'm scared that she doesn't feel the same way. Perhaps she thinks I'm too old for her, or too boring, or not clever enough? Or just not good enough?'

'Rocky Berryman! Never say that. Any woman would be lucky to have you.'

'So why won't she talk to me?'

Olivia glared at him, wondering how this man whom she loved like a brother could be so spectacularly dim at times. 'I'll make a suggestion, shall I? How about you go and see her, face to face, and ask her for yourself?'

'Hiya! Anyone about?'

Olivia hadn't expected to be so relieved to see Finn Nankivell appear round the corner of the farmhouse with the rest of Rocky's team. Having spent the last twenty minutes listening to her best friend confiding in her how he felt about Kitten and working through how he could actually tell her, she was glad of the distraction.

'All right, Olivia? Long time no see.' Finn's handsome face beamed down at her. 'How are you doing?'

She took his proffered hand and smiled back, noticing his bare arms. 'Good, thanks. Although it's a bit chilly up here today, isn't it?'

He laughed. 'And I've only gone and left my work fleece at a customer's. So trust it to be nippy today, eh?' He turned to Rocky. 'Shall we get on with things here, mate, before the sun goes down?'

'You do that, while I go and talk to the Woodbridges about the timeline. I'm sure they'll be delighted to hear we're ahead of schedule.' She stood and picked up her plan tube. As she headed off towards the house, Finn called out.

'Could I have a quick word when you've finished, Olivia?'

Well, that worked perfectly. 'Of course.'

* * *

Olivia's chat with the clients lasted longer than she'd expected, and Finn was waiting for her when she returned to Rocky and his giant Jenga set. Finn signalled for her to move away from the rest of the men, and they ended up by the same pile of reclaimed bricks she'd occupied with Rocky. For a few moments they sat in silence, watching the dairy cows in the field below them making their way to the farm's automated milking parlour. Jago had explained to her time and time again how it all worked, but it still made Olivia sad to think that the milking parlours she remembered from her childhood were all changing. *Progress, eh?*

'Look, I'll cut to the chase. Louisa told me she'd been confiding in you.'

Olivia listened carefully for any hint of hostility in his voice, but heard none. She nodded.

'And no doubt Jago told you he saw me at Amanda Burrows's salon on Monday? I recognised him immediately, but I wasn't sure he clocked who I was. I tried to keep my head down'

'It was your branded fleece that identified you. You dropped it.' She gave him a sheepish smile, which he returned.

'And you've put two and two together and come up with what?' His eyes locked onto hers.

'I haven't come up with anything,' Olivia confessed. 'I just think a lot of people are talking at cross purposes.'

'How d'you mean?'

She came to a decision. 'Look, Finn. I'm going to be honest with you. I don't like all the secrecy and intrigue that seems to be rife in Penbartha at the moment. I've known you since I was a little girl, and George and Mollie always spoke very highly of you.'

He nodded. 'They were good to me. George really supported me when I set up on my own all those years ago. He got me a lot of work.'

'That sounds like George. And how long have you and Louisa been married?'

He screwed up his face, reminding her of Rocky. 'About thirty years. Give or take.'

'I'm twenty years younger than you, and I'm not married. So, I don't really think I'm best placed to give you marital advice, do you?' She pulled a face. *What a morning this was turning out to be.*

A twinkle appeared in Finn's eye, and Olivia could understand why Amanda Burrows would find him attractive. He was one of those men who had become more attractive as he'd aged. And the complete opposite of Rafe. 'But you're going to anyway?'

She reddened. 'Not really. All I'll say – and I'd rather this didn't get back to Louisa, because I don't want her to think I'm betraying a confidence – is that she thinks you're actively involved in the FHO campaign.'

He did a double take. 'The FHO campaign?'

'First Homes Only.' She clarified. 'The anti-second homes group.'

'I know who they are.' He looked confused. 'I don't understand why she thinks I'm so involved with them.'

'Louisa told me that you blame Rafe Burrows for encouraging your mother-in-law to buy her home here, that you now can't sell to pay for her care home fees. And that you've started rushing off to clandestine meetings at all times of the day and night and have become very secretive.'

Finn narrowed his eyes and then suddenly widened them. 'And Lou's put two and two together and made five?'

Olivia frowned. 'What do you expect? Would you rather she jumped to the even more bizarre conclusion that you're having an affair with your arch-enemy's wife?'

He winced. 'Touché.' He recovered himself. 'Sorry, you're right. I do despise Rafe Burrows, and I totally blame him for the situation we've ended up in and the financial pressure we're under now. So, I suppose it was easy to jump on the FHO bandwagon and throw insults at the type of people Burrows makes money out of and paint them all with the same brush. And I have supported the various campaigns against them, from the sidelines anyway.' He glanced at Olivia. 'But I haven't deflated any tyres or painted houses with graffiti, if that's what you're getting at.'

'What about the fire at Gillan Cottage? Louisa said you were out until very late that night, supposedly helping a mate with his electrics.'

Finn reddened. 'Okay, I was at Amanda's. She and Rafe had a massive row before he went off on some golfing jolly. So I went to comfort her.'

'So the wife of your arch-enemy is your alibi for the night of the fire? Nice.' Olivia couldn't keep the sarcastic note out of her voice. 'And you're sure you know nothing about the fire at Gillan?'

'For God's sake, Olivia! Jasper Swift's my mate. We grew up in the village together, and we still keep in touch. I was talking to him online just the other day. I'm hardly going to set fire to his house, am I? I'm not an arsonist.'

No. Just a cheating bastard. Olivia thought for a horrible moment that she'd spoken out loud, but the look on Finn's face was one of indignation, not anger or guilt.

'Okay, I get it. And I don't want to know anything about your relationship with Amanda Burrows. That's a matter for you and Louisa.'

Unfortunately, Finn was keen to explain, despite Olivia's protestations. 'Look, I'm not gonna lie. It felt good to be getting one over on Rafe. All Lou and I seem to do is argue these days, and it made a nice change to have fun with someone.' He sighed. 'Amanda was keen too. He's not a very nice husband, by all accounts.'

'That doesn't surprise me.' Olivia spoke with feeling. 'What d'you reckon will happen?'

'With Mandy? Nothing. I reckon I'm just her bit of rough. I'm nowhere near rich enough or refined enough for her. I'm sure if someone with better prospects came along she'd be off like a shot. In the meantime, we're both going through a rough patch in our marriages, and we want some no-strings fun.'

'Do you think Louisa will see it like that?'

A closed look crept over his face. 'Are you going to tell her?'

Olivia shook her head. 'No. That's up to you. But you're going to have some explaining to do.'

'Why's that?'

'Because it really upset Louisa to think you might be a vandal or an arsonist.'

'So I'll tell her I'm not.'

'And what are you going to tell her that will explain away all her suspicions?'

'I'll think of something.' Finn was starting to look worried.

'Good.' Olivia spoke firmly. 'Because the police may well ask you about an alibi for Wednesday night, and if Louisa was that upset by thinking you could be a vandal or an arsonist, how is she going to react to finding out you're having an affair?'

18

'I suggest you have a day off relationship counselling, Liv, and hopefully you'll be in a better mood.'

'Thanks very much! I was completely out of my depth. Give me buildings any day – they stay where you put them and they don't answer back.'

Jago glanced sideways at Olivia who sat at the refectory table in the orangery, flicking through the newspaper and doodling on a pad in front of her. She'd been subdued since her chats with Rocky and Finn the day before, and her plans for a long early morning run with the dogs hadn't come to pass. Unusually strong westerlies had brought rain lashing against the windows and gushing down the drainpipes, and the wind whipping through the fronds of the palm trees in the garden was making an almighty din. It was weather like this that made Jago almost wish he was back in London where it didn't seem to impact everyday life so much.

'I take it we're working from home today?'

Olivia nodded, still scribbling away.

They had an unwritten rule that on Wednesdays – trustees' meeting permitting – they didn't go into their respective offices at the station site to work. It gave Alice full rein as the Goods Shed manager without feeling she had to defer to Olivia, even though there she was repeatedly told there was no need, and

Jago had his own deputies at the Signal Box, who covered for him while he was in London and were more than happy to keep their hand in one day a week.

Austol Berryman, who was Rocky's grandad and Brian Pascoe, his friend, had been only too delighted to step into Jago's shoes and help out with his railway memorabilia business when he first returned to the London Bar. Both men had been junior porters at Penbartha station before the Beeching cuts of the 1960s had led to its closure and their jobs had been transferred to Truro station. Now in their eighties, they had jumped at the chance to help Jago and relive the golden age of steam together. The two friends had reorganised the Signal Box with military precision. The wooden floor and the wall-to-wall windows gleamed, and all the auction catalogues and magazines were neatly filed in the bookcases. The Signal Box gardens had also been transformed under their watch into a wonderful cottage display, with all the best seasonal flowers and plants now making their well-timed appearances, as nature intended. Jago knew that Kitten had enlisted their help to decorate the station and Signal Box gardens for the now legendary Hallowe'en trail on Saturday. They would be busy there today, and he preferred to leave them to it.

'We've got to clear Alfie's name. So we need to regroup,' Olivia announced, looking up at him and shoving her reading glasses up into her curls. It was her unspoken signal she meant business. 'We've been barking up completely the wrong tree, and we need to start again.'

Jago nodded. 'I think you're right.' He sat down opposite her at the table, his mind already whirring as he processed all the facts and organised them in his mind before he began speaking, just like he did when he was preparing a case for court. He cleared his throat and ignored Olivia's raised eyebrow. 'Okay, so what do we know so far?'

'Is that a rhetorical question, or may I reply?' She jumped in with a definite glint in her dark eyes.

'Be my guest. I'd like to hear your take on it.'

She looked at him, and then spoke. 'Well, it all started at the beach clean, which seemed to unleash a wave of anti-second home sentiment, the deflated tyres, the graffiti on the Old Foundry, the blue plaque stickers on second homes, and culminated in the fire at Gillan Cottage. Which was a pretty big leap from the earlier antics.'

Jago nodded. 'Or has all the FHO stuff been going on for much longer, and we were simply unaware of it? Things like that don't just happen spontaneously, do they? They take a lot of organising.'

Olivia frowned and made a note on her pad. 'Let's come back to that. So far, we have a pretty good idea that Caroline, Alfie and Finn have all been involved in the FHO group to a greater or lesser extent.'

'Well, Alfie admitted he was forced to get involved in the fire, unwillingly,' Jago reminded her. 'But we don't know who was behind that. And Finn claims that although he supported the group from the sidelines, he was with Amanda that night. We need to check his alibi too.'

Olivia scribbled some more notes. 'Is Finn's strange behaviour, as reported by Louisa, down to his affair with Amanda, or is it a cover for what he might be getting up to with the FHO group?'

Jago rocked back on his chair, running his hands through his hair in exasperation. 'And for some reason, that we don't know yet, Rafe Burrows took it upon himself to erect that board at Gillan Cottage, without Jasper Swift's knowledge or consent.' He took a quick look at Olivia's face and hurried on. 'Was that to whip up local resentment? Or was he doing it to hide something more sinister?'

'And Grace never mentioned anything about it?

'No, but she had every opportunity.' Jago sat up straight. 'Although she did say Trenow had been asking questions. Perhaps he asked her about Gillan Cottage, so she decided not to mention it to me. Just in case it got her into trouble.'

Olivia pulled a face. 'So remind me what she said about Marcus not being at the golfing event.'

'She said she didn't see him, so assumed he'd been called back to London early to deal with a high-end contract. That happens a lot in their business, apparently'

'So Finn was with Amanda on the night of the fire, and Rafe and Marcus were allegedly at the golfing event together, but we have absolutely no proof of that yet.'

'Perhaps we need to be looking closer to home. Alfie claims that someone was blackmailing him to set the fires, but has no idea who. And that person knew Caroline had been involved with other FHO stuff, and was threatening to tell the police if he didn't do what they demanded.'

'Have the police come up with anything more concrete to link him to the fire?'

'Not yet. But they seem to accept that he was one of four people who lit small fires, around the garden, but nowhere near where the body was found. And as they were all wearing masks, Alfie claims not to know who any of the others were.'

'Do you believe him?'

'I believe he thought he was just lighting a few small fires.' Jago chose his words carefully. 'It's a big garden, and it's been quite wet, so he didn't think they would do that much damage.'

Olivia sighed. 'I think we should talk to Caroline again.'

'Good luck with that.'

'Not me! You're her knight in shining armour, remember? And you can always use the excuse that you're asking for more information in order to help Alfie and the best way to do that is to find out who actually did it.'

Jago started to laugh. 'I can't believe that my ball-busting fiancée is actually scared of someone.'

'I'm not scared of Caroline!' she started to protest and then subsided quickly. 'Well, I suppose I am. A bit. She's always been a bit off with me, and I'm not expecting a complete reversal in her attitude. Whereas, on the other hand, you are her hero. Apparently, she was singing your praises to Willow only yesterday.' The sparkle that had been missing from Olivia's eyes for the last few days was suddenly back, and she started to laugh, a deep, musical, infectious sound that melted his heart. 'She was waxing lyrical about your courtroom successes. Said she'd been googling you and hadn't realised Penbartha had such a brilliant legal beagle in its midst. And that she couldn't have asked for anyone better to represent her grandson.'

Jago felt his face warm. 'Oh God, no. I hate it when people say that.'

Olivia laughed again. 'Oh, there's more. She couldn't resist being Caroline and made some catty remark about now understanding what I see in you, even if she still can't work out what the attraction is for you.'

Jago was horrified, but a quick scan of Olivia's face reassured him that she wasn't offended at all. He stretched his arm across the table and squeezed her hand. 'Do you want me to remind you what I find attractive about you?' He looked at his watch. 'How long have we got?'

'Stop it!' She batted his hand away with a smile. 'This isn't about you. Or me. It's about Alfie, remember?'

'Oh yes. It's just that I deal with crime all the time in London and sometimes it would be really nice to come home and just be normal, you know?'

Olivia looked like she was forcing a smile onto her face. 'I do know. And I agree. But the sooner we get to the bottom of this, the sooner we can get back to normal. Yes?'

'Okay.' He got to his feet and went over to the Aga and then turned to face her. 'Now here's an idea. Why don't we ask Cassie if she's heard anything on the grapevine?'

'Cassie?' Olivia's mouth practically fell open.

'Yes, Cassie. What's the problem?'

Olivia definitely looked awkward. 'I feel really bad about Cassie, actually,' she confessed. 'I've been keeping her at arm's length since Sam said all that stuff about looking into a link between me and the FHO group and it left a bad taste in my mouth. I know it's silly, but I don't want her to feel she's caught between the two of us.'

'Isn't that my decision to make?'

Jago spun towards the boot room door, from where Cassie had appeared. 'Cassie!'

'The very same.' She walked into the orangery, dressed in her customary gardening dungarees, fleece and waterproof, fussed the dogs who rushed over to greet her, and sat down next to Olivia. 'Are you putting that kettle on, Jago?'

'Of course. Your usual?' He set about making tea, just the way she liked it, and kept his ear firmly on the conversation taking place at the table.

'Thanks for considering my feelings in all this, Olivia.' The older woman put her arm round Olivia's shoulder and kissed her cheek. 'But as much as I love Sam, I still feel my loyalties lie with you two more than they do with the police.'

He could see Olivia blink away her tears.

'I'm sorry, Cass. I just didn't want to put pressure on you and Sam so early on in your relationship.'

'You should have given me more credit. We agreed early on in our relationship that we wouldn't let his job come between us. But he mentions things occasionally, and I hear him on the phone to Ross. You'd be amazed at how little they have learned from the locals. They're coming up against brick wall after brick wall.'

Jago carried a tray across to the table. 'So what's your take on the situation, Cass?'

Cassie brightened. 'Sam has never asked me that question. He's a firm believer in keeping his personal and professional lives completely separate.'

'I don't blame him for that,' Olivia commented with feeling. 'But he's neglecting a great font of inside information.'

Cassie's cheeks pinked. 'I wouldn't go that far, perhaps. But I am quite friendly with Caroline Pellow.'

'I didn't know that!' Olivia leant forward.

'Well, Mollie always had time for her. Said her bark was much worse than her bite. And after Mollie died, Caroline and I would meet up to reminisce about her, swap recipes and so on. And Caroline was very good to George.'

'She was?' Olivia sounded bewildered.

'Yes. She'd come here to play him at chess.'

'I didn't think he played after Mollie died. She was his greatest opponent.'

'Yes, but Mollie asked Caroline to take over from her. She said chess helped to keep George's mind sharp. Caroline suggested I did it, but I can't play, so she came every week. And they became good friends.'

'I didn't know that,' Olivia repeated, and Jago could see her mentally re-evaluating what she felt about Caroline Pellow. 'Why is she always so frosty with me then?'

Cassie shrugged. 'Like Mollie said, her bark is much worse than her bite.' She looked away briefly. 'And she couldn't understand how Mollie and George were happy to let you fly the nest and leave Penbartha. She was always desperate to keep her daughter near.'

'Mollie and George encouraged me to move away for my career,' Olivia said faintly. 'But Tresillian was always my home.'

'Roots and wings. That's what Mollie said. They gave you roots so you always knew where home was and wings to let you fly off and live your life.' She sighed. 'I don't think Caroline could cope with the wings part. That's why she was so devastated when her daughter moved to Exeter.'

'I thought that was to do with house prices down here.'

'That's what she tells people. And why she manipulated the scholarship place at Treave School for Alfie, so he had an opportunity his parents couldn't turn down. Caroline just couldn't bear to lose her whole family.'

'How did she do that?'

'She submitted Alfie's art work without his parents knowing, and the school invited him to sit the exam. They didn't think he would pass but he did, so they agreed he could stay in Penbartha.'

Olivia's dark eyes widened. 'She must have been devastated about them all leaving if she went to those extremes. And must still be, given Alfie's not that happy there at the moment.'

'Caroline's husband had only recently died, and Alfie was the apple of their eye. That's why she's so grateful to Jago now.'

Jago's heart sank. 'I'm not sure I'm helping much at the moment.' A thought struck him. 'Do you think Caroline would talk to you about the FHO group?'

'First Homes Only?' Cassie chuckled. 'They're a pretty harmless bunch, I think.'

Jago was taken aback. 'I think they're getting themselves in some pretty serious stuff with the fires and potential murder.'

'Look, Jago. I know about the body from Sam because I can keep a secret. I also know the Penbartha FHO group wouldn't ever get themselves involved in anything as serious as that. I don't believe it was them for a minute.'

Jago watched Cassie closely. He had come to respect her judgement over the last couple of years. And she had arrived at the right conclusion about the events at Peneglos Hall the previous year at the same time Olivia had. In his opinion, not much got past Cassie Polmere. Her quiet manner led people to confide things in her that they might not say to anyone else. And, at a time like this, that could only be a good thing.

'So who do you think was behind the fires at Gillan?'

Cassie scrunched her face up as she thought. 'I don't know, but I can talk to Caroline if it helps? She knows everything about everyone who has lived here over the past forty years.'

'That would be great, thank you.'

She nodded. 'What I'm struggling to understand is why they picked on next door. It's been empty for a long time, so why now? It's all very weird.'

'I know what you mean,' Olivia agreed. 'I don't think anyone round here thinks of it as a second home. It's just the Swifts' place.'

'And the other thing I don't understand is why Jasper hasn't sold it, given that it's been two years since Peggy died. He's lived in Canada for years and rarely makes it over here any more, other than for the odd weekend.'

'D'you think it might be for sentimental reasons?'

Cassie shrugged. 'Perhaps, but when I offered to oversee the maintenance of the gardens, he said he'd got some general lawn-mowing business from Truro to keep the grass down.'

'Well, I suppose if his life's now in Canada and he's caught up in the sailing world over there, it must be tricky to get back,' Jago offered. 'Is he married? Family?'

'Yes, to both,' Cassie replied. 'Twin daughters, I think, who must be in their early twenties now. Finn Nankivell will be able to tell you more. He and Jasper are still great mates. Finn keeps an eye on Gillan for him. I see him there every now and then, and we have a chat.'

Jago and Olivia exchanged a look. 'Can you remember when you last saw Jasper?'

'Not for ages.' Cassie had just opened her mouth to speak

again when the front door bell jangled, and the dogs let up their usual volley of barks.

'I'll go.' Olivia got to her feet. 'I have a horrible feeling I know who this will be.'

So did Jago. Not many people used the front door. Unless it was bad news. Olivia reappeared followed by a tense looking Trenow and O'Driscoll. They refused to sit down.

'Look, I'm just going to cut to the chase. You can ask questions later. We now know the identity of the body found at Gillan Cottage.'

Jago realised he was holding his breath.

'Dental records have confirmed that it's Marcus Walker-Smith.'

19

'Just trust me, okay, Kitten?'

Kitten shot Olivia another suspicious look and then settled down into the passenger seat of her friend's car with a heavy sigh. 'You know I don't like surprises.'

'Since when?' Olivia almost stalled the car. 'You've always loved surprises!'

'Well, I've gone off them. Particularly ones that aren't nice.'

'This one will be nice, I promise.'

Kitten could feel her friend watching her out of the corner of her eye, but she kept staring ahead. Olivia had arrived at her flat, insisting that Kitten brush her hair and change out of her Waiting Rooms uniform, and said that she was taking her out for a treat. Although she was feeling a little better, thanks to her medication, she was still taking it easy. She had spent most of the morning in the office, sorting through orders and invoices and leaving the hard work to Jasmine and Ned, and then agreed with Jasmine that she would take the afternoon off. An afternoon she had been planning to spend sorting out the staff rotas for the following week when Jasmine, Alfie and Mya were back at school and no longer available to work. At least her assistant manager, Izzy, would be back from her holidays and she was always willing to take on extra shifts. Kitten sighed. She was going to have a very honest conversation with Olivia soon. But not today. She just wasn't up to it.

'It doesn't feel like I've seen much of you lately,' Olivia commented easily as they drove out of Penbartha. 'Are you sure you're feeling better now?'

'I'm getting there, thanks.'

'That's good. We need a proper catch up. So much has been happening, you wouldn't believe it.'

'This is Penbartha, Olive. I'd believe anything.' Kitten was too tired to ask the questions she knew Olivia was expecting. 'But I'm glad Jago's helping Alfie. He's a good kid.'

'We think so too. But there are still some pieces missing from the puzzle.'

As Kitten mulled over her words, thinking about her own conversations with Alfie, Olivia drove through a neighbouring village at the furthest point of the headland and then pulled up at a lay-by in a lane that led down to a tiny sandy beach surrounded by mature woodland, that was so well-hidden only locals knew about it.

'Right. Out you get.' Olivia turned to her with a big smile on her face.

Kitten froze. 'What? Here?'

'Yes, here. Just walk down to the beach. Your surprise is waiting for you there.'

Kitten looked towards the beach and then back down at her legs. *Would they make it that far?* Then she heard Olivia's mobile buzz.

'I've got to dash. Off you go.' Olivia practically shooed her out of the car, and before she knew it, she was standing at the side of the road while her friend did a quick three-point turn and drove off.

Shit. I suppose I asked for that, she told herself as she stood gazing down the path towards the beach. *Mollie was right when she said lies had short legs. There was no way she was going to get away with not being honest for much longer.*

'C'mon, Polmere. You can do this.' And she made her way slowly and carefully down the path, feeling like an eighty-year-old. As she turned left and crossed the band of pebbles and shingle at the top of the beach to reach the sand where the cove widened out, there stood Rocky, in his customary jeans, fisherman's sweater and rigger boots hopping from foot to foot. And at his feet he'd spread out a tartan picnic blanket, cushions and a wicker picnic basket overflowing with goodies.

Kitten was stunned. The realisation hit her that she had been so worried about having to walk any distance, she hadn't given a moment's thought to what, or who, might be waiting for her. She must have gasped out loud, because he turned towards her, his dark, piratical looks, black eyes and well-defined muscles, earned from honest hard labour and playing rugby rather than hours at the gym, making her heart race faster. The sea breeze blew the black curls away from his face, revealing an expression she had never seen before.

Kitten swallowed hard. The sucking and sighing of the frilly waves as they lapped against the sand felt deafening, and the warm October sun burned into her skin. Her heart lurched. This was going to be their last moment together before everything changed.

As soon as Rocky spotted her he hurried across the beach and caught her in his arms. She breathed in his signature scent of aftershave mixed with wood shavings, felt the soft stubble against her face and realised she loved this man so much she had to let him go. When he leant in to kiss her, she couldn't bring herself to turn away from him.

'Right, let's sit down.' He ushered her onto a cushion and opened the basket. 'I could have brought champagne, but I know you're not keen. I thought you'd prefer hot chocolate – and it will keep us warmer when the sun goes in.'

Kitten nodded, turning her head away so he wouldn't see her tears. *She hated champagne and the bubbles always made her sneeze. How many men would be thoughtful enough to put practicalities before a grand, romantic gesture?* Rocky poured the hot chocolate into chunky mugs and sprinkled mini marshmallows onto hers, just as she liked it.

'Here's to us!' He handed her the mug and clinked his against it and then settled down on a cushion, leaning into her. 'I've brought you here for a reason.'

The band that had settled round Kitten's heart squeezed more tightly.

'I wanted to talk to you away from Penbartha. I love that place, but sometimes you can't do anything or go anywhere without bumping into someone you know.'

Kitten nodded.

'Do you see that house there?' He pointed along the beach to where the red roof and tall chimneys of a house could just be seen peeking through the trees in the huge gardens that surrounded it, the gulls whirling and wheeling in the blue sky above. 'There's a beautiful story behind it.'

Kitten loved hearing Rocky's tales. His deep voice with its rounded Cornish vowels rumbled through his body. She swore she could even feel it through his shoulder, nestled against hers. *Just one more story,* she promised herself.

'Tell me.'

'It was originally built in Sussex in the 1600s, but was moved here, brick by brick, three hundred years later. All for love.'

'For what? How?'

'The lady who lived in it met and fell in love with a Cornish sea captain. And when he proposed she wanted to say yes, but she couldn't bear to leave her home. So, because he wanted her to be happy, he moved every brick and timber from Sussex to Cornwall by sea and rebuilt it for her here, overlooking the harbour where his ship was based. That's how much he loved her.'

Kitten felt tears prick her eyelids. 'How romantic!'

Rocky smiled, his teeth white against his olive skin and black stubble. 'I'd do that for you Kitti-Kat, you know. That's how I'd show you how much I love you. I'm not a champagne and diamonds kind of guy.'

The band squeezed her heart again, and she shook her head quickly, turning so she could wipe away her tears before he saw them. He grabbed her hand, his touch sending shivers through her body, just like it always did. She couldn't bear to look back at the house that had been rebuilt with such love, and stared instead over the water towards Falmouth and its rows and rows of colourful houses, rising in terraces like a football stadium, all jockeying for the best view of the Penryn river.

'What's going on, Kitten? I know something's up. You haven't been yourself for weeks now. And that flu-bug story's beginning to wear a bit thin. So now I'm worried. Please just tell me.'

She froze. *She couldn't do it.*

'Are you pregnant?'

'No!' Her voice was a squeak, and she turned back to him in time to see the excitement in his eyes replaced by a flash of disappointment. Her heart squeezed again. Rocky would make a wonderful dad. That would be something else she might be depriving him of if they stayed together. She hadn't asked the consultant about having children when she'd seen her the day before. Mainly because she was scared of the answer.

'Oh, okay.' He pulled his hand through his black curls, dislodging a cloud of sawdust and wood shavings, and then winced when he caught a blood-blistered thumbnail in his hair. Then, he looked back out to sea, and his olive cheeks turned a shade of pink she had never seen before.

He cleared his throat. 'Look, you know I'm not good with

words. So I'm just going to come out and say it. I'm in love with you, Kitten Polmere. Totally and utterly in love with you. And I have been since the day we started working on the Waiting Rooms together. I want to spend the rest of my life with you.'

Kitten couldn't speak. Those were the words she'd been longing to hear. And now the timing just felt cruel.

'I didn't know how to tell you. I tried to think of some big, romantic gesture, but you know that's not my style. I hoped you'd prefer this – something simple.'

Kitten's eyes were so full of tears, she couldn't see. Nobody had ever said anything like it to her before, and all she wanted to do was throw her arms round his neck and say the same things back. But she couldn't. Everything felt wrong.

Rocky caught hold of her hand, his strong fingers calloused by all his manual labour curling round hers. 'Well, Kitti-Kat, how do you feel about marrying me?' The look on his face made her heart break all over again. He looked just like a hopeful little boy on the brink of receiving the present of his dreams. And she was the horrible person about to snatch it away from him.

She inhaled sharply and pulled her hand away. She wanted to say yes, yes, yes, but there was a bigger part of her that knew he deserved better. She could try lying and tell him that she was moving away, perhaps back to Manchester, but he wouldn't believe her. He knew she wouldn't leave her mum and Olivia and Penbartha. *No, she couldn't lie to him. He deserved to know the truth. To have a choice, a get-out clause. She owed it to him.* A tear slid down her cheek.

'Hey, what's up?' His blistered thumb brushed away her tear in a touch so gentle and caring it almost broke her resolve. 'I wanted to cheer you up, not make you cry.' He smiled. 'You haven't been listening to more of Olive's stories about our misspent youth, have you? Because you shouldn't believe at least half of what that woman says about me.'

His attempt at humour fell flat. For once Kitten, who usually loved Olivia's greatly exaggerated tales of their teenage years, failed to manage a smile.

'Talk to me, Kitten. You're worrying me now. I need to know what's bothering you and don't say nothing, because you're a really hopeless liar.'

She squeezed her eyes shut, promising herself that when she opened them, she would tell him the truth. And she knew that when she'd spoken the words there was no way of taking them back. She would have to face the enormity of what she said, something she hadn't even admitted to herself yet. She had an incurable disease and no one knew what its trajectory would be. All anyone knew was that was no cure, little hope and she would slowly lose control over her body.

'I've not been honest about what's wrong with me.'

He caught hold of her hand again, but stayed silent. When Kitten opened her eyes, the whole world had fallen silent too; the distant thumping from the docks on the opposite bank of the river stopped, the wind dropped, even the gulls were quiet.

'I had a few weird symptoms, which I thought was that bug, but they didn't go away, so I went to see Dr Kitson.' She swallowed. 'He did some tests and then referred me for an MRI.'

He nodded and she could see a whole range of emotions flit across his face, before it settled in a worried frown. 'And?'

'I've got multiple sclerosis.' She watched his face turn pale and then his arm snaked round her shoulders and pulled her close.

'We'll get through this, Kitti-Kat.'

She pulled away and burst into tears. 'This isn't something you get through, Rocky. It's not a broken arm that will mend. It's a lifelong, incurable disease, and I could end up in a wheelchair, dribbling. This changes everything between us. Can't you see that?'

In true Rocky form, he stayed calm. 'What are you saying?'

A massive spasm ran through her legs from sitting in one position for too long, and she bit her lip against the pain. 'I'm saying that I think we should split up. Go our own ways.'

He reached for her hands again, grasping them tightly. 'I thought you loved me.'

Her heart broke again. 'I do love you, but I can't offer you a future when I don't know what mine might be. I don't want you to feel responsible for me, or be my carer.'

'I think you're massively racing ahead of yourself and planning for something which might never happen.'

'Perhaps. But what if it does happen? Loads of things could go wrong. I can just about cope with going through it myself, but I'm not putting you through it.'

'You're overreacting.'

Kitten tried to get up from where she was sitting, but her legs had gone numb and she couldn't move. She collapsed back onto the sand with a howl of frustration. 'Look at me! I can't even stand up on my own. Do you want to spend the rest of your life lifting me up, carrying me to the bathroom, stuff like that? I'm giving you a get out here, Rocky. I'm trying to do the right thing. Can't you see that?'

'Have you told anyone else? Your mum? Olive?'

'No. Well, Emily Hogan caught me at a weak moment and I ended up telling her. It was easier talking to her actually.'

A look of confusion crossed his face. 'Easier than talking to people who love you?'

'Yes. She doesn't really know me. She isn't invested in me, so I didn't have to deal with her emotions when I told her.' Kitten paused. 'And Olive's my employer.'

'So?'

'What if she decides I can't do my job anymore and gets rid of me?'

Rocky stared at her, like he was baffled. 'Olive treats you like a sister. She wouldn't do that.'

'You read about it all the time. People are diagnosed, and their bosses decide they'll be in a wheelchair by the time they're thirty and so let them go.'

'They can't do that, surely? Aren't there laws against that sort of thing?'

'Yes, but it happens. Believe me.'

'Kitten, stop it! You're jumping to worst-case conclusions. Let's just deal with one thing at a time. I don't know much about MS, but I can find out, do some research. I'm sure there are things they can do – medication, therapy. We can go to the best doctors in the country, get a second opinion—'

Kitten burst into tears, refusing to look at him. *This was typical of Rocky. He'd gone straight into saviour mode, trying to fix things that were unfixable, without even asking her how she was feeling or what she needed.*

'Stop it, Rocky, please. This is exactly what I don't want – people making a fuss. I can't stand it. I need to work things out for myself first. Can't you do that for me? Give me some time?'

'How much time?' His voice was flat.

'I don't know. It's a lot to get my head round.'

'Okay.' He started packing up the picnic basket. 'Let me know when you've made your decision.'

'You need to think it through, too. You have to realise what this diagnosis means. For me. For us. There's no way we can just carry on as before.'

He turned a stricken face towards her. 'So you keep saying.'

She hated herself. Was this how her life was going to be from now on? Constantly having to ask people for help. She wanted Rocky to be her lover. Not her carer. She swallowed another sob. 'Will you give me a lift home, please?'

'Of course.' Ever the gentleman, he helped her to her feet and led her to his pick-up as though he had been doing it all his life. They drove home in silence, and once again, he helped her up the stairs to her flat.

'I'll leave you to it then,' he said brusquely, bending to kiss her cheek as she sat exhausted on the sofa.

'Thanks.' She caught hold of his hand and when he turned back to her, the tears in his eyes reflected those in her own. 'I'm sorry. But you need to think about it.'

He nodded. 'Sure. Let me know when you're ready to talk.'

Kitten waited until the door closed behind him before she let the tears fall freely. She cried for everything she'd already lost and all that she stood to lose in future.

WHATSAPP GROUP – #FirstHomesOnly

@CoastalCrusader: No idea whts goin on. Thnk we all need to lie low

@BanSecondHomes: Not until I say so

@Homes4Locals: It's getting out of hand.

@BanSecondHomes: That's what u think

@KernowCurrent: WTF?

@BanSecondHomes:I know who u all are. Where u live. Who yr families are. U don't have a clue who I am

@PlasticFreePioneer: Ur a fkn nutjob. I'm outta here

@PlasticFreePioneer left the group

@BanSecondHomes: We'll see. Got more jobs for u.

@Homes4Locals: Not now

@BanSecondHomes 1. do more FHO stuff – spray houses/smash windows. Don't care what. Just do it Need to distract from Gillan

@BanSecondHomes 2. scare that Wells woman off. She's bn sniffin around. Or her chap. Or her mates.

@KernowCurrent: NO WAY. This is getting ridiculous

@BanSecondHomes: So scare someone or something close to her. Your choice

@CoastalCrusader: And if we don't?

@BanSecondHomes: You'll soon find out. Watch ur backs

20

Jago leant back in his chair, feet resting on the desk, sipping his cup of tea and relishing his favourite radio news programme. Setting his mug aside, he glanced through the legal section of *The Times*. He always enjoyed this early-morning peace before the Goods Shed tenants, dog walkers and Waiting Rooms customers arrived.

He'd left Olivia eating her breakfast at Tresillian in a much-improved mood. She'd been for a long run with her dogs and was due at the Goods Shed to oversee the installation of two more EV charging points. Since more used electric cars were coming on the market, an increasing number of tenants now owned one, and the single charging point at the station site was no longer sufficient. All three dogs were spending the day with Cassie at Peneglos Hall. Olivia hadn't left Mylor and Zennor alone since Caroline had warned them they may be in danger, and although Jago thought she was over reacting, Olivia refused to take any risks when it came to her precious pets. The memory of Zennor's attempted abduction was still ingrained in Olivia's memory, and Jago doubted it would ever be fully erased.

He'd pleaded a date with an online railway memorabilia auction in which he was bidding on behalf of a client for a dark green 1929 Bognor Regis railway station totem sign. He had no idea why Bognor Regis was so special to this client, but it was up to him to buy it for a good price, not question his judgement. He registered his opening bid and then, with one eye on his computer screen, he had a quick scan for any signal box name boards from his own personal favourite, the North Cornwall Railway line, that may have come up for sale. He now owned ten out of the thirteen, and he turned to look at the wall behind his desk where the large but slim rectangular cast-iron nameboards graced the walls with a sense of satisfaction that was short-lived. Marcus Walker-Smith's murder was still very much on his mind and his killer still at large.

Trenow hadn't enlightened them in any way about how Walker-Smith had died. And despite his promises, there hadn't been any time to ask him questions. Another phone call from the pathologist had sent him and Sam rushing back to the station, and much of the remainder of Jago and Olivia's day had been filled with unanswered questions and endless speculation.

Happy with his bid in the online auction which wouldn't close until after the weekend, Jago began scribbling down all his new questions and theories. He was still steadily working his way through them when the sound of footsteps hammering up the external wooden staircase gave him permission to put his pen down.

Detective Inspector Trenow, closely followed by Olivia, walked through the door. Jago was pleased to see both of them. *Perhaps now we'll get some answers.*

Trenow helped himself to the chair on the other side of the desk from Jago and sat straight-backed as ever, in business mode. Olivia pulled up a chair alongside him.

'I'm sorry we were interrupted yesterday.' Trenow pulled his notebook from his jacket pocket. 'The pathologist just wanted to run through a few more details.' He turned his dark, intense gaze on them and waited.

Jago sent a warning look to Olivia who had just opened her mouth, and then quickly shut it again. *Two can play at that game.*

Trenow sighed. 'You're not going to start all that as well, are you?'

Jago adopted his best innocent look. 'All what?'

'Adopting the same approach as everyone else in this bloody place.' Trenow's retort was sharp. 'Seeing nothing, hearing nothing and saying nothing. This village is apparently full of wise monkeys.'

Jago exchanged another look with Olivia. 'Can we just establish in what capacity you're here?' He saw a look of confusion cross the policeman's face and sighed. *Did he really have to spell it out?* 'Is this just a chat between friends, or are you talking to me as Alfie's legal representative? Because if that's the case, shouldn't we be having this conversation at the station?'

Trenow's face cleared. 'Of course. I'll be talking to you and Alfie in a more formal setting later. I just wanted to run a few things past you both. Off the record.'

'Okay.' Jago sat back in his chair. 'Fire away.'

'But before we start, I want to tell you that Marcus Walker-Smith had to be identified by his dental records, not because of the fire but because he'd been killed by blunt force trauma to his head that rendered him unrecognisable.'

Jago glanced at Olivia who had gone pale. 'From the For Sale board?'

'The pathologist thinks it's unlikely that the wooden stake was sufficiently strong to cause the fatal injuries. They've done extensive tests on the wound site and the fragments contained within it.' He flipped back through his notebook. 'She thinks he was impaled post mortem. Probably as some kind of sick gesture.'

'What? By someone with a grudge against estate agents?'

Olivia gasped. 'Bloody hell!' She paused. 'Does that let Alfie off the hook?'

'We all very much doubt that Alfie has the strength to do that much damage to another human being, and that's backed up by a lack of forensic evidence on his clothes and arms and hands.' He nodded at Jago. 'We'll talk more about that later.'

Olivia let out a sigh of relief and smiled briefly at Jago. She turned back to Trenow with a frown.

'Marcus was an estate agent in London, and not many people would know him here. Could someone with a grudge against him have followed him from London to settle a score?'

'Unlikely. But it's an avenue we're exploring. The Met have sent some of their people to interview his work colleagues. Meanwhile we're looking for people he may have upset here.'

'Well, you can add Olivia and me to that list,' Jago volunteered. 'He was incredibly rude to both of us. And he was shouting his mouth off about buying a place here in the Ship the night they had their tyres let down, apparently. Perhaps he upset someone then.'

'What about other parents at Treave School?' Olivia suggested. 'I bet he's upset a few of them over the years.'

'Sam's checking that out.'

Jago looked down at his list of scrawled questions. 'Did you ever find out for certain whether he'd made it to the golfing event with Rafe Burrows? Did you speak to Rafe?'

'Yes. I eventually tracked him down at his office on Tuesday, apparently blissfully unaware of everything that's been going on. He says Marcus was driving them both to Plymouth when he got a call from his office insisting that he rushed back there to sort out an urgent issue regarding a sale. So Marcus dropped him off at the event, then went on to London. And that was the last time he saw him.'

'Did his wife know about that?'

'No, when I spoke to her at the time she thought he was in Plymouth and had no concerns that she hadn't heard from him. That was usual, apparently.'

'So Rafe thought Marcus was in London, and Marcus's wife thought he was in Plymouth,' Jago clarified.

'Yes, so we had no reason to think the victim was Marcus until the dental records came back. It came as a bit of a surprise, I can tell you.'

Jago sat up straight. 'So why would Marcus have come back to Penbartha?'

'And why change his shoes?' Olivia asked.

'I beg your pardon?' Trenow looked confused.

'His shoes. When we saw Marcus and Rafe in the lane in the day before the fire, they were both wearing brown leather shoes. And the victim was wearing old gardening wellies, that looked like they hadn't been worn for years. And they certainly weren't the designer wellies I'd expect Marcus to wear.'

Trenow scribbled in his notebook. 'I'm sure forensics will have examined them. I'll see what they came up with.'

Jago steered the conversation in a different direction. 'Did Rafe say what he and Marcus had been arguing about when Olivia and I saw them in the lane the day before the fire?'

'He said he "couldn't remember, and therefore it couldn't have been anything major." Those were his exact words.'

Jago thought back to the raised voices they had both heard. 'It sounded pretty major. Did you believe him?'

'Perhaps not about that. But he looked genuinely shocked when we told him Marcus was dead. And his alibis at the golf place check out.'

'What about time of death?'

'That's what I mean. It's a pretty wide window of time. But Rafe allegedly arrived in Plymouth on Thursday, before the fires were set and seems to have alibis for the whole time he was there.'

It was Jago's turn to scribble something down. 'So what happens now?'

'We're waiting for a few more tests to come back. And I need to speak to Alfie to let him know he's no longer a person of interest in this case.'

'That will be such a huge relief,' Olivia admitted. 'For everyone in Penbartha.'

Trenow frowned. 'Do you think anyone is likely to suddenly remember anything that could help us, now one of their own is no longer in the frame?'

'If you're looking for someone who doesn't like estate agents, there's probably quite a long list, particularly if they're involved in second homes.'

Trenow looked around the room, and his gaze eventually came to rest on Olivia. 'What do you know about the First Homes Only group?'

'More than I did before all this started,' she admitted. 'Everyone's being pretty cagey. And from what I can make out, although what they've done is petty and not very nice, I don't think they've broken any laws.'

'Apart from letting down car tyres which could have resulted in catastrophic accidents,' Trenow muttered darkly. 'Which is criminal damage.'

'That was a different group, apparently.' Olivia replied, unhelpfully.

'Oh yes.' Jago spoke up. 'I understand Amanda Burrows omitted to tell you that the culprits left large warning notices on all the targeted car windscreens, informing them of their objections to SUVs and similarly unnecessary cars, on health and environmental grounds.'

'She most certainly did.' Trenow narrowed his eyes. 'And

I don't think I want you to tell me how you know that.'

'Fair enough. And while the notices don't alter the offence of unlawful interference with a motor vehicle, they could be seen as a mitigating feature if it came to litigation.'

'Thank you for explaining the law to me.' Trenow sounded riled. 'I don't want to know how you found out about the posters because you wouldn't want to be accused of interfering in a police investigation, would you?'

'Certainly not.' *They weren't interfering in Trenow's investigation. They were conducting their own.*

'But you're perfectly happy use our local knowledge to find out about the FHO group?' Olivia jumped in. 'Talk about double standards!'

Trenow's face was a picture. 'As you've just pointed out, Olivia, what your little group is doing is petty and not very nice. But not illegal. So we'll park all that shall we? The two issues aren't connected, and thinking they are is just muddying the waters. On the other hand.' His face hardened. 'I think we're all in agreement that murder is another matter altogether. And you should leave the investigation of that to the professionals. I don't want to hear of either of you instigating conversations with any of the people involved. By that, I mean Rafe and Amanda Burrows, Juliet Walker-Smith, their children, or anyone involved in their businesses. Do you understand?'

Jago bristled. He wasn't used to being spoken to in that way. Particularly by people who weren't actually doing their job very successfully. He glanced over at Olivia, whose expression was one of mixed fury, indignation and concern. 'Understood,' he said curtly. *Two could play at that game*. 'Now if you'll excuse us, Olivia and I have Goods Shed matters to discuss.'

Trenow looked taken aback. *Perhaps he wasn't used to being dismissed. Touché.*

'Fine.' The policeman stood up and walked to the door. 'I'll be in touch.'

'Who's rattled his cage?' Olivia turned puzzled eyes to Jago, who felt a sudden surge of resentment towards Trenow.

'Oh, you know Ross.' He waved a dismissive hand, in an attempt to downplay the situation. 'He's happy to use us when it suits him, but he gets antsy if we get closer to the meaty stuff than he is. And it still really gets to him that people round here won't talk to him.'

'He's probably getting it in the neck from his superior officers as well,' Olivia observed. 'Isn't that what usually happens at this stage in an investigation ?'

Jago shrugged. 'Not our problem.' He reached across the desk to catch hold of her hand and squeezed it. 'I think he's wrong though.'

'About what?'

'I think the second-homes issue and Marcus's death are connected. And whatever the connection is, it's important enough to be hidden. We just need to find out what it is.'

'I think you're right.' The tall, angular body of Caroline Pellow slipped silently into the room, the usual unfriendly expression on her face. Her critical gaze swept over them, coming to rest on their joined hands, and she tutted in disapproval. Jago felt a tug on his hand as Olivia tried to pull hers away and increased his grip.

'Caroline!' He gave her his biggest smile. 'We should be getting some very good news later today. Inspector Trenow has just told me that Alfie's no longer a person of interest in their investigation.'

'Tell me something I didn't already know,' she snapped, and then the fierce expression on her face softened slightly. 'But it will be good to be told formally.' She crossed her arms across her chest. 'I just watched him leave. I need to talk to you.'

Olivia succeeded in tugging her hand away and stood up. 'I'd better leave you to it, then.'

'No need.' A frown crossed her forehead. 'This concerns you too.'

Olivia sat back down, but Caroline remained standing, her body radiating tension.

'You know I told you about the FHO Whatsapp group?' She directed her question at Jago.

'Yes.'

'Well, it's taken a turn for the worse.'

Talk about getting blood out of a stone! She really was the most taciturn woman he had ever met. 'In what way?'

'One member is trying to ramp up the violence. Asking people to spray houses and smash windows.'

'Do you know who it is?'

'Everyone has codenames. But this one's not been in the group that long, I don't think.'

He tried again. 'Have you still got the messages?'

'We delete them straight away. Always have done. But I kept this one, so I could show you, and now it's disappeared.'

'Disappeared?'

Caroline let out a snort of annoyance. 'Yes. It's not there. Reckon it's an automatic thing someone's put on the chat, just in case.'

Jago had never heard of such a thing, and judging by the look on Olivia's face, neither had she. An increasingly familiar feeling of concern began to coil in the pit of his stomach. 'That's not all the message said, is it?'

'No. Can't remember exactly. I should have taken a screenshot of it, or whatever you call it, but didn't.' She took a deep breath. 'They said Olivia's been sniffing around, and she needs to be scared off.' She stretched out a bony arm to pat Olivia awkwardly on the arm. 'Sorry, love.'

Jago couldn't work out if Olivia was more shocked by Caroline's words or her show of affection. Her mouth opened and closed a couple of times, but no words came out. Then she turned to Jago. He came to a quick decision. There was no need to alarm Olivia by overreacting to what they'd just heard and she was safe while she was with him. And he couldn't imagine Trenow offering her any kind of protection when he had just made his position on the FHO group clear. On the other hand, he needed to get as much information out of Caroline as he could while she was being amenable.

'Did the message say anything else?'

'I think there may have been something else, but I don't remember.' Her face pulled into an expression of distress and she sniffed. 'I'm sorry. I just wanted to warn you.'

'And we're grateful for that. Do you know who else might have received the message?'

She shook her head. 'Like I said, everyone has codenames.'

'Can you give it some thought and let us know? Or if anything at all comes back to you?'

She nodded and turned towards the door, before turning back. 'I know I haven't always been very nice to you, Olivia, and my words last week might have sounded like a threat. But I didn't mean them. I was trying to warn you.'

Jago watched as Olivia jumped up from her chair and crossed the room in a flash. For a horrible moment, he thought she might try to hug Caroline, but she stopped herself just in time, and settled for placing a hand on her arm.

'It's fine, Caroline. Really—'

'I'll be off then.' Caroline pulled the door open as the owner of a shouting, hysterical voice hammered up the stairs.

'Kitten's fallen down the stairs. I think she's dead!'

21

Olivia had never felt so helpless in her life. Kitten had been blue-lighted to Treliske Hospital, with Olivia at her side, her eyes fixed on the pale and bloodied face for the whole journey, constantly looking for any sign of the slightest twitch; waiting for a squeeze of her hand; listening for any change in the beeping of the monitors which seem to be attached to every part of her battered body. Once at the emergency department, Kitten's stretcher had been whizzed into a specialist area with paramedics shouting numbers and scores at the staff, and Olivia had been ushered into a relatives' room where she sat alone in muffled silence, her eyes glued to the small window through which she watched the hurried movements of nurses and doctors. The strong smell of antiseptic and disinfectant was doing a poor job of masking the far more unpleasant smells seeping under the door. She didn't think she'd ever want to eat again.

The only piece of news Olivia had received so far was that Kitten was still alive. Just. The image of her body lying crumpled in a pool of blood at the bottom of the stairs leading up to her flat, with one arm bent at a horrible angle, would be forever imprinted on her mind. And had stopped time. Olivia no longer had any idea how long it had taken for the ambulance to arrive, or how long she'd now been waiting for news. All she remembered was Jago taking over and organising everyone. She was to go in the ambulance with Kitten, Dylan at Peneglos Hall was driving Cassie straight to Treliske, and Jago was collecting Rocky from the Woodbridges and would meet them there.

So where was he? Olivia pulled her phone out of her pocket for the fifteenth time to check the tracking app she and Jago used for each other. But it was reliant on internet connection which was notoriously unreliable in certain parts of the county. And in order to avoid the traffic Jago was probably using back lanes, which were usually internet blackspots and explained why the app just showed him to be somewhere in a ten-mile radius of Truro. *Useless.*

Her fingers automatically moved to the shiny, smooth gemstone that hung at her neck from a slim brown lace. Her godmother had given it to her because the obsidian mahogany stone matched her unusual eyes and because it was known as the stone of strength. Olivia clasped the stone tightly as her heart squeezed again at the thought of Mollie and how much she'd loved Kitten. *Please Mollie, help us all get through this and let Kitten be okay.* She really couldn't bear the thought of losing someone else she loved.

She sat breathing in and out slowly, just as Mollie had always done with her when she was upset. When she eventually felt calmer, she took another deep breath and stepped into the corridor, hoping to attract someone's attention. The nurse who'd first spoken to her rushed past, but then turned on his heel and walked back to her, a look of concern on his face.

'Are you okay?' He peered more closely at her. 'You don't look too good.'

Olivia waved his question away and noticed his yellow name badge. 'I'm fine, Toby. Just want to know how my friend, Kitten, is.'

'Is her next of kin here yet?'

'No.' Olivia could hear her voice rising and she struggled to keep it under control. 'Her mum and her partner are both on the way, but they've got quite a distance to come. Can't you tell me anything? She's like a sister to me. Is she going to be all right?'

Toby took her by the arm and guided her back into the relatives' room. 'Look, I'm only supposed to talk to next of kin. What I can tell you is that Kitten's got a severe head injury and several broken bones. She's currently being scanned to see if she needs surgery. As soon as I hear any more, I'll let you know, but I can't go into detail. But I'll see if I can get one of the HCAs to bring you a cup of tea. We could do without you passing out as well.'

Olivia sank back down onto the uncomfortable plastic chair and noticed a scratched stainless-steel mirror on the pale green wall opposite. Thinking back to Toby's words, she glanced across at it and flinched at the distorted, blood-spattered face that stared back. There was no sink in the room so she scrubbed ineffectually at the dried blood with a tissue from the box on the table, leaving her face looking sore and red. She sat back down to wait, still clutching her pendant and breathing slowly, for what felt like an eternity before the sound of heavy, running footsteps propelled her to the door, and she saw Rocky barrelling down the corridor.

'Hey, Rocky, in here.' She caught hold of his arm as he raced past, bringing him to a sudden halt. He spun back round and then scooped Olivia into a hug so tight it practically lifted her feet from the floor.

'Is she…?' His voice broke.

'She's alive.' She hugged him back. 'Hold on to that.' She repeated what Toby had told her and led him into the room, where she sat next to him in silence, her hand firmly clutched in his as he gazed fixedly at the floor. Having been desperate for someone else to arrive, Olivia now felt even worse. The levels of anxiety and fear in the room had more than doubled, and she didn't know what to do to help other than just sit there, her arm stretched around his wide shoulders and holding his hand.

It seemed another age before Jago burst through the door, took one look at their faces and then slid onto the chair the other side of Olivia, his hand resting comfortingly on her knee. She breathed out for the first time in what felt like hours. *Thank God for Jago.* She attempted a smile for him and failed. But it didn't matter. There was no jealousy between Jago and Rocky. He'd been more like a brother to her for twenty-five years, and Jago didn't have a jealous bone in his body, which had always been part of his appeal. Most of the other men who'd been in Olivia's life, however temporarily, hadn't known what to make of Rocky. Yet Jago had simply accepted him as the quasi-brother he was. As had Kitten. The image of Kitten lying at the bottom of the stairs flashed back into her mind and she gulped.

'Any news?' Jago asked.

She repeated Toby's words again, and Jago squeezed her knee. His mobile buzzed.

'Right.' He checked his screen. 'That's Dylan. Cassie will be here any second, so I'll go and meet her. Dylan thinks he'll just be in the way here, so he's going back to Peneglos to look after the dogs.' He exchanged a look with Olivia. 'He says Cassie's beside herself, so we all need to be strong for her. Okay?'

Olivia nodded and then nudged Rocky. 'We can do that, can't we?' She nudged him again. 'Can't we?'

He visibly pulled himself together in front of them and stood up. 'Sure. Let me go and find her. You stay here with Olive.'

'Is he okay?' Once Rocky had left, Jago pulled Olivia into his side and kissed the side of her face gently.

'I'm not sure. He's not been himself lately, so I staged a bit of an intervention yesterday, which I'm not sure went that well.'

Olivia suddenly realised she had not spoken to either Kitten or Rocky since then, and her stomach clenched.

Jago groaned. 'What sort of intervention?'

'I told you I was being treated like some sort of relationship counsellor by both Rocky and Finn Nankivell the other day while I was at the Woodbridges. Rocky said that Kitten wasn't talking to him at the moment, and I suggested he was a bit more open with her about their future.'

'And?'

'He asked me to drop her off at the secret beach yesterday as a surprise. So I did. And no, I didn't ask him any questions, but I got the feeling that love was in the air.'

'And did you find out what happened? Have you seen either of them, or heard from them?'

Olivia felt tears prick at her eyelids. 'No, but it's only been a day and they're not kids.' She dropped her head into her hands. 'Oh, Jago. What kind of friend am I?'

'A busy one, who's got much more on her mind than her friends' love lives. Like you said, they're both adults, Liv. It's not your job to sort everything out for them.'

'But Kitten hasn't been well and I haven't spent enough time with her. I feel really bad now that I haven't been there for her.'

'She didn't want you to know.' Rocky and a sobbing Cassie, still wearing her gardening dungarees, came into the room together. 'We've just seen a doctor, and she says she'll be with us shortly.'

'What was it that Kitten didn't want us to know?' Cassie demanded between sobs.

Rocky signalled for her to sit down, but he chose to remain standing. 'Look, I only found out yesterday, when she refused to marry me.'

Cassie sobs grew louder, and Olivia's heart broke for her best friend. She felt Jago's hand squeeze hers and glanced at him. For once, he didn't look at all like his usual calm self.

Olivia could tell Rocky was struggling to form his words. He shifted from foot to foot and eventually cleared his throat.

'Kitten's been diagnosed with multiple sclerosis.' His voice broke on the last word.

Olivia's world rocked on its axis, and a stunned silence filled the room. Cassie stopped sobbing. All eyes fixed on Rocky, who just stood with tears rolling down his cheeks, his shoulders heaving with emotion.

Olivia stared at him, speechless with shock.

Jago recovered first. 'Shit, mate! When did this happen?'

'She got the formal diagnosis last week, after an urgent MRI.'

'Why didn't she tell me? I'm her mum,' Cassie whispered.

Rocky looked helplessly round the room. 'She said she couldn't face dealing with the emotions of people she loves. Not until she's got it sorted in her own mind.'

'Fair enough.' Jago didn't sound convinced.

'No it's not!' Olivia burst out. 'We love her and want to help her, to share the pain—"

'I'm her mother',' Cassie whispered again. 'It's my job to be there for her. She should have told me.'

'Since when has Kitten done anything because it's what she *should* do?' Rocky retorted. 'That's not her way. She told me she needs time to think it all through before she decides what to do. All she said was that she doesn't want to be a burden and won't marry me because she doesn't want me to be her carer.'

'I'll look after her,' Cassie declared.

'She doesn't want to be looked after. That's the whole point! She's trying to take control while she still can. Even I can see that.' Rocky's voice rose to a level Olivia had rarely heard before, and she threw an anxious glance at Jago. He got the message, stood up and got Rocky to sit down next to Olivia, who immediately put her arm round him again.

'We get that, Rocky. And I sort of understand her reasoning.' Jago still sounded shocked. 'If we're reacting like this now, imagine what we'd be like if Kitten was here. Jumping to all sorts of conclusions without having the facts we need.'

Olivia glared at him, but he ignored her.

'I don't know that much about MS, but what I do know is that it's a spectrum disease and there's a huge variation in how it presents in different people. There are benign forms and more aggressive ones. I know a woman at the Bar in London who lives a perfectly normal life with her MS thanks to medication and some life adjustments.'

'You're right. I've been googling and they've made huge leaps in its treatment and management over the last couple of years.' Rocky's voice was quieter. 'It's not always the life sentence people used to think. But Kitten's got to reach that conclusion herself.'

'How did it start? What were her symptoms? How did we not notice?' Cassie began to sob again. 'If I hadn't been so preoccupied with Sam, I might have noticed things were wrong.'

'We're all guilty of that,' Olivia agreed. 'I thought she just had some kind of bug.' She paused. 'What made her go to the GP?'

'I'm not sure, but I know she's been having problems with her sight, and pain in her eyes for a while. From what I've read since, people also often develop balance problems and have falls—"

'Falls?' Olivia pounced on his words. 'Is that what happened today? How she fell down the stairs? Did she lose her balance and fall?'

'Did Kitten tell you she was having those symptoms?' Jago asked.

Rocky shook her his head. 'I can't remember much of what she said. It was all such a shock.'

'Does it matter why she fell?' Cassie turned on Jago. 'My

daughter's fighting for her life because she fell down a steep staircase and probably bashed her head on every step before landing on a hard floor. What matters is that we could have prevented it, if we'd known.' She turned her blazing gaze on Rocky. 'You should have told me. You had no right to keep it from me.'

'That's not fair, Cass.' Olivia rushed to defend her friend. 'You can't blame Rocky for doing what Kitten asked him. We all should have noticed that Kitten really wasn't well and it was more than a bug.'

'It's no one's fault and we're not helping anyone by falling out among ourselves.' Jago's calm voice was back to its usual soothing level, and Olivia shot him a grateful look. 'Kitten did a good job of keeping her symptoms from us and that was her choice. And it might explain why she fell in such a catastrophic way.'

'I don't think it does.' In the heightened emotion of the room, no one had noticed Sam O'Driscoll slipping through the door. Cassie fell into his arms, and he patted her back while his gaze travelled round, assessing everyone. His eyes met Olivia's and he just nodded at her, his own concern written across his face.

The door opened, and a doctor walked in, seemingly unbothered by the number of people in such a small space. She spied Cassie.

'Ah, Ms Polmere. I have some news for you. Can I have a word?'

Cassie seemed to shrink in front of Olivia's eyes and she clutched Sam's hand. 'You can say it to everyone. We're all family here.'

The doctor nodded. 'In addition to a broken arm and a few other minor fractures we're not concerned about, your daughter has experienced a severe head injury. The good news is she appears to have a very tough skull, which has probably been the saving of her. We haven't found any skull fractures or intercranial bleeds as yet.'

A sigh of relief rippled round the room.

'The not-so-good news is that once we scanned her brain and cleaned all her injuries up, we became aware that they weren't caused just by falling down the stairs. She's still unconscious so we're moving her to a specialist unit here where they can keep her under very close observation and take her to theatre immediately if her condition worsens.'

'Worsens in what way? Why is she still unconscious?' Cassie demanded, through yet more tears.

'Head injuries can be unpredictable. We're just taking every possible precaution.'

Jago cleared his throat, and Olivia prepared herself for his question.

'You said Kitten's injuries weren't caused by the fall.' He'd adopted his most serious court voice. 'Do you know what happened?'

'The most serious injuries to her *head* weren't caused by *just* a fall.'

'What?' Five pairs of eyes fixed themselves on the doctor's face. But it was Sam who replied.

'Kitten's fall wasn't an accident. It would seem that she was attacked with the fire extinguisher on the landing outside her flat.'

22

Jago turned his face up to the warm October sun as he stood by the creek in Tresillian's garden and took several deep breaths of fresh creek air, seasoned with the woody smells of autumn. His mind sifted and sorted through the previous day's events and revelations, and it didn't take long before the peace and calm of his morning so far was replaced by a gnawing worry.

He and Olivia had left the hospital, both feeling punch drunk from the news of Kitten's diagnosis and subsequent attack, and driven to Peneglos Hall to collect the dogs. Ruan and Dylan persuaded them to stay for dinner and then the night, and their head chef, Lexie, lent Olivia some sports kit so she could change out of the bloodied clothes she'd been in all day. After a surprisingly good night's sleep, they'd received the welcome news that Kitten had regained consciousness during the night, responded well to all the doctors' initial stimulus tests and was now sleeping peacefully.

To celebrate, Dylan had taken them on a walk around the gardens, admiring the autumn colours and breathing in the intoxicating scents of fir, pine and spruce mixed with dusty smells coming from the crispy leaves scrunching beneath their feet. He told them proudly how successful their forest-bathing experiences had become and explained how science had proved that spending just two hours in woodland soaking up the phytoncides released by trees could boost the human immune systems for several days. Feeling better, both mentally and physically, they agreed to leave the dogs with Ruan and Dylan while they sorted things out in Penbartha and said their goodbyes.

Jago checked his watch and took a last, deep breath of Tresillian's own phytoncides before heading back indoors. He met Olivia as she was coming out of the utility room.

'I've left our clothes from yesterday in the laundry bag Lexie gave us, I'll sort them later.'

'I suppose we'd better ask Sam if the police want to check them for trace evidence of any sort.'

Olivia winced. 'I'll let you do that. I don't want to even think about someone hurting Kitten in that way at the moment. I just want to concentrate on what we can do for her from now on.'

'Well, Alice was pretty insistent that we meet her and Jasmine at the Waiting Rooms at 10.30, and I got the definite impression it was to do with Kitten.' Jago ushered out of the back door and along the drive. 'We'll find out what they've got planned then.'

He could feel Olivia shudder as they walked past the driveway to Gillan Cottage, the blue-and-white police tape stretched between the gate posts and fluttering in the morning breeze.

'I feel like death's stalking us again.' She spoke so quietly he could hardly hear her. He slipped his arm round her shoulders and pulled her close. 'Or we just have an unfortunate knack of being in the wrong place at the wrong time.'

He stopped suddenly. 'Or the right place at the right time, depending on which way you look at it. We did the right thing on the last two occasions and hopefully made our little corner of the world a safer place.'

She shuddered again. 'It doesn't feel very safe at the moment, what with the FHO stuff, Marcus's murder and now Kitten's attack. It's incredible that the police don't think there's a link between the first two, and heaven only knows what they're thinking about Kitten's assault. I don't believe for a moment that what happened yesterday was a coincidence.'

'Neither do I,' Jago agreed. 'If only there was CCTV in this village and round the station, life would be so much easier. We could check people's comings and goings. But there isn't, and people don't even have those doorbell cameras.'

'Locals will say they don't need, or want, them.' Olivia pointed out. 'I suppose some of the bigger houses may have security cameras, but they'll only cover their homes, not the roads and lanes.'

'So we're back to square one and completely dependent on old-fashioned detective work. And by that, I mean finding and talking to the people who have the information we need. Because it's definitely out there,' Jago thought out loud as they carried on walking down the unusually quiet lane, nodding to the various walkers they passed who were making the most of the beautiful day. 'The first thing we need to find out is who the other members of that FHO WhatsApp group are; do some asking around.'

'And how do you suggest we go about that?' Olivia didn't sound convinced.

'We keep our eyes and our ears open and hope that someone is guilted into talking to us about what's been going on. And it doesn't matter how much or how little they think they know. It can all be put together to show us the real picture, like a jigsaw puzzle.'

'I've never liked jigsaw puzzles,' she muttered unhelpfully.

'What!' Jago was amazed. 'Who doesn't like jigsaw puzzles?'

'Me. You start with a box of pieces, organise then into a pretty picture and then deconstruct them back into a box of pieces. What's the point? Why not just look at the complete picture and enjoy it for what it is?'

Jago sighed. *With Olivia in this low mood, it was going to be a long day.*

Olivia's mood seemed to improve slightly when they met Alice and Jasmine on the Waiting Rooms platform, the unmistakeable sound of happy children having fun tinkling through the doors and windows.

'We decided to shut the café to the public today so we could concentrate on the pumpkin-carving workshops Kitten organised. The online booking system went crazy after news of her accident went round. And lots of people have volunteered to help out,' Jasmine explained after throwing her arms around Olivia and setting her tears off again. 'We've now got two morning sessions and two afternoon sessions for the kids. Then we decided to put on an adults' one this evening and that's fully booked too. Everyone wants to show their support for her.' Jago watched Olivia scrabble around for a tissue and wipe the tears from her cheeks.

'We thought it would be a good idea to get all the pumpkins carved today, so people can create the pumpkin trail for Hallowe'en, where they'll be judged in situ tomorrow night,' Alice added, patting Olivia on the arm. 'We did think about cancelling the whole thing, but then we decided Kitten wouldn't want her accident putting a stop to such a worthy cause. Poor girl.' She patted her arm again.

Jago saw a look of confusion cross Olivia's face at the second mention of Kitten's 'accident'. *The police must have decided to withhold information about the real cause of Kitten's fall. Good of Trenow to let them know.*

'That's a great idea and it looks like you've already got a houseful, so we'll leave you to it.' He managed to speak before Olivia had pulled herself together and formed her words. 'We'll be over in the Signal Box if you need us.'

*

'I can't believe the police aren't telling people the truth about Kitten's assault!' Olivia didn't sit in what had become her usual seat on the brown chesterfield sofa which took pride of place beneath the wall of windows overlooking the walkway. Instead she perched on a tall vintage GWR stool, which Jago had recently bought at an auction, and hooked her legs behind the brass footrest. With her back straight against the wall and her arms folded tightly across her chest, it gave her the perfect bird's-eye view of the old station building on the opposite side of the walkway, and she could monitor all the Waiting Room's comings and goings closely. It was a view Jago loved and one which countless railway signalmen would have enjoyed over the years.

He retreated behind his desk and picked up the previous day's newspaper so he could observe both Olivia and the Waiting Rooms more discreetly. The low morning sun filtered through the increasingly leafless trees that lined the walkway and softened the edges of the attractive old building. Any other day he would have taken delight in both her company and their surroundings, but there was too much going through his mind.

'Remind you of old times?' He attempted to lighten the mood in the room and immediately regretted it. Olivia spun round, two spots of colour bright against her pale cheeks, and then turned her face away quickly, but not before Jago had seen her eyes filling with tears.

'I still think about Libby every day. The image of her slumped over her desk, the letter opener sticking out of her chest and the surprised look on her face seems to be imprinted on the inside of my eyelids.' She turned back to Jago. 'I thought I loved Penbartha, but now I'm not so sure.'

He was beside her in an instant, caught hold of her arm and guided her to the sofa. At least he could hold her now and comfort her; she was no longer the prickly, unhappy woman he had met eighteen months ago.

'C'mon, Liv, we need to stay strong for Kitten. And Rocky and Cassie. This isn't about us, and it isn't personal.'

'It feels personal.' She sniffed, but didn't pull away. 'You can't get more personal than someone who's more like a sister than a friend.' She nodded her head in the direction of the Waiting Rooms. 'Just look at all the people who've turned out to support her. And that's without them knowing she was assaulted. Never mind that she's been diagnosed with a horrible disease that she hasn't told anyone about.'

'I know, I know,' he murmured into her hair and felt her relax a little. 'I think we need to let Kitten explain her reasons for that in her own time.'

'I just wish we knew what the police are playing at.' Her body tensed again at a sudden commotion outside and they both craned their necks to look out of the window behind them. It was obviously change-over time for the morning session as there were parents and children milling round, but above the general chatter they could hear the raised voices of a man and woman.

'Bloody hell! It's Trenow and Jasmine. Having a right old stand-off.' Jago got to his feet, pulling Olivia with him. 'I think it's time for us to intervene.'

By the time they'd crossed the walkway, most of the onlookers had dispersed, and as soon as they saw him and Olivia approaching, the rest beat a hasty retreat.

'I'm sorry. But I was just trying to help.' A tearful Jasmine was standing up to a very angry-looking Trenow.

'By destroying every last scrap of evidence at a crime scene. In what world would that be helping anyone? Are you stupid or what?'

Olivia jumped in before Jago could. 'Please don't speak to Jasmine like that, Inspector Trenow. It's not helping anyone.'

She stood firmly beside her employee, like the mother tiger she could so easily turn into if anyone threatened her nearest and dearest. She was back to her old self. Other people's needs put firmly before her own.

Trenow spun round on his heel. 'Have you any idea what this stupid woman's done?' The look Olivia sent him would have made many other men quake, but the policeman was too angry to notice. 'She's only gone and got her sodding mop and bucket out and washed and bleached the stairway and vestibule to Kitten's flat.'

Boy, was Trenow going to get bollocked by his superiors for this.

'I thought I was helping. I didn't want anyone else coming in and finding all that blood everywhere!'

'Exactly! God only knows what other evidence you've destroyed!'

Jasmine burst into tears. 'I don't know what you're talking about. What evidence? Why would there be evidence? Kitten lost her balance and fell down the stairs. You told Alice it was an accident.'

Jago stood the other side of Jasmine. 'That's what I heard too.' He raised an eyebrow. 'Interesting choice of words, given the circumstances.'

'I'm not prepared to be cross-examined by you over this, Jago. We're not in court.' Trenow was clearly rattled. 'I'm focused on the fact that when the SOCO team arrived at eight o'clock this morning to examine the scene, it had already been cleaned. Very thoroughly.'

'It's not Jasmine's fault that your team only work office hours.' Jago pointed out. 'Or that no one else had thought to drop by to secure the scene. Or that someone, in their infinite wisdom, decided to tell people Kitten had just had a fall.'

Jasmine's brown eyes widened in her round face. 'Wasn't it just a fall? Oh my God!'

'See what you've done?' Olivia demanded. 'This could all have been prevented if you'd managed the situation properly.'

'Did you clean the fire extinguisher at the top of the landing, Jas?' Jago asked her.

Jasmine thought quickly. 'No. It was attached to the wall, so I didn't give it any thought. I just concentrated on getting the blood off the stairs, the walls and the floors.' Her face crumpled. 'It was a horrible mess.'

'So there might still be some evidence on the fire extinguisher, or some fibres or hairs that have caught on the handrail or skirting board. You need to call your SOCOs back. And secure the place so no one else drops in to do a bit of housework.' Jago lessened the bite of his words with a small wink at Jasmine.

'Thanks for telling me how to do my job,' Trenow muttered through gritted teeth. He pulled his mobile out of his pocket and stabbed angrily at the screen.

'And what am I supposed to do?' Jasmine spoke up. 'Go back in to the workshops and pretend Kitten just had a fall?'

'I think you're probably the only person who works here who's capable of doing that.' Olivia squeezed her arm.

'I agree,' Jago said with a reassuring smile for Jasmine. 'You don't need to say anything to anyone, other than that Kitten's had a nasty fall, but all the signs are good. If the noise that's coming out of the Waiting Rooms is anything to go by, everyone's having such a good time I doubt they're talking about what happened.' He turned to Trenow. 'Don't you agree, Inspector?'

Trenow mumbled his reluctant consent.

What on earth was the matter with the man? He'd blamed a member of the public for his own schoolboy error and been incredibly rude to her and wasn't really taking control of the situation the way he should. Jago resolved to catch up with him when this was over and see if he was okay.

'Could anyone else be in danger?' Jasmine's quiet voice spoke up. 'A murder in a place like this is bad enough, but folks are just putting that down to him being a Londoner who'd probably upset someone upcountry. But if Kitten's been attacked, that puts a whole different spin on things. Was it personal? Random? Are there going to be more attacks?' She turned to Trenow, her face full of concern. 'And what exactly are the police doing about it?'

'I couldn't have asked a better question myself.' Jago smiled brightly as a sudden movement on the walkway caught his eye. 'We'll leave it to you, Inspector, to explain to Jasmine exactly what you want her to do now. In the meantime, Olivia and I have to be somewhere else.'

'What are you doing?' Olivia whispered furiously as Jago pulled her past the Goods Shed and further down the walkway. 'We can't just abandon Jasmine like that.'

'Wait and see,' he whispered back.

Slightly further ahead along the path, Olivia could see someone sitting on a bench. As they got closer, the straight-backed figure of Caroline Pellow came into focus.

'Did anyone see you coming here?' There was no mistaking the anxiety in her voice.

'I don't think so.' Jago glanced around. 'Why all the secrecy, Caroline?'

The sharp face glared at them both. 'I think you might be in danger, and I don't want anyone to see me talking to you. In case they think I'm warning you.'

'Nice to hear you're so concerned about our welfare.'

Caroline reddened. 'Do you want me to tell you or not? I could be putting my neck on the line here.'

'Sorry, Caroline,' Olivia spoke up. 'We do appreciate your help.'

'Like I said, you're a good girl. Mollie would be proud of you and she'd want me to help. I wanted to let you know that the FHO group chat has disappeared.'

'How d'you mean?'

Caroline shook her head. 'It's been completely deleted. Without trace.'

'Perhaps they've decided enough is enough and they're drawing a line under everything?' Olivia suggested, without much conviction.

Caroline looked at her as if she was slightly simple. 'And more of that last message from the FHO group has come back to me.'

'Oh good. We wanted to ask you if you'd had any further thoughts about who the other members could be. That's even more important for us to know now the chat's gone.'

'Ssh, Jago. Let Caroline speak.'

'It said Olivia and you had been sniffing around and if we couldn't scare her off, we were to scare someone close to you. I'm really sorry, love.'

Olivia's face paled. 'So you think Kitten was targeted because of us? As a warning?'

'I'd say so. Wouldn't you?'

23

Olivia spent an unplanned Saturday morning sorting out a listed building query that had arrived via email late the day before. It involved some precise measurements and materials choices for an upcoming project, and while Rocky would have known the answer immediately, there was no way she was going to bother him with it. Since she had a long run scheduled on Sunday, this was her only opportunity to get it done, and she headed off to her studio in the Goods Shed to find the exact drawing and hunt through their files and samples. She wanted the reply to be in the conservation officer's inbox when they got into work on Monday.

As often happened, she got chatting to two newer members of the Goods Shed who were also busy at work, despite it being a Saturday. They were young entrepreneurs who were collating an eco-conscious online directory which showcased a curated selection of local enterprises committed to sustainability, green practices, and ethical principles in the area. Olivia loved the way the Goods Shed members spoke, buzzing with infectious enthusiasm about the work they did, their plans, hopes and vision for the future. Just listening to them talk reminded her why her godfather had worked so hard to create this collaborative and dynamic environment and always made her feel inspired.

It also made time fly. A phone call from Jago, who'd decided to check on how Jasmine was doing, and was now suggesting a late lunch in the Waiting Rooms, eventually dragged Olivia away from the Goods Shed. They managed an entire meal without talking about everything that was going on, but as they walked back to Tresillian, she felt her mood dropping.

'I don't know what I feel worse about,' Olivia confessed. 'The fact that Kitten's been diagnosed with a life-changing disease or that someone attacked her as a warning to us. How am I ever going to look her in the face again? Or Rocky? Or Cassie?'

Jago put his arm round her shoulders. 'We don't know for sure that her attack had anything to do with us. And no one, other than us and Caroline, knows that she may have been attacked as a warning to us.'

She snuggled into his side for a moment. *Thank God for Jago. He always knew just what to say to calm her down.* The feeling didn't last long.

'But all the others in the FHO group – whoever they may be – will have read the message with the warning in it.'

'If the police are keeping the real reason behind Kitten's fall quiet, I doubt they'll put two and two together. It does prove one thing, though.'

She sighed, a dark, heavy feeling beginning to pool in the bottom of her stomach. 'I know. That the FHO group is connected to both Marcus's murder and Kitten's attack. So, what do we do now?'

'I think we carry on. But more under the radar. 'What choice have we got?'

'Won't Trenow be looking for whoever pushed her?'

'Yes, but he has to follow procedure. That's why I reckon we have a far better chance of getting to the bottom of things than they do. We can do whatever we want and don't have to answer to anyone.'

'But can we?'

'Look what we've found out so far – far more than Trenow has. And that's because we've been able to cherry-pick the people we talk to. We just need to carry on. The answer's here in Penbartha, I know it.' He pulled her to him again. 'Look, Liv, we've done it before and we can do it again.'

'I can't bear the thought of anyone else getting hurt.'

'Believe me.' He caught hold of her hands. 'If anyone else gets hurt, it won't be because of us. Whoever's behind all this has an agenda. And they're not going to let anyone get in the way of it.'

Olivia started walking again. It was mid-afternoon, but because of the low cloud, daylight was disappearing fast, and the earthy scents of autumn mingled with woodsmoke and the unmistakable tang of coal were heightened by the sudden chill in the air. It brought back a rush of vivid memories of her younger years in Penbartha that felt like a punch to her stomach. She pushed her hands deeper into her pockets and came to a decision.

'I don't want to talk about all this anymore today, Jago, let alone think about it. Can we just get the pumpkin trail this evening out of the way and take lots of photos to show Kitten, please? It will be good to see the village coming together.'

'Fine.' They carried on walking, their breath beginning to cloud in front of them. 'Since when has Hallowe'en become such a thing in England anyway? Something else the Americans are to blame for?'

'Hallowe'en here isn't anything like it is in New York!' Olivia insisted. 'It's in places like Penbartha where we're lucky still to have quite a few elderly people, that the old, proper traditions of Hallowe'en still survive. It's so much more genuine and real. Like it really means something.'

'But pumpkins?'

'Hallowe'en is the night when the barriers between the worlds of the living and the dead are at their thinnest and the souls of the departed spirits are allowed to return to earth. The Celts carved turnips to ward off evil spirits on that night, but when so many Irish emigrated to North America they struggled to find turnips, and as pumpkins were more readily available and much easier to carve, they used those instead.'

'Who knew?' Jago looked impressed.

'If you lived with Mollie you'd know more about the pagan Wheel of the Year and its festivals than you could ever imagine. Not the commercialised plastic and nylon version you see in the shops. She always celebrated Samhain, as the pagans call it, because it was all about remembering and honouring your ancestors.'

'Is that why so many photographs of Mollie and George have suddenly appeared around the house?'

'It's tradition. I don't need photos to make me think of them, but it was one of her favourite times and they always had a celebration. Family meant so much to her.' She paused, her voice suddenly choked. 'I miss them both, but especially Mollie, even more at this time of year.'

'Put your faith in Mollie, then.' He squeezed her gently. 'She was a very wise woman, and she'll show you the way.'

As they reached the drive to Tresillian, Olivia gasped out loud. There in the gateway was a collection of pumpkins of all sizes, with suns, moons, stars, flowers and leaves carved into them and all lit by LED flameless candles casting a warm glow across the drive.

'Aren't they beautiful? I wonder who put them here?' Olivia followed Jago's arm, pointing to the Coach House, near the top of the drive, where Sam's car sat outside. 'D'you reckon Cassie's home?'

'Only one way to find out.' He stood looking at her expectantly.

Olivia felt sick. 'What if she hates me for what's happened?'

'She won't, but avoiding her isn't going to help anything. The sooner we see her, the better.' He held out his hand and led her down the drive to the Coach House.

'Oh my lovely!' Cassie had barely opened the door when she threw her arms round Olivia and drew her inside. 'And Jago!' He received an equally big hug and gave Olivia the thumbs-up sign above Cassie's head.

'C'mon up.' She eventually let Olivia go. 'Sam's making tea. We've been at the hospital since this morning and haven't been back long.'

'How's Kitten doing?' They followed her up the stairs into the cosy open-plan area that took up the whole of the first floor of the old coach house.

'Well, thanks. Still very sleepy and not saying much, but the doctors say it's all going in the right direction.' Cassie turned tired eyes on them both. 'Rocky's with her now. We've told the hospital that we'll do shifts until she's completely out of the woods.'

Olivia's heart lurched. 'But she will be okay?'

Cassie clasped her hand. 'We hope so. They keep warning us about the unpredictability of head injuries. And they won't let the police question her yet.'

'But they also say she's doing as well as can be expected.' Sam joined them, handed out mugs of tea and sat down next to Cassie, his hand resting on her upper thigh. 'Which I reckon is about as good we're going to get from the medics for now.'

'That sounds promising.' Olivia could feel Jago's eyes on her, but she still needed to come clean.

'Look, Cassie, I'm really sorry if you or Kitten or Rocky think that anything we did could have made someone attack her.'

Cassie's tired green eyes turned to her. 'Why would we think that?'

'Because of all the stuff that's been going on in the village and the murder.'

'There's no evidence to suggest there's any connection between those two things,' Sam said quickly.

'Couldn't Kitten's attack be seen as evidence, or even the link?' Jago asked, very politely.

'How do you mean?' Cassie was on the edge of her seat again, clutching her tissue tightly.

'I think we can agree that all the anti-second homes stuff led to the fires at Gillan Cottage and Alfie's arrest for the murder of Walker-Smith. Kitten always made her support for Alfie very clear, and she asked us to help him by finding the person who was blackmailing him. Although we haven't managed that yet, Alfie's subsequent release without charge has left the police without a viable suspect and a killer still at large.'

'I can't accept that Kitten was attacked by someone who knows she's close to Olivia and was warning her off. Despite what that supposed message said. If it even existed,' Sam said crossly. 'Really?'

'Stranger things have happened here, believe me.'

Olivia looked at Jago quickly. She could tell from the set of his mouth that he wasn't impressed with the policeman's response.

The two men continued to glare at each other across the room. Cassie dropped her head into her hands, but when she lifted it back up, her face was dry and her eyes bright.

'I know for a fact that Kitten wouldn't blame you for what's happened. I also know that she'd want you to find the person responsible.' She spoke firmly. 'And so do I.'

'That's our job, Cass,' Sam said. 'Leave it to the professionals.'

'And what have you achieved so far?' she demanded, tears filing her eyes again. 'Nothing! Zilch! Trenow's so useless at the moment, he didn't even bother securing the entrance to Kitten's flat and Jasmine cleaned all the evidence away!'

The jungle drums had been jumping!

'That wasn't really his job,' Sam said feebly.

'But it was his job to make sure someone else did! He told you to take time off, that you were too close to everything to be of any help.' Cassie was in full flow, and Olivia watched in admiration. 'And why is he so reluctant to let it be known publicly that that Kitten just didn't fall down her stairs, that she was attacked with a bloody great fire extinguisher?'

Sam looked up at the ceiling. 'I have no idea,' he confessed. 'The boss will have his reasons, I'm sure. He just hasn't shared them with me. But I do know that SOCO have retrieved the fire extinguisher, so hopefully something will come of that.'

'Has he taken you off the case?'

'Unofficially, yes. He's waiting for a replacement.' Sam ran his hands over his unshaven face. 'I don't want to talk out of turn, but I'm not sure what he's playing at. And now Rafe seems to have disappeared completely.'

'The sign of a guilty conscience?' suggested Jago.

'And meanwhile, my poor little girl is coping with two of the most awful things that could ever happen to a person.' Cassie's tears started to fall again, and Olivia put her arms round her and sent a pleading look to Jago.

'Right.' He took control. 'Your job, Cassie, is to concentrate on Kitten and only Kitten. We don't want you worrying about anything else. Carry on the shifts with Rocky, and we'll fit in when needed.' He turned to Sam. 'Until you know where you stand with Trenow, I suggest that you support Cass.'

Sam grimaced. 'And what about finding the bastard that did this to Kitten?'

'Leave that to us, for now,' Jago declared. 'But if you find anything out that might help us, it would be good if you could share it.'

'Right. So you're happy for me to slip you any inside information I might have, but not help directly?'

'Please don't be offended, Sam, but people round here aren't going to talk to you,' Olivia explained. 'And I'm sure Cass would like your support, wouldn't you, Cass?'

She nodded gratefully and caught hold of Sam's hand. 'Please.'

There was no way Sam would deny her that. Olivia smiled as she saw the gentle expression cross his face.

'I still think you might be conflating two separate issues here.' Sam wasn't going to give in without a fight.

'And Kitten's attack was a complete coincidence, was it?' Jago retorted. 'I don't think so, Sam. And we'll get the evidence to prove it.'

Olivia glanced at Jago. She could tell he was getting frustrated with the policeman, but she also knew that was not going to help anyone. She stood up and gestured to Jago to do the same.

'Okay. We'll be off.' She smiled at Cassie. 'But we'll be back at about half past four so we can all go on Kitten's pumpkin trail around the village and thank everyone for their support.' Half of her wondered whether Cassie would agree or if she'd shy away from people's concern.

Cassie's face brightened. 'Yes, and did you see that beautiful collection of pumpkins at the top of the drive? They're so pretty!'

'Aren't they? My money's on Jasmine for those.'

'Mine too. I must thank her when I see her. I'm going to check how Kitten's doing with Rocky, and if everything is okay, I'll definitely come along. We can take lots of photos and show them to Kitten later. She'll love that.'

The sun was just setting as the four of them walked up the drive to the lane which was carpeted in swirls of fallen leaves the colours of an upmarket toffee selection. The dark sky slowly brightened with stars, and a sliver of a moon hung among them, hinting at sharp frosty weather to come. They were all in a more light-hearted mood as Rocky's update about Kitten had been full of hopeful news. As they passed the gateway to Gillan Cottage, Cassie stopped for a moment and peered into the gloom of the garden. 'Oh, I forgot! I had a message from Jasper this morning, saying he was planning on coming back any day to sort out the house. I must reply and invite him to dinner. Poor man – I hope the housekeeper he uses has made it comfortable for him, and it doesn't smell too much of smoke.'

'I can't see any lights on, so it doesn't look like he's back yet.' Jago peered through the hedge as they carried on walking. 'I don't envy him sorting all that mess out.'

'Oh, wow!' Olivia squealed. 'Look at all the pumpkins lighting up the gateways all the way down the lane!' Her excited words distracted the others from their thoughts of Gillan and they all hurried ahead drawn by the orange glows in driveways, and as they got further down the lane and the houses got smaller and closer together, in many cottage windows and porches the intricately patterned hollowed-out pumpkins glowed prettily into the twilight.

'They are all so beautiful!' Cassie exclaimed. 'And not an evil one among them.'

'It was agreed at the workshops yesterday that there wouldn't be any spooky or scary ones this year,' Olivia explained. 'It was Kitten's idea that this year we'd concentrate on the more positive aspects of Hallowe'en.' She fumbled for her mobile, deep in the pocket of the warm winter jacket she was wearing. 'Jas said she'd send me a digital map of the trail, so we can make sure we see everything.' She squinted at the screen. 'Got it. And it looks like there are various charity collection points along the way. Jack's doing mulled wine and snacks at the pub and then there's a display of extra pumpkins on the playing field where the bonfire's being built for next weekend. Oh, and you need to pay careful attention, Cass. Apparently you're doing the judging. Jas'll meet you in the village with a clipboard.'

'Really? Oh, that's so kind of them. Kitten will be thrilled.' Cassie's eyes filled with fresh tears. 'Right, Sam, get your notebook out. If I'm going to do this, I'm doing it properly.'

It took two hours before Cassie announced that she had seen all the pumpkins on offer, apart from those on the playing field. Not only because there was a bumper number of entries, but because concern for Kitten had enticed people out of their homes on the first really cold evening of the season and they wanted to chat and send messages of support. Everyone was wrapped up in their cosiest coats and boots, often stomping from foot to foot to keep warm as they exclaimed happily over the carved pumpkins and threw coins into the buckets being rattled by various members of the Goods Shed who had turned out to show their support. Once Olivia had lost the feeling in both feet, she suggested they retreat to the pub to thaw out and allow Cassie to study her notes before she declared the overall winner.

The Ship Inn, with its low beams, smooth flagstone flooring and crackling fire was crammed, mainly with locals, but there were a few tourists determined to get their money's worth out of their half term holiday, and no doubt wondering what all the fuss was about. It wasn't long before the mulled wine went to Cassie's head, and they set off back down the hill to the playing field to complete the rest of their duties. There were even more people there than in the pub, and they soon saw the reason why – Willow and Fraser had set up trestle tables and were serving coffee, tea and hot chocolate along with pumpkin-shaped iced cookies. It took a long time to reach them. Everyone with children seemed to be on the field, even Emily and Silas with Darragh.

'This is so good of you!' Olivia threw her arms round her friend as soon as she could get near. 'What a brilliant idea.'

'It was the least we could do.' Willow hugged her. 'And we're donating all the profits to Kitten's charity. How is she doing?'

'They seem to be pleased with her progress.' Olivia trotted out the line they'd all agreed on and then changed the subject quickly. 'Where's my handsome godson?'

'Caroline offered to look after him.'

Olivia did a double take. 'I'm sorry?'

Willow smiled. 'She said she thought you'd really appreciate seeing both me and Fraser showing our support for you. And then offered to babysit Dougie.'

'How's that going?'

'She's so good with him, and he loves her. You wouldn't believe it.'

Olivia was lost for words and went to stand with Jago and Fraser while Willow served the next person in the queue.

'What's going on over there?' Jago asked.

'Oh that's where the wood's being collected for the bonfire,' Fraser told him. 'Folks have been bringing driftwood, fallen branches and old pallets all week. Finn Nankivell is organising the building of it on Thursday, if you want to come along. It's going to be extra big as we're having silent fireworks this year.'

'About time too. All those poor animals and pets who are sacred witless by the noise,' Olivia declared. 'We're looking forward to Penbartha proving it can be done in much more environmentally friendly way, aren't we, Jago?'

But Jago wasn't listening. His eyes were focused on a pile of what looked like rags and mannequins next to the neatly stacked wood.

'Oh, that's just the guys. Awaiting their gruesome fate.' Fraser topped up their mugs of hot chocolate. 'I wouldn't look too closely if I were you. Some are horribly realistic.'

Jago ignored the advice and wandered off across the field. He was back in minutes, his face white. 'Where's Sam? We need him here. Now.'

'He's over there. I'll call him. What's the matter?' Olivia could feel familiar prickles of concern march up her spine.

'I've just had a quick look at that pile of guys, and I'm pretty sure Rafe Burrows's body is among them.'

24

November dawned bright, sunny and cold. The creek was quiet, although there were a few locals on the opposite bank, out for an early dog walk. Jago sniffed at the woodsmoke as it drifted upstream from the village, and the few boats still moored out in the creek bobbed on the gentle swell of the tide, their mooring ropes creaking gently.

Jago sat on the small quay, his back against the stone balustrade that was covered with lichen and weathered by centuries of storms, enjoying the beautiful views up the creek towards the village in one direction and out to the Carrick Roads estuary in the other. He'd adopted it as his favourite place to sit and think, just as Mollie had in her day and Olivia did now. She'd gone for a long run with the trail running club she'd recently joined. They met at weekends and went further afield and ran much longer distances than she usually did by herself. After a sleepless night she'd told him that she needed to run long and hard to clear her head and get her thoughts and feelings sorted. Happy that she was with company, Jago had contemplated getting his kayak out of the boatshed and doing his own workout, keen to rid his own head of the images of Rafe's bloated face and staring eyes, but the sharp chill in the air had soon convinced him that sunshine and fresh air would suffice

Although he was still convinced that the two murders,

Kitten's assault and the FHO issues were all connected in some way, he was at a loss as to how. Someone, or something, was the link that tied them all together, and once they knew what that was, the pieces of the puzzle would fit together. But for now, all that he was sure of was that the person or persons responsible were irrational and therefore unpredictable, and they all needed to tread very, very carefully. And as for the police…

'Morning, Jago!' Sam walked across the lawn, a thermos mug in each hand. He handed one over. 'Cass doesn't want you getting cold.'

'She's a good woman.' Jago stood up and took the mug with a grateful smile. 'Always putting others first.'

'That's my Cass.' The wistful note in his voice made Jago's ears prick up.

'How's the patient today?

'Rocky's called to say she had a good night and they're all pleased with her. He'll wait for us to take over and then he'll go home to get some kip.'

'How's Kitten's arm?'

'She's got a definite fracture of the left radius and ulna, but it doesn't require surgery, thankfully. They reckon she'll be in a cast for about six weeks.'

He frowned. 'She's left-handed isn't she?'

Sam shrugged. 'No idea. Why?'

Jago glanced at him, but he was watching three kayakers racing up the creek and being cheered on by people on the opposite bank. 'No reason.' He paused. 'She is going to be okay, isn't she? I'm not sure how Olivia would cope, or Cassie, if—'

'I reckon so,' Sam cut him off. 'They breed them tough down here. I know she's got her MS diagnosis to deal with, but she's also got a lot of people who love her.'

'I know Olivia really wants to see her. Me too.'

Sam nodded. 'I know. And Cassie thinks it will do Kitten good to see you both. Maybe tomorrow, if all goes well today.'

Jago brightened at the thought. 'That would be great. Thanks. I need to warn you about life in this village, Sam, it sucks you in. In a good way.'

He laughed. 'I'm beginning to find that out. But I'm afraid I'm already in too deep with Cass to get out now.'

'I understand that feeling. Life has certainly been a hell of a lot more complicated since I got involved with Olivia, but I wouldn't have it any other way.' They exchanged a conspiratorial look, and Jago felt the air between them had cleared.

He sipped his coffee and looked round the lawn, covered in a carpet of red and golden leaves. 'Do you think I could help Cassie by sweeping up some of these leaves? I know the garden's her domain, but I fancy doing some manual labour.'

Sam sucked in his breath. 'Not if you value your life. I offered to do the very same the other day and got a half-hour lecture on how a leaf-sprinkled lawn may look a mess to humans, but it's a vital source of nutrients and shelter to wildlife and insects.'

'Ah.'

'I could tell you more about how the insects and worms love the leaves and the birds and hedgehogs love the worms and so on, if you like.'

'I get the picture.' Jago grinned. 'I can certainly see where Kitten gets it from, sometimes.'

Sam turned. 'Look, about last night.'

Jago raised an eyebrow. 'Before or after the grisly discovery?'

'Both really.'

'Fire away.'

'Look, I know I said I wasn't convinced that everything that's been going on round here is connected, but I'm beginning to agree with you now.'

Hallelujah! Jago felt ridiculously pleased that Sam was finally on board. 'Dare I ask what's changed your mind?'

Sam looked away. 'I don't want to talk ill of Trenow. He's my boss, and I respect him. Usually. But he's going for a promotion and so has to do things by the book. Not that he doesn't normally, but he's particularly fussy and difficult at the moment.'

'It's a pity he wasn't a bit fussier when it came to the scene of Kitten's assault,' Jago retorted. 'God knows what evidence was lost when that was cleaned.'

Sam grimaced. 'Indeed. God only knows how his mind is working at the moment. But as far as I'm concerned, there's a definite link between the two murders and Kitten's attack. I'm even beginning to agree with Olivia that perhaps Kitten was attacked as a warning that the perpetrator means business.'

Jago took a sudden interest in a pile of fresh leaves that had settled over his shoes. 'I agree. But I still think the FHO stuff is connected somehow, or it was in the beginning. More importantly, I think that the group, or at least the person or persons behind it, is the link we're looking for. The blackmailer is either the murderer or will lead us to him.'

Sam shook his head. 'I think they are separate issues.'

'No.' Jago stood his ground. 'That's not how things work round here. I'm sure the final piece of this puzzle is closer to home than we realise. It might not make sense now, but once we know what it is, everything else will slide into place.'

'Have it your way. I think Trenow wants to talk to Kitten today if she's up to it. If I hear anything that could be of use, I'll let you know.' He looked at his watch and then held out a hand for Jago's empty mug. 'And speaking of which, I'd best be off.'

Well, that was an interesting change of direction. Jago shoved his hands further into his waxed jacket as a sudden gust of wind blew along the creek, and he hunkered back down behind the stone balustrade, mulling over Sam's words. He could understand why Trenow was being so cautious if his career was at stake, but he also knew the detective wouldn't solve the case that way. At least they had Sam on their side now.

'Ahoy there! Permission to come alongside!' A stranger's voice jolted Jago from his thoughts. He looked around in surprise, expecting a dinghy or a RIB. Instead, two sea kayaks, the paddlers sitting low in their enclosed cockpits, pulled up next to the quay.

'I'll leave you to it then, Jasper,' one man said to the other. 'I need to get home.'

'Thanks for the invite, Finn, and the loan of the kayak. It's in good hands.'

'It's great to see you again. Don't be a stranger.' The two men bumped fists across the water and Finn Nankivell took off down the creek towards the village.

So this was Jasper Swift. Jago remembered his manners. 'Shall I haul you up our slipway?'

A grin split Jasper's face. 'Please. The one at Gillan's been damaged by the fire.'

Once on dry ground, the two men shook hands, introduced themselves and quickly lapsed into chatting about kayaking and sailing in general. Jasper certainly matched the image Jago had created of him in his mind from what he'd heard about him. The full extent of his career as an experienced yachtsman who'd sailed and raced all over the world just shone out of the way he spoke and was reinforced by his slight, wiry figure, close-cropped grey hair and beard and weather-beaten face. He exuded a quiet confidence and strong determination, and Jago, despite his earlier misgivings, found himself warming to Jasper.

'Do you want to keep your kayak in our boat shed while you're here?' Jago offered. 'There's only my stuff in there, and I can give you the combination lock code.'

'That would be great, thanks. Especially as it's not mine.' Jasper unzipped the top of his drysuit and wriggled his arms out of it, revealing a fleece top underneath. 'In the good old days I just left all my stuff out in the garden, but with what I've heard about what's been going round here lately, I think I'd better take you up on that offer.'

'Probably for the best.' Jago led the way to the boat shed and helped Jasper stow his kayak away. 'It's been a bit of a full-on time.'

'So I gather. Finn's been filling me in. I'm sorry it's taken me so long to get over here, but I had a publishing deadline for my next sailing book, and you know what they're like.'

Jago didn't, but could imagine.

'And then I struggled to get a flight. I only landed at Heathrow yesterday afternoon, and it was really late by the time I'd driven down. Tresillian and the Coach House were in darkness, so I thought I'd be better catching up with you all today.'

'You can't have had much sleep then, if you've been up and about already.'

'All the solo, long-distance sailing I've done means I'm used to operating on not much sleep,' Jasper explained. 'But the jet lag's a killer. I'll try to keep going today, and then after a good night's sleep, I'll be as fresh as a daisy by tomorrow.'

Jago nodded in the direction of Gillan. 'You've certainly got your work cut out there.'

'Tell me about it. Fortunately, the smoke damage inside is mainly superficial. Although it will still be a nightmare to sort. The outside is a complete mess.' He closed his eyes for a moment. 'Mum and Dad would be heartbroken. They put their hearts and souls into that garden.'

'So I understand. I'm sorry.'

Jasper cleared his throat noisily. 'But I suppose two murders put a damaged garden into perspective, don't they?' He shook his head. 'Who'd have thought it in a peaceful place like this? It certainly sounds like things have changed round here.'

'Have the police spoken to you lately about their investigation?'

'No. I had a message to say the crime scene investigators had finished in the garden, but there's been a deafening silence ever since. That's another reason I decided to come over. I thought it would be easier to deal with them and the insurance people and then sort out repairs in person, rather than from four thousand miles away.'

'Sounds sensible.'

'And I suppose I'll have to go through how I have absolutely no idea who the two murdered men were. Or why one of them had apparently shown an interest in buying Gillan and the other had taken it upon himself to erect his For Sale board on my property.' He turned his bemused face to Jago. 'You hear about people selling houses they don't own, but you don't think it will happen to you.'

Jago racked his brain. 'I think it's quite rare, fortunately. It must be a legal nightmare.'

'But it does happen. Especially with properties that are empty. I've been looking into it this last week, trying to work out what could have been going on.'

'Do you think it was targeted because it's empty?'

Jasper rubbed the back of his neck. 'It's all I can come up with so far. I know this anti-second homes group has been active recently, but Gillan's my only home in this country, and if they're local, they should know that. Besides, it's not as if the average local person could afford to buy it, even if they wanted to, is it?'

'Have you ever thought about selling it?'

'At times. But it would be such a wrench. My parents put a lifetime's work and love into the house and garden, and they always said they wanted it kept in the family. I just can't see that happening. My sailing takes me all over the world and my kids are in Canada, and I doubt they'll want it.' He pursed his lips and turned to Jago. 'To be honest, it can feel like a bit like a millstone at times. And now I feel like I've landed in an episode of *Midsomer Murders*!'

Jago chuckled. 'I can relate to that.'

'And besides, from what I've heard from Finn the bottom has completely dropped out of the property market in this country and it's flooded with expensive houses that no one wants to buy. Look at the position Finn and Louisa are in. It's a nightmare for them.'

'It's a weird old time for lots of people, I think. I suppose the best thing you can do is make sure the house is safe from fraudsters from now on.'

'That's first on my list of jobs.'

They walked up the garden towards the drive in a sombre silence, but as they passed the Coach House, Jasper stopped. 'I really must call in on Cassie and see how her daughter's doing. Finn just told me she'd been hurt.'

'Cassie's at the hospital visiting Kitten – that's her daughter.'

'Ah yes. I'm not sure I've ever met her. I moved to Canada years before George and Mollie had the foresight to employ Cassie. I wish my parents had done something similar. Things might have turned out very differently.' He looked across at Jago. 'So how's Kitten doing?'

'To quote the medics, "as well as can be expected".' Jago trotted out his usual line, without thinking.

Jasper stopped. 'That doesn't sound good. Finn said she'd just fallen down some stairs. How bad is it?'

Jago felt he had to reassure him. 'No, she's doing okay. Really.'

'Do they know what happened yet? What caused her to fall?'

'Not yet.' Jago hated himself for being so guarded and vague. 'The medics hope she might remember more as the days go on.'

'Poor girl! I do hope she's okay.' They reached the lane. 'And how's Olivia? I can't believe I haven't asked about her yet!'

'She's fine thanks. Out with a trail-running group that go out for fifteen, twenty-mile runs at weekends. But at least the dogs have a day off.'

'And where are they?'

'On a spa break.' That was another line Jago and Olivia had decided to trot out when anybody asked about the dogs. 'We're both really busy at work at the moment, so it's better for them to be spoiled rotten.'

Jasper laughed. 'It really is a dog's life, isn't it? Right. I'd better be off and start on my enormous list of jobs. But why don't we all get together in the Ship one evening for a proper catch-up?'

'Sounds good to me. Let's just see how things go with Kitten today, shall we?'

'Of course. God, I'm not sure if it's the shock of all that's happened here or this jet lag which is playing with my manners.'

With an apologetic wave, Jasper walked off down the lane to Gillan, and Jago wandered back to Tresillian, lost in thought.

25

Kitten swallowed her painkillers with a gulp of water and lay back on her pillows with a sigh of relief.

'Well, that's not the best way to start a new week, but at least the police interview is out of the way now,' the nurse said, smoothing her bedcovers. 'Although, how you were supposed to have seen anything when you were hit on the head from behind, I don't know.'

Kitten agreed. 'That's what I said.' She knew she hadn't given Trenow much information, but she was desperate to get out of her hospital room, with its antiseptic smells, electronic beeps and call bells constantly ringing and get back to the peace of Penbartha. The police interview was another box that had to be ticked before the doctors would consider discharging her, and she wanted to get it out of the way.

'Why don't you have a rest before that gorgeous boyfriend of yours comes in?' The nurse smiled. She and her colleagues hadn't even tried to hide how much they liked Rocky and admired his obvious devotion to her. It had made her think about things she hadn't thought she was ready for yet.

Kitten smiled back. Despite still having the headache from hell, the assault had put everything into perspective for her, and she was pretty sure she now knew where her future with Rocky lay. What was really bothering her was the feeling that there was something niggling at the back of her memory, tantalisingly out of reach, and every time she thought she was about to grasp it, it floated away again. 'I think I will, thanks.' And still trying to capture that elusive memory, she drifted off.

Kitten woke to the feeling of Rocky's soft stubble brushing against her cheek as he kissed her. She lifted her unplastered arm to hug him, and he clasped her firmly to him.

'Hey,' he whispered into her hair. 'How's the head?'

'Still sore, but a bit less, I think.'

'That's so good to hear. Everyone's asking about you. Even Jasper, who's back to sort out Gillan Cottage. Jago saw him yesterday.'

'I'm glad he's back. That beautiful house needs looking after properly.'

He settled her back on her pillow and fussed around her, until she flapped his hands away. 'Stop it, Rocky. We need to talk.'

A look of devastation crossed his tired face, and she mentally kicked herself. 'I'm just going to ask you something, and I want you to be honest with me.' She held his hand tightly.

He nodded.

'Have you thought any more about my diagnosis?'

He swallowed. 'Not a lot. I've done a bit of research online, but I've mostly been preoccupied with the idea that you could have been killed.' He paused. 'And it's like I said last week, I love you, and I want to be with you. No matter what. That's never going to change.'

'But have you thought about the implications? We need to look at our options, plan round my symptoms, that sort of thing. I need to be in control of my own life, as much as I can be. Do you understand that?'

He kissed her hand, and when he looked up, his black eyes were glistening. 'I'm just so glad you're alive, Kitti-Kat. We can do this. Together. We can cope with whatever life throws at us, as long as we're together.'

Kitten nodded and chose her words carefully. 'I know I could have died in that fall, Rocky. And that's made me realise how lucky I am. In all sorts of ways. Okay, an MS diagnosis isn't the best news in the world at my age, but it's by no means the worst.' She grasped his hand. 'A specialist nurse came to see me earlier, and she was amazing. I hadn't realised there was so much support out there, medications, options. It's not necessarily the life sentence it used to be. I feel so much more positive now.'

'Good. I'm not going anywhere. We'll sort it. We'll sort everything. I promise.'

'Baby steps, Rocky. We need to take things slowly.' She gestured at the bandage on her head. 'Especially with this. But I'd like you to be there.'

'Always.' He caught her up in a tight hug, and lying there, her arms wrapped round the man who had calmed her down and loved her for who she was, accepted all her passions and shared her dreams, Kitten felt very lucky .

'Hey, I'm not sure that sort of thing is allowed in hospital.' Jago's deep voice interrupted their moment, and they pulled apart, both laughing.

'Kitten!' Olivia threw her arms around her friend and then apologised. 'Have I hurt you?'

'Not at all. It's just lovely to see you.' Kitten lay back on her pillows and beamed at them both.

'We've been so worried about you!' Olivia explained, her voice full of emotion. 'For all sorts of reasons. And I just want to say to you now, in front of witnesses, and before I say anything else, that I was shocked to hear about your MS diagnosis, but I will bend over backwards to ensure that any adjustments you may need now, or at any time in the future, are made both at the Waiting Rooms and the flat. Or anywhere.'

'Thanks, Olive. That's good to know. And I'm sorry I didn't tell you in person.'

'I'm sure you had your reasons.' Olivia squeezed her good hand.

'I did. I needed to be able to deal with my own emotions before I could handle other people's reactions. It was the only bit of control I had left.'

'That makes sense.' Jago smiled at her. 'A diagnosis like that is a lot to handle, and you need to do it your own way.'

'How are you feeling about it now?' Olivia sat down in the chair Jago pulled up for her, still holding Kitten's hand.

'The diagnosis made sense of a lot of things, and the steroids are doing a splendid job,' she admitted. 'And at least I know what I'm dealing with now.' She took a breath. 'But I'm going to be honest with you that I'm a bit scared about what might happen in the future and how much of a difference it will make to my life and the choices I make.'

'We'll all take it slowly and not do anything rash,' Rocky spoke up firmly. He exchanged a look with Olivia, and Kitten smiled. She really did have the best people on her side, and she knew they would all be there for her. *Thank God she had decided to make her life in Cornwall.* She hated to think how things might have turned out if she hadn't.

'Can you promise us one thing?' Jago said. 'That you will always tell us what we can do to help. We may get things wrong, or forget. But it won't be because we don't care. It'll be because we don't know what's the right thing to do at that particular time. So we need you to tell us. Deal?'

'Deal.' Kitten felt hot prickles at the back of her eyes. 'And I'm going to start as I mean to go on. Can we change the subject now, please?'

*

They lapsed into general chat, and safe in the knowledge that Kitten was in good hands, Rocky went to check on progress at the Woodbridges' orangery. As soon as he'd left, Kitten changed the subject again. 'The police came to interview me this morning.'

'Ah.' Jago spoke first. 'Sam said they might. How did it go?'

Kitten scowled. 'It was that Trenow and some young woman who kept looking at me pityingly and spoke to me like I'd got brain damage. So, I might not have been that cooperative.'

'That's a shame,' Olivia sympathised. 'I think he's under pressure at work, but that's really no excuse for the way he's behaving.' Kitten watched her glance at Jago, who nodded back. 'Have you remembered much about what happened?'

Kitten ran her right hand over her face. 'I know I didn't just fall, so it didn't come as much of a surprise when he turned up to ask questions,' she said firmly. 'I'd been down to the Waiting Rooms to see Jasmine and then I went home and stopped halfway up the stairs for a reason I still can't recall. Then I got to the landing at the top, and the last thing I remember is opening the front door.' She closed her eyes, trying to summon up a clear picture of what happened. After a few moments she sank back onto her pillows. 'No, nothing.'

Olivia squeezed her hand. 'Don't worry about it, Kitten. You're safe now.'

Her eyes flew open. 'I got the impression he doesn't have much of a clue about who might have done it and was hoping I could help him. I know I'm not everyone's cup of tea, and I call people out on their behaviours sometimes, but really? And I definitely don't believe that anyone in Penbartha who cares about the second-home issue for the right reasons had anything to do with the awful things that have been happening. It's just a smokescreen.'

'How do you mean?'

'Can you remember any real anti-second home stuff in Penbartha itself before now? Apart from Caroline Pellow? Because I can't. I reckon someone's jumping on the bandwagon because it's been all over the news and it's an ideal screen to hide behind.' She looked at their faces. 'I've been thinking about it a lot. Even though it hurts my head.'

'I think we need to change the subject,' Jago soothed her. 'We just want you to concentrate on getting better quickly.'

'Yes, we were wondering whether you, or you and Rocky, want to come and stay with us while you're recuperating? We've got plenty of room, and you'll be close to your mum. But not too close.'

Kitten saw the twinkle in Olivia's eye. 'That sounds like the best of both worlds,' she admitted with a sigh. 'I'm not scared of going back to the flat, but it will be nice to have company and not to have to deal with so many stairs.' She waved her plastered arm. 'And I suppose I'll need more help with some things.'

'Well, that's sorted then,' Olivia said with a satisfied smile. 'And Cass will be perfectly fine with it.'

Kitten relaxed and then caught Jago's eye. 'What's up?'

He pulled a face. 'I don't want to put you through any more stress, Kitten, but can I just ask you one more thing?'

Kitten ignored Olivia's glare. 'Fire away.'

'It's just that I read somewhere that most people instinctively use their non-dominant arm to break a fall. But you're left-handed, so you should have had your right hand out.'

'I didn't.' She waved her cast around.

'Exactly, so the most obvious reason you didn't would be that you were already holding something in your right hand. You said you stopped on the stairs on the way up to the flat…'

Kitten closed her eyes, desperately trying to remember. A

sliver of a memory danced round the edge of her brain, and she grabbed hold of it. Her eyes flew open. 'That's it! I saw something on the stairs that shouldn't have been there. So I picked it up thinking I would take a proper look when I got in.'

'Do you remember what it was?'

'It was a man's wallet. Or travel pouch, or something. And it was bulging with various bits of paper and some had fallen out, so I collected them up so I could track the owner down when I got the chance to have a proper look at them.'

Jago turned to Olivia. 'Did you see any papers or anything lying about when you got to the scene?'

Kitten noticed Olivia wince and then screw her face up as she racked her memory. 'I don't think so… I can't remember… there was just so much blood everywhere…' she trailed off. 'I'm so sorry, Kitten.'

Kitten waved away her apology. 'So what did you do with your clothes?'

'I think they're probably still in the utility room in the laundry bag Lexie gave us. I was waiting to hear if the police wanted them.' Olivia turned to Jago. 'Did Sam say anything about them?'

He shook his head. 'I'll get onto him again.'

Kitten caught hold of his hand. 'Before you do, why don't you have a quick look through them? See whether Olivia picked anything up—'

'I really don't remember seeing anything.'

'But you thought I'd just had an accident and fallen down the stairs. You weren't looking at it as a crime scene. You might just have thought they were flyers or something. And shoved them in a pocket, to recycle later?' Kitten could feel herself getting worked up, and then saw her friends exchange another glance.

'Okay, okay. We'll look when we get home,' Olivia promised

her quickly. 'Although those clothes will be pretty grungy by now and only fit for the bin.'

'Don't throw them away!' Kitten was horrified. 'That's just wasteful. Promise me you'll wash them. And then give them to charity if they bring back unhappy memories.' She paused and then smiled ruefully. 'Although, perhaps I'll manage to do that all by myself.'

'Never!' Olivia declared. 'We can't wait for you to come home, can we, Jago?'

'Of course we can't. Penbartha isn't the same without you. It's far too quiet.'

'Where's quiet? I want to go there, right away,' a friendly voice asked from the doorway, and a large bump appeared, closely followed by the rest of Emily Hogan.

'Emily!' Kitten was thrilled to see her. 'Come in!'

'I don't want to intrude. I was just over in the maternity wing and thought I'd try and get to see you.' She glanced at Olivia and Jago and then back at Kitten.

'No, that's fine. Come in.' Jago offered his chair, and Emily sank down into it with a grateful sigh.

'Silas not with you?'

'No, it was just a routine appointment. He's busy collecting up all the pumpkins from Hallowe'en.'

'Is he okay with doing that?' Jago asked. 'I've never seen so many pumpkins in one village!'

'Oh, it's all sorted. Some will go to various local farmers for feed, and we'll make sure the rest are all chopped up properly and composted at the flower farm.'

'That's good of you.'

'Not at all! Silas is definitely up for the challenge and is already bragging that we'll have the best compost in Cornwall at this rate!' Emily smiled at Kitten. 'So how are you doing?'

'I'm doing as well as can be expected, thanks.' She smiled and then turned to Olivia and Jago. 'Emily and I are going to talk baby stuff now, so why don't you two get off, and sort that washing out?'

26

Olivia and Jago parted company at The Goods Shed. Olivia had a final meeting with a new client who lived near Peneglos Hall and had commissioned a garden studio built from sustainable materials. It was a smaller project than they usually took on, but she and Rocky had decided they could fit it in before Christmas as their last project of the year. Then, they'd agreed she would fetch the dogs from Ruan and Dylan, as they missed them being around.

Olivia's plans suited Jago. He needed to check if his online bid for the Bognor Regis totem sign had been successful. He was relieved to see it had and contacted the auction house and his client to arrange its delivery. Then he turned his attention to several other phone calls he needed to make and possibly a visit or two, as well. He sat down at his desk and opened his laptop, his heart suddenly beating faster. He was back in barrister mode.

* * *

Everything took longer than expected, and Jago was tired and frustrated when he finally got home. He let himself through the boot room door and breathed in the delicious smell of whatever was cooking in the Aga.

'Cassie must have been round earlier and put a casserole in

the Aga to keep warm,' Olivia called to him from the kitchen, but the dogs beat her to it and he was vigorously greeted by three very excited, and apparently affection-starved, dogs, running round his legs in circles and yapping excitedly until he made it to the sofa and they could all jump on him for a fuss.

'Don't believe a word they say.' Olivia laughed as she handed him a glass of red wine. 'They've had a wonderful time and been spoilt rotten by everyone at Peneglos. The guests loved them apparently, and Lexie doesn't think it will be long before the boys get a puppy.'

Jago pulled a face. 'Can you imagine the havoc a puppy could wreak in a place like Peneglos? I reckon they're better off just borrowing ours when they feel the urge.'

'That's what I said.' She set the table, and within a few moments they were sitting opposite each other in the candlelit orangery, the shutters closed against the dark evening and the wood burner glowing brightly, enjoying Cassie's delicious casserole. By unspoken agreement they chatted about inconsequential matters, and Olivia entertained him with an account of her afternoon's client visit. She was a gentle and funny mimic and as she sat opposite him, her dark eyes shining with laughter, he realised it had been a long time since he'd seen her smile properly. He felt the same. It was only two weeks since he'd been preoccupied with the lack of progress in their wedding plans. Now he was totally focused on keeping them all alive. Okay, that might be a bit of an exaggeration, he admitted, but all he wanted was to have a romantic evening with the woman he loved rather than trying to identify and track down a killer.

'It's only when you're at risk of losing someone that you realise how much they mean to you and how lucky you are, isn't it?' Olivia's mood had plummeted with his, and she pushed her empty plate away from her.

'Kitten will be fine,' Jago said firmly and caught hold of her hand and kissed it. 'Look, I've been doing some digging around. Can I talk things through with you?'

'Of course! We really don't seem to be getting very far, do we? We just keep coming up with dead ends.'

'It certainly feels like that. So I decided to try a different route.' He topped their glasses up. 'Jasper Swift mentioned that he'd been reading about people who'd had their empty houses sold without their knowledge, and he was wondering if Rafe Burrows might have been trying that.'

'Really? That's not very likely, is it?'

'That's what I thought. So I spoke to a planning silk friend of mine from Chambers, called Mel, and she said that these days most people register their empty homes with a Land Registry property alert service which is free and notifies you whenever there's any attempt to change anything on the title deeds. In fact, she went as far as to say that she thought property owners who didn't do that were very foolish.'

'In Jasper's defence, perhaps he isn't aware of it, as he lives thousands of miles away.'

'Perhaps. Anyway, she suggested I take a look for myself. So I did and fell down a huge Land Registry rabbit hole, but the long and short of it is that I ended up paying for digital copies of the title plan and the title deeds to Gillan Cottage.'

'Can you do that? Won't Jasper find out somehow?'

'He won't find out as I'm not changing anything. And anyone can buy copies.'

'And?' Olivia sipped her wine, never taking her eyes off his face.

'Well, here's the interesting bit. It looks like Rex and Peggy Swift bought Gillan Cottage from the local council in 1966.'

'Really? Was that usual back then? Why was the council selling it?'

'Apparently it was left to the council by someone who had no family. But it had a restrictive covenant that it could only be sold to locals who had lived in Cornwall for three years, and on condition they lived in it full time.'

'I didn't know that. George and Mollie never mentioned it as far as I can remember.'

'They might not have known. They didn't buy this place until the early seventies, did they? And there was no reason why Rex and Peggy should tell them. But looking at the title deeds, there's no evidence that they ever tried to get the covenant lifted.'

'That doesn't surprise me. It's usually a nightmare.'

'Indeed. Property owners have to formally apply to the local authority – in this case Cornwall Council now – to get it released. And wait for this, it looks like Jasper's tried. Repeatedly. And failed every time.'

'What a two-faced toad! He's always said he can't bear to part with Gillan because it meant so much to his parents.' Olivia leant forward, her face furious. 'Thank God they've said no. Is that the end of it?'

'Unfortunately, he does have another option,' Jago said flatly.

'Does he?'

'He could apply to the civil equivalent of the High Court to get the covenant discharged or modified.'

'That sounds complicated. And hopefully very expensive.'

'Absolutely. According to Mel, the court fees alone can be up twenty thousand pounds. And with all the expert reports and barrister's fees on top, you could be talking six figures.'

'And presumably it can take years?'

Jago nodded. 'Yes. But Mel said there have been some cases in recent years where these antique restrictive covenants have been ruled to be obsolete and removed. You just have to have the money, the time and the patience to see it through. What we have to ask ourselves is, why hasn't Jasper started the process?'

'Do we know for sure that he hasn't?'

'There's no record of it.'

'Don't these things always come down to money? Perhaps he just can't afford to go to court.'

'And he obviously can't afford to sell it at a lower price to a local. Can you imagine the ridiculously low offers he would get in the current property market?'

Olivia chewed her bottom lip. 'I always thought he was really rich. He gives that impression with his elite sailing clothes and the things he talks about.'

'People don't make money by giving it away,' Jago observed. 'Even to worthy causes like barristers.' He ignored her rude gesture. 'Besides which, who was it who said that yacht racing is like standing under a cold shower and ripping up fifty-pound notes?'

Olivia shuddered. 'I can't think of anything worse.'

They both fell into a contemplative silence, which Olivia broke by draining her wine glass and fetching a jug of iced water from the fridge.

'This is all very interesting, but I think we're going off at a tangent. Are we getting tied up with Jasper and his problems just to take our minds off the bigger issue?' She filled a glass tumbler with water and drank from it, crunching an ice cube between her teeth. 'Jasper told us he had never heard of either Rafe or Marcus, remember?'

Jago held her gaze. 'He also told us he couldn't sell his parents' house because he was too attached to it. I'm afraid the gloves are off now when it comes Jasper Swift.'

Olivia dropped her head into her hands. 'I hate it when this happens. And it always does. Just when you think you can trust someone, the mask comes off and bam! So I suppose the next step is to find something that links him definitively to Rafe?'

He felt his lips twitch, and she narrowed her eyes at him. 'What aren't you telling me?'

'I might have gone along to Burrows Prime Property Search earlier, to pay my condolences to Grace Evans.'

'The one he was having an affair with? Jago!'

A sliver of guilt ran through him. 'I felt a bit sorry for her really, having to pretend she was perfectly okay despite her lover having been murdered. Amanda is refusing to let any of them have time off, or even shut the office for a period of respect. Apparently, when it was suggested, she asked if any of them knew how expensive funerals are these days. So, it's business as usual.'

'Rafe and Amanda really were as bad as each other, weren't they?' Olivia reflected. 'Even I'm beginning to feel sorry for Grace now.'

'Well, it worked in our favour. She was so angry with Amanda, she sang like a canary about all sorts of things.' He filled his own water tumbler. 'She's known about Gillan Cottage for nearly a year.'

'So why didn't she mention it to you?'

'Rafe had sworn her to secrecy. Apparently, Jasper approached Rafe out of the blue and asked him to find the easiest way to get the covenant lifted in return for a lot of money.'

'And he couldn't do that through his existing company because he was a buying agent and not an estate agent?'

'Exactly, so Rafe decided to set up a shell company, Prestige Coastal Properties, and list it as an estate agency. Grace created a website for it, which hasn't been published.'

'And what would that achieve?'

'Well, it just so happens that one of the best pieces of evidence you can present in court to get a restrictive covenant removed is being able to prove that it's been for sale for a continuous period of twelve months, with no interest shown. Which now they could.'

Olivia let out a slow whistle. 'Wow, that's crafty. Do we know how much money Jasper offered him?'

'No, but this is where Grace was particularly helpful. Rafe was in debt up to his neck. He'd got into a lot of financial trouble in his business arranging the purchase of houses that didn't have the necessary planning permission, building regulations, you name it. And like you said after the beach clean, second-home owners were realising they couldn't sell their properties without the paperwork, and the law suits were beginning to pile up. Grace said he was becoming desperate.'

'I wish I could feel some satisfaction at that, but the man's dead.' Zennor pawed at Olivia's leg and then jumped on her lap, kissing her cheek with her little pink tongue. 'And so is Marcus. How do you reckon he got involved?'

Jago shrugged. 'I'm not sure.'

Olivia eyed him. 'Didn't the grieving Grace have any theories?'

He felt his face warm. 'She did say that Rafe owed Marcus quite a bit of money. Unpaid backhanders if you like, from Londoners Marcus had introduced to him who were looking for second homes in Cornwall. Apparently, Marcus could be quite aggressive towards Rafe and never let him forget he owed him money.'

'I can believe that.' Olivia played with Zennor's silky ears. 'So we know Jasper's a sneaky bastard, trying to sell his parents' house without admitting it to anyone, but that's hardly the crime of the century, is it? And we're no further forwards in working out who killed Marcus and Rafe.'

'Well, as much as I hate to say so, it looks like we can rule Jasper out of the running for the murders if he was still in

Canada at the time. And we still have no idea if there is any link between the murders and the FHO group, do we? I think that's what we need to pursue next.'

They lapsed into another silence; both lost in their own theories and thoughts. Olivia suddenly turned towards him, eyes shining. 'Finn Nankivell!'

'What about him?'

'Finn Nankivell must be the link between Jasper and Rafe! And if he's not part of the FHO group, he's certainly a sympathiser. Think about it.'

'I don't think Finn would have recommended Rafe as an estate agent, do you? He hates him.'

'Exactly! I bet Finn had been mouthing off to Jasper about how unethical and dishonest Rafe was over his mother-in-law's house. And Jasper must have decided he would be the perfect man to be part of his dastardly plan.'

Jago felt his mouth twitch. 'Did you just say dastardly?'

'It is dastardly!' she protested. 'It's worse than dastardly.'

'Okay, okay.' Jago moved on. 'You might be right. Jasper and Finn are mates and keep in touch, so it would make sense for Finn to vent at him. Do you reckon Finn is in on it?'

Olivia shook her head. 'I hope not. He's totally against second homes, so I think it's really unlikely he'd support Jasper in getting the covenant lifted. And he certainly wouldn't support anything that would make Rafe money. I think Jasper's used Finn.'

Jago felt a stirring of excitement. 'I agree. And I don't think he stopped there. I reckon that he used Finn as a way into the FHO group.'

'Why on earth would he do that?'

'To strengthen his case to get the restrictive covenant removed?' he suggested. 'If he could prove that second homes in Penbartha were coming increasingly under attack from locals, perhaps he hoped the council would support him? They know how important tourism is to the Cornish economy, and wouldn't want to be seen as giving into people who could be seen as terrorists. And, besides which, they'd benefit financially from the extra taxes if it was sold as a second home.'

'So you reckon Jasper somehow infiltrated the group and got them to up their game against second homes in the area, just to support his case?' Olivia caught hold of her gemstone, the way she always did when she was troubled. 'That's not just dastardly, it's totally far-fetched!'

Jago bristled. 'I'm not so sure. I reckon Jasper and Rafe were up to their necks in this together. Perhaps Rafe thought he could get Marcus a good deal on Gillan, if he was genuinely looking for a second home here, and that might pay off some of the money he owed him. How that escalated into two murders is another question.'

'All these questions and not enough answers.' Totally frustrated, Jago began clearing the table and loading the dishwasher, and Olivia went off to sort the laundry.

Twenty seconds later there was a shriek from the utility room, and she rushed back in flourishing something in front of her, breathless and gabbling incoherently.

Jago dropped his tea towel and held out his hand. 'What is it?'

'I've just been through the laundry bag from Peneglos Hall. With my bloodied clothes in it.'

'And?' His pulse quickened.

'I must have picked up whatever Kitten had been lying on at the bottom of the stairs… I didn't think anything of it because we thought she'd just fallen… and I automatically put it in my pocket… read it – I haven't got my glasses on so I can't make it all out—' She held a creased and blood-stained slip of card out to him.

He took it carefully. 'It's an Air Canada boarding pass.' He looked at her triumphantly. 'It's in Jasper's name. And it's dated three weeks ago.'

27

Olivia and Jago didn't get much sleep that night, after talking long into the early hours about what they had learned and what they needed to do. Top of the list was talking to Sam. They were up before sunrise, walked the dogs around the headland so they could avoid passing Gillan, and then they sat at the refectory table together and made copious notes about what they had learned, any gaps in their knowledge that they needed to fill and a list of questions they still needed answers to.

It was mid-morning before Jago had got his notes into a format he was happy with. He'd explained to Olivia that they needed to develop their theory and present both supporting and challenging facts and arguments, alongside a chronological timeline. Olivia didn't really care. She just wanted to hand everything over to the police to deal with. It was too big for them now.

'Right, that should do it.' Jago replaced the cap on his fountain pen with a satisfied click. 'There are still quite a few questions to be answered, but I think that will give Sam enough to be going on with.'

'You're not presenting a case in court,' Olivia squeaked, unable to contain her frustration. 'Will you just get on with it? We could be wasting valuable time with all this faffing about.'

He shot her a hurt look and gathered his papers up. 'It will save time in the long run. Trust me. And while Jasper has no idea we're onto him, which he doesn't, we'll be fine.' He dropped a kiss on her cheek. 'I'll just scan these, then there's no chance of losing anything.'

'Most people would just do it on their laptop in the first place and then email it.' She muttered to his back as he left the room. 'And reduce the amount of paper needed. The trees will thank you.'

She turned to the window and gazed out over the gardens and sighed again. Despite only being mid-morning, the sky was darkening and matched the moody greyness of the creek. She'd need to put the lights on soon. *God, she hated days like this.*

A sudden movement in the garden distracted her, and Finn Nankivell appeared at the door. 'Hi, Olivia, have you got a moment?'

The dogs rushed to greet him as Olivia pushed away the prickles of concern that had begun creeping up her spine. *Finn was one of the good guys. Even if he did have dubious taste in friends and extra marital affairs. Wasn't he?*

'Hey, Liv.' Jago dashed back into the kitchen, waving his mobile about. 'The alarm's going off in the Signal Box and Sam's called too. Some kids are trying to break in, so we're going down there together.'

'Do you want a hand?' Finn offered.

'It sounds like they're just kids, so I think we'll be okay, thanks. But I'll call if I do. You stay and keep Olivia company.' He ignored the anguished glance she sent him and tossed his notes onto the table. 'It's unlikely they'll get in, but we better check. And I'll talk to Sam while we're there.' And before Olivia's sleep-deprived brain could process what was happening, he was off.

'I don't know what's happening to Penbartha at the moment,' Finn said sadly as he sat down at the table. 'All I do know is that

I'm getting loads of queries about fitting burglar alarms. And it's not something I thought we'd ever need here.'

Olivia smiled weakly at him. 'What can I do for you? You said you wanted a word.' *Please, please don't mention Jasper. It's too soon.*

'Oh yes.' Finn shook himself. 'Look, Olivia, I wanted to talk to you. About Amanda Burrows.'

She managed to swallow her sigh of relief. 'How's she doing?'

He shrugged. 'I don't really know. She called it off. The day before Jago found Rafe's body. And she hasn't replied to any of my messages since.'

'Oh.' Olivia's mouth dropped open. 'What do you think's going on there?'

'I have no idea.' Finn must have read her expression of surprise. 'I'm not bothered about her calling it off, I just didn't think she'd ghost me so quickly.' He looked away. 'But now I'm worried that if I tell Louisa about our affair she might think I had something to do with Rafe's murder.'

'No way!' Olivia was so shocked she nearly laughed, but after one look at Finn's face, she changed her mind.

'It was you who told me she thought I might be responsible for all the vandalism and arson in the village, remember?'

Olivia's mind started racing. Had they missed something? They'd been so focused on Jasper being the villain had they overlooked the idea of any one else being involved? *Was Finn, Jasper's oldest friend, in on it all too?* She looked quickly round the quiet orangery, the silence broken only by the sound of Mylor's gentle snoring. She clicked her fingers at him and within seconds he was at her knee, wagging his tail. She forced a smile onto her face. 'And you were adamant that you weren't a vandal or an arsonist. So how likely is it that you'd be a murderer?'

A loud jangling at the front door interrupted Finn's reply, and

Olivia jumped up in relief, eager to follow the excited dogs out to the front door and put some distance between them. There was no one there but the prickles of concern that had begun creeping up her spine assumed a strict battle formation and marched up to her scalp and back down both arms.

Should she run for it? She shook herself and straightened her shoulders. She was being ridiculous. *There was no way she was running from her own home.*

She tapped out a quick message to Jago, on her mobile that fortunately was still in the back pocket of her jeans, and fixed a smile on her face and walked back down the hall, the dogs at her heels. Before she'd even reached the eerily quiet kitchen, her senses started to tingle again. From where she was, she could see that Finn wasn't there anymore. She hissed to the dogs to stay close by as she moved slowly forward, flicking on the light switch as she went. And gasped.

There, sitting at the table was Jasper Swift, cool as cucumber. On the floor beside the window lay Finn Nankivell, in a pool of blood. The dogs pressed against her legs, Mylor growling softly at the back of his throat.

'Sit down please, Olivia. And then the dogs will be fine.' Jasper spoke quietly. 'I'm afraid Jago and the policeman friend of yours will be tied up for a while yet. Literally, hopefully.' He laughed at his own joke. Olivia did as she was told, her pulse quickening. *Was he mad?*

He gazed down at Finn's lifeless body. 'I saw Finn driving past, and I gathered he'd come to talk to you.'

'He came to talk to me about Louisa. That's all!'

'Do you expect me to believe that? He never could keep things to himself.' A cruel smile flitted across his face. 'Especially when it came to women like Amamda Burrows.'

Olivia looked at him, and suddenly she didn't see the sailing hero she'd known all her life who regularly regaled them with stories of his daring escapades, but a pathetic, weasel-like creature who was on the verge of losing everything.

'How do you know Amanda?'

'Finn had told me about her some time ago, so when I got here, I met up with her. And we realised we had quite a lot in common.' Jasper's attention was diverted to Jago's pages of neat notes, and he sifted through them casually. He stopped at the photocopy of the boarding card and swore under his breath. 'The bastard! I wondered where that had got to.'

'You dropped it on the stairs after you attacked Kitten with the fire extinguisher and nearly killed her.' Olivia spat the words at him. 'Remember?'

'That wasn't me. It was Rafe.' His stare was intense, unsettling.

'How convenient, now he's dead and can't defend himself.'

'Don't feel sorry for him, Olivia. It's all his fault we're in this mess. Kitten saw me and Rafe at Gillan the morning of her accident. I wanted to know what he was playing at with the For Sale board. I thought she might have recognised me and she definitely clocked Rafe, so he said he'd deal with her. I didn't realise he was going to try to kill her – you have to believe me!' He pointed at the boarding card. 'But he made sure he left evidence that linked me to the accident. Bastard.'

Olivia blinked. 'How did he get hold of it?'

'He nicked my wallet. The card must have been in it. He gave me the wallet back, and said he'd picked it up by mistake. I didn't notice the pass had gone until later.'

'Why didn't you go to the police when you realised what he'd done to Kitten?'

Jasper rubbed the back of his neck. 'It was too risky, Rafe had become a liability by then and I was scared he'd come for me. Or Amanda. He'd already killed Marcus, for God's sake!'

Olivia's right hand automatically went to her necklace. 'Do you know he killed Marcus? I thought he was his friend.'

Jasper's eyes darted round the orangery, rested momentarily on Finn's inert form and then darted back to Olivia.

'All's fair in love and war. He only told that prick Marcus about Gillan because he owed him a shed load of money and thought he could keep him off his back for a while longer with empty promises about getting him a good deal on the house.' He looked at Olivia. 'Rafe said they had a massive row.'

'About the money Rafe owed him?'

'What else? They only ever talked about money. All I know is that he was getting desperate and he had a nasty temper – ask his wife.' He didn't explain. 'Just said he was out of the financial equation.' Jasper stared at her. 'And the bastard swapped his shoes for a pair of my dad's old gardening wellies that were in the potting shed as a clear warning to me. He knew I'd recognise them. If that's not the action of a man with a sick mind, I don't know what is, do you?'

Olivia's eyes widened. *Talk about taking one to know one.*

Jasper's attention turned back to Jago's notes and he started reading through them. Unsure of what to do, she glanced down at Finn, who was lying facing her and with his back to Jasper. One of his eyes suddenly opened. Then closed. And opened again. Her spirits rose. *She just had to keep Jasper talking while Finn came to. If she could.*

'These are quite good actually.' Jasper sat back in his chair and pointed at the scattered papers. 'Your chap obviously knows his stuff. It's no wonder barristers charge so much.' His eyes wandered back to her. 'Do you want me to fill in the gaps?'

She bent to pat Mylor and risked another glance at Finn. This time he managed a nod. 'If you like.'

He pointed at the first page. 'Well you're spot on about the restrictive covenant at Gillan. God knows why it didn't occur to my parents to get it lifted in the first fifty years they lived there.

And by the time I found about it, it was too late and it's nothing but a bloody millstone round my neck.'

'Couldn't you try to get it lifted? Go to court?'

He sighed. 'Have you any idea how much that costs? Only a bloody blood-sucking barrister, with their extortionate fees, could afford to buy Gillan Cottage.' He seemed to realise what he'd just said. 'No offence.'

'None taken,' Olivia said smoothly, with another glance at Finn. 'Besides which, criminal silks only earn about a quarter of what planning silks do.'

'Shame.' He brightened. 'But even then, Jago could probably still afford to buy it and live next door? Isn't living-apart-together all the rage these days? Perhaps I'd still be married if I tried that. Have I told you about my wife, or rather ex-wife?' His voice rose.

Olivia's heart began to race. She needed to calm him down. 'Why don't we talk through the rest of Jago's notes. You can tell me what else we've missed.'

He picked the papers up. 'You're also right about how I got to know Rafe. Finn was always raging about what a crook he was, so I thought he'd be just the man for the job. He agreed to put Gillan on his books for a stupidly high sum as he said that would count as evidence towards me being unable to sell it. He also said he reckoned it would be a good move to get some anti-second homes protestors to up their game against homes in Penbartha. He hated them and reckoned it would kill two birds with one stone. They'd get into trouble with the police and it would provide more evidence to support my case.'

'And you knew Finn was kind of involved in the FHO?'

A sly look crossed his face. 'Yes, and I thought it was quite clever to use him to get me added to their WhatsApp group. He's always been easy to wind up, and I knew exactly what buttons to press. We all had code names so no one really knows who anyone is.'

'And then you egged them on to the things they did?'

'It wasn't hard. I also used a few lads I know from years back, who are always up for a bit of edgy stuff.' He smiled. 'They're the ones who are looking after Jago and the policeman as we speak.'

Olivia's stomach went cold, and she tightened her hold on Mylor's collar, risking a quick glance at Finn. He nodded again.

'So they organised the graffiti and other things?'

'Yes, but not the tyre extinguishing. That could have been dangerous. I wouldn't get involved in something like that.'

Olivia blinked. *He really was mad!*

'What about blackmail?'

He gave her a sideways look. 'Well that took a bit of an unexpected turn. I saw the lad's gran posting those stickers on houses and told him I'd tell the police if he didn't set a few fires for me at Gillan. I didn't know that Rafe was planning to murder Marcus, did I? Or that the lad would be arrested. You can't blame me for that. And besides the cops soon let him go, didn't they? So no harm done.'

Olivia couldn't believe what she was hearing. *Who was he trying to convince?* She tried to get him back on track.

'Are you sure Rafe murdered Marcus?'

'Positive. The bastard swapped Marcus's shoes for a pair of my dad's old wellies as a crystal-clear warning message to me. He just kept needling me, flexing his muscles if you like.

He had that For Sale board made a year ago so he could put it up outside Gillan, take a photo of it and then remove it straight away, as part of the proof we needed to say it was for sale. But he left it up there this time because it was all part of his plan to inflame the locals and could then be used to cover his tracks. No one would expect someone to use their own board in a murder, would they? I reckon he thought it would look like another anti-second homes move – which I suppose was quite clever really.' He took a breath and wiped the beads of sweat from his brow. 'When I found out what he'd done to Kitten, I decided I needed to get him off my back once and for all. If he'd killed Marcus and then tried to kill Kitten, it was obvious I was next on his list. Can't you see that?' He gazed at Olivia with unseeing eyes, tapping the papers on the table.

'So we met again at Gillan, on the night before the pumpkin trail. Before anyone was supposed to know I was back. We were meant to be discussing next steps, but he'd found out I'd been seeing Amanda behind his back. It was okay for him to have affairs but not her, apparently. She'd told him we had plans for Gillan that didn't include him. He went for me in a fit of rage, so I just grabbed the first thing that came to hand and hit him over the head with it.' He started to laugh. 'It was one of those bloody awful Cornish serpentine lighthouse carvings that every person over eighty seems to own. Dad loved it, he always said it was a "symbol of Cornwall's maritime identity". It's quite ironic to think that Rafe had his brains bashed in with a bit of rock from the county he's exploited so badly over the years, isn't it? And then it was just a matter of putting the body into Dad's old boat trailer, taking it down the field at night and adding it to all the guys that were piling up for the bonfire.'

Olivia was too shocked to speak.

'I reckon I've done everyone a favour, really, don't you?' He laughed again and then sobered quickly. 'So the question is, what happens next? You probably know a bit too much for your own good now, unfortunately.'

Olivia shot a desperate look down at Finn who nodded and mouthed, 'now'. In a flash, she jumped to her feet, deliberately knocking her chair over, and commanded 'get him' to Mylor. The faithful black dog launched himself, teeth bared and snarling, at Jasper at the exact time Finn pulled the chair from beneath him, and the two men ended up in a big tangle of arms and legs on the kitchen floor.

For a moment, Olivia couldn't work out which limb belonged to who as Finn and Jasper thrashed around on the floor together, hurling insults and blows at each other, with all three dogs circling them like referees in a boxing ring. Every time Jasper tried to get away, Mylor herded him back into Finn's grasp, his teeth bared. Olivia hovered anxiously on the sidelines, removing any items that Jasper could use as weapons from his reach, and sending SOS mobile alerts to everyone she could think of. In spite of his injury, Finn began to overpower Jasper, undoubtedly helped by Mylor's carefully timed interventions, but it was only when the sound of sirens got closer and louder that Jasper gave up the fight.

By the time Tresillian was invaded by the police, emergency services and half the village, Jasper was sitting quietly in the corner, penned in by three excited dogs.

28

Three weeks later…

'Only Kitten would want a beach party in the middle of November to celebrate her recovery.' Jago spoke his thoughts out loud as he sorted through their warmest coats, scarves and beanie hats in the boot room.

'Ah, but it's not just any old beach party, it's been meticulously planned and timed by her, Jasmine and Izzy, to get the tides and stars aligned,' Olivia told him as she accepted her waxed jacket with a fleece lining from him. 'And if we dress up warmly, we'll be fine, so stop being such an old grump.' She reached up to kiss him and then looked at her watch. 'We need to get a move on. She wants us there by five o'clock.'

'And why on earth is it starting at precisely five o'clock?' he asked as he pulled on his own winter clothes and then patted his pocket, checking for poo bags, dog treats and other essentials. He could think of plenty of ways he'd rather spend the evening, all of which involved just him, Olivia and a bottle of red wine. But he could tell Olivia was excited about the party, and he would always put her happiness first. Her eyes were shining as she turned to him.

'Because the Beaver Moon is at its most powerful thirty

minutes after sunset.' She whistled to the dogs and ushered everyone out of the back door. 'Just look!'

A huge golden moon, seemingly perfectly round, hung in the sky above Penbartha. It was the biggest and brightest moon he had ever seen, cushioned against a dark blue velvet sky, its brightness overshadowing the stars nearest to it, but the ones further away put in a showstopping backing performance.

'That is beautiful,' he conceded. 'I don't think I've ever seen anything like it before.'

'Well, it's a perfectly clear night, so we get a fabulous view and it'll get even bigger and brighter in about half an hour, so let's go!'

She locked the door, and they set off with the dogs down the moonlit lane, their feet crunching on the already frosty leaves and their breath clouding in front of them. 'Wow!' Jago was impressed. 'It's like having our very own floodlight.' He put his torch away. 'So why's it called a Beaver Moon?'

She turned to him. 'Sometimes, I struggle to believe you're a farmer's son and lived in Cornwall until you were eighteen. How do you not know about these things?'

'Probably because my family stopped living by the sun and moon cycles when artificial light was introduced, so about one hundred years ago,' he replied with a smile. 'And of course, we didn't have any witches in our family who held on to the old ways like Mollie did.'

Olivia shook her head in mock horror. 'You have such gaps in your education, Mr Trevithick.'

'Apparently so.' They paused, listening to owls hooting in the ancient oak trees that lined the lane, while the dogs had a good sniff in the leaves. 'So tell me, briefly, about this moon.'

'It's called that because it was the time when beavers began preparing for winter by building their dams and storing food.

And it's called a supermoon because it's a full moon that occurs when it's at its closest point to the earth, which is why it looks so big and bright. Is that brief enough?' They carried on walking, getting closer to the village where lights were beginning to twinkle in the windows of the cottages.

'Perfect. So, I might regret saying this, but that doesn't sound a big enough reason for Kitten to insist on this party tonight. There must be more to it.'

'You're right. As always.' Olivia tucked her arm through his as they walked, watching their breath cloud and rise into the starry sky. 'The Beaver Moon has huge spiritual significance for people like Mollie and Kitten. It's all about reflection, preparation and transition. Just as the beavers adapt to their new winter environment and get prepared for what's ahead, for Kitten it's a time to let go of past troubles, adapt to the changes she's facing and make plans for the new year.'

They lapsed into a comfortable silence as they walked, each lost in their own thoughts. Jago would have preferred to forget all about the events of the previous weeks, but that wasn't going to happen any time soon. By the time he'd arrived at Tresillian following his eventual release from the Signal Box by the local uniformed police, Jasper had been unceremoniously carted off to Truro police station and hadn't been seen since.

He didn't envy Trenow and his superiors, who had now been drafted onto the complex case of getting to the bottom of who had killed whom and why. The police had mountains of statements and forensic, medical and expert evidence to sift through. Jasper was behaving increasingly irrationally by all accounts, and Jago was beginning to doubt if he'd be well enough to stand trial. But that wasn't his problem, he was very relieved to know, although he felt a pang of pity for the judge who found himself hearing that trial.

The whole village was still reeling from Jasper's betrayal of so many people and his shocking actions. In true Penbartha style, everyone had closed ranks to protect their own, and Jago had no doubt that tonight's party would be well attended.

'And talking of new plans.' He squeezed Olivia's hand, glad to move on to more practical matters. 'I have some news.'

'About what?' She pulled on his arm. 'Have Jasper's daughters been back in touch?

'Yes. Well, we're communicating through solicitors now. It turns out that Gillan was left equally between Jasper and his daughters, not just to him. And there are various clauses in the will that allow two of them to sell without the agreement of the third, so they've offered to sell Gillan Cottage to me at a very reasonable price. I'd be mad to say no.'

'You would! It's an ideal house to be adapted for any future needs Kitten may have.' Olivia's shining eyes held his. 'And are Rocky and Kitten still on board with this?'

'Absolutely. We're just working through how it's going to pan out, but it looks like our plans are all falling into place.'

She leant up and kissed him, her lips warm against his cold cheek. 'It's the most wonderful solution all round, thank you so much!'

He felt a surge of happiness. 'Well, it's not going to be a quick process, but Rocky and Kitten can lease it from me and we can come up with some payment agreement that suits us both. Perhaps a peppercorn rent in return for renovating it; something like that.'

Olivia's eyes gleamed. 'Ooh, I'm so looking forward to getting my hands on that house. We can make it absolutely beautiful, energy-efficient and make sure it's perfect for any future needs Kitten may have.'

Jago laughed. 'That's what Rocky says. And if all goes well, they could buy it from me eventually, if that's what they want.'

'And what about the restrictive covenant?'

'Mel says she'll take on the case to get the covenant removed, or at least amended in our favour, if I do most of the donkey work for her. She reckons if we do it properly, there shouldn't be a problem. And that clears the way for any future sales, if they're necessary.'

She threw her arms around him. 'You buying Gillan Cottage really is the perfect news! See, the Beaver Moon's casting its magic already.'

* * *

'This is going to be such a wonderful night,' Kitten declared as they walked to the party. 'Everything's coming together, and I feel really positive for the first time in ages.'

'Oh wow! Look!' Rocky was speechless. Kitten, still not fully in control of all her emotions, burst into tears of delight.

Against the backdrop of the golden full moon, the beach looked enchanting, dotted with braziers burning brightly with firewood. Finn Nankivell had strung colourful lights between makeshift poles and a small sound system, giving it a real party feel. It was slowly filling up with familiar faces, some of whom had brought camping chairs and others were already taking full advantage of the temporary dancefloor before the tides reclaimed it. At the back of the beach, Willow and Fraser had set up their trestle tables and were getting ready to serve soup, rolls and hotdogs, helped by Alfie and Mya who looked like they were now much more than friends. Next to them, Jack from the Ship was cheerfully accepting help to man the free bar. The whole village seemed to have been enticed from their cosy homes to celebrate with her.

'Isn't it all amazing!' A squealing Jasmine and Izzy launched themselves at Kitten, and they all did a little happy dance together, as the girls pointed out various people across the beach and what they were doing to help.

'I don't know how I'm going to thank everyone!' Kitten gasped. 'There's just so many of them!'

'They don't expect thanks. They just want to show their support. Now and in the future,' Jasmine declared. 'Now do you want me to get you a seat?'

'Not yet, thanks!' Kitten stated very clearly, knowing she had to be careful about pacing herself as well as other people's expectations of her. 'Ask me again in half an hour, will you?' She blew kisses at her friends. 'Hey, there's Emily!'

Kitten rushed across the beach to where Emily and Silas were standing in a huddle with several locals, a pram and a stroller.

'Meet Roisin – Rosie for short!' Emily pushed the pram towards her, with the sweetest, most perfect little baby Kitten had ever seen swaddled in several cosy blankets inside. 'She's a week old today.'

Kitten dropped to her knees so she could examine the newest addition to the village properly, and her heart squeezed with a sudden rush of love and wonder. 'Oh, she's so beautiful!'

'Silas and I would like to ask you to be her godmother.'

Kitten felt her eyes fill with tears. 'No one's ever asked me that before.'

'You were one of the first people to offer me real kindness and friendship here. We want Rosie to grow up being kind and can't think of a better role model for her.' Emily peered at her. 'I haven't upset you, have I? That's the last thing we wanted to do. Are we being insensitive?'

Kitten understood immediately. *Really that bash on the head seemed to have knocked some empathy into her.* 'Not at all! I'm honoured.' She reached out a hand, and Silas helped her up. 'Thank you so much.' She suddenly realised that the person holding onto the stroller and talking animatedly to Darragh about all the lights and fires on the beach was Caroline Pellow. She raised an eyebrow at Emily.

'And Caroline's going to be Rosie's other godmother,' Emily explained with a huge smile on her face. 'You may have heard that my waters broke while I was in the Bakehouse and Caroline's the one who took me to hospital and stayed with me until Silas arrived. And then she collected Darragh from playgroup and took him back to the Old Foundry until Tressa finished work. She and Darragh are quite the besties now.'

Wonders would never cease! Kitten smiled at the older woman, with whom she shared so many similarities.

'Between us we should see this young maid right, eh Kitten?' Caroline said gruffly. 'And I'm proper glad you're on the mend.'

Kitten stood, mouth open, unable to find the words.

'You'll be the dream team, won't you?' Emily came to her rescue.

'Well, we can't leave it all to old Margaret Chynoweth at her age. So I'm here to even the playing field if this one starts leading young Rosie down the militant path. Especially as Alfie is spending so much time with that Mya girl, who's perfect for him.' Caroline managed to stretch her mouth into a smile, which lit her whole face up. Kitten smiled back, her streak of mischief as strong as ever.

'You'll be pleased to know my militant days are over, Caroline. No more chaining myself to the top of trees to stop them being felled unnecessarily. I'm all about gentle activism now. I'll still have all the same causes, but I'll be going about things in a very different way from now on. Watch this space!' She blew kisses at them all and rushed off to hug someone else. The little bubble of hope that had started deep down in her stomach when the steroids took effect, and had got bigger after their most recent, very positive visit to the neurologist, was still and growing, and now it felt she might burst with happiness.

*

'Did I just hear Caroline Pellow tell someone that Kitten's bash on the head has finally knocked some sense into her?' Louisa Nankivell spluttered with laughter as she recounted what she'd been told to Olivia. 'Something about "gentle activism", whatever that might be.'

'Ah.' Olivia moved aside from Jago who was deep in conversation with Sam. 'Apparently it's more about using thoughtful action and respectful dialogue to influence hearts, minds and policies rather than anything aggressive and shouty.'

Louisa chuckled. 'Isn't that what the rest of us are already doing?'

'Well yes, but the more the merrier, and I should imagine Kitten will bring a whole new vibe to it and keep us all on our toes.'

'I'm happy to support her in any way I can. That's the beauty of this village. People come together when one of their own is in need.' Louisa turned back to the beach, which was full of happy people. 'Finn's done an amazing job with the lighting and the music, hasn't he?' She lowered her voice. 'Between you and me I think he's trying to make up for everything Jasper did, even though he's not responsible for him.'

'No, and I'm pretty certain he saved my life. God knows what would have happened that day if Finn hadn't been there.'

'You'd have managed, Olivia. Especially with Mylor's help. He was quite the hero by all accounts.' They both laughed as the black hero thumped his tail proudly against the hard sand at the sound of his name. 'And just for the record, I know about Finn's affair with Amanda. Thanks for getting him to tell me.'

Olivia felt her cheeks warm. 'I thought it would be better coming from him. I didn't know what else to do.'

'We've decided to work things through. I don't want to throw away thirty years of marriage for a fling. I'm not saying it will be easy, but we're going to try. And Amanda's going back to

London, so that should help. She and Marcus's wife are probably in line for huge life insurance payouts when the police have finally decided who did what.'

Olivia pulled an awkward face. Louisa was getting very close to the unwritten rule that no one was to talk about the murders at the party, but then she changed the subject. 'And we've just had a good offer on Mum's place so if it all goes through, everything should be okay.'

'Oh, Louisa, that's such good news, I'll keep everything crossed for you.'

The sound of a spoon being clinked against a glass interrupted them. Rocky and Kitten stood on a large rock, so everyone could see them.

'I'll keep this short,' Rocky announced, with a huge smile plastered across his handsome face. 'Kitten and I just want to say thank you to everyone here tonight, and for all your cards, gifts, messages of support. We've been really touched by your kindness.' His voice sobered for a moment. 'There may have been a bit of a cloud over Penbartha for a few weeks, but I'm pleased to say it's definitely been lifted, and we can dance once again in the moonlight.'

The beach erupted into cheers and applause and only quietened down when the spoon was clinked against the glass again. This time it was Kitten who spoke.

'I'm sure you all expect me to say something.' The cheers broke out again. 'So here goes: I'd like to add my thanks to Rocky's. Especially to Mum and Sam. And Olivia and Jago. Between them, they've got me through. I realise I'm going to have to make some pretty big changes to my life. But the biggest change for me is also the happiest – Rocky and I are getting married!'

This time the beach exploded with cheers and applause, and everyone rushed to congratulate them. Cassie was crying with happiness, and Olivia could feel tears on her own cheeks. Jago's arms slid round her waist, and she leant backwards into his solid warmth.

'Happy?' he whispered into her ear.

'So happy.' She turned and let him move her away from the crowds. Only then did he speak again, his face serious.

'I'm not stealing their thunder, promise. But I made such a hash of proposing back in the summer, I thought I'd try again.' He rummaged through his pocket and produced a small dark blue box, which he opened with fumbling fingers and held out to her. 'Will you marry me?'

Olivia gasped. Inside the box was the most beautiful art deco-style diamond engagement ring.

'It's beautiful!' She held out her hand. 'Can I try it?'

'Of course.' He slid it onto her ring favour and it fitted perfectly.

'How did you know?' She guessed immediately. 'Cass.' She looked at the ring more closely. 'Hang on, it's a bit like Mollie's, except this is platinum and the diamonds are bigger.' She looked again, and a warm feeling spread through her. 'I always said I wanted an engagement ring just like Mollie's. Did Cass tell you that as well?'

Jago smiled. 'Yes. And I know how much you love Mollie's ring and all the memories it contains, so I want this one to mark the start of our own memories. If we can be anything like as happy as George and Mollie were for all those years, we'll be okay.'

'Oh, Jago. It's perfect.' She stood on her tiptoes, snaked her arms round his neck and kissed him.

'Is that a yes?'

She pulled away slightly. 'It's a yes.'

'Do you want to tell people, as we've got them all here?'

'No,' she answered instinctively and smiled at his sigh of

relief. 'This is Rocky and Kitten's night. We have all the time in the world.'

A sudden shout came from down the beach. 'Tide's on the turn!'

'One of Mollie's favourite sayings was that a turning tide washes everything clean,' Olivia told him as they headed towards the part of the beach where everyone was starting to clear up.

'She was a very wise woman,' Jago said with a smile as they arrived at the group, his glass aloft. 'Let's put these last few weeks behind us and look to the future!'

'To new beginnings!' It sounded like the whole of Penbartha beach was taking up the toast. 'For all of us!'

Acknowledgements

This book has been a major part of a rollercoaster year of my life, and I'm still reeling in many ways. I started 2025 in a pit of despair, having undergone two cancer surgeries in three months, and I was facing much uncertainty. I'd completely forgotten I'd even entered the RNA awards, when in February last year, I discovered that I'd been shortlisted for the Romantic Thriller Award in the RNA awards. And although I didn't win the award, I won a literary agent and a four-book publishing deal!

So I owe a great deal of thanks to Francesca Riccardi, my agent, who has taken a huge amount of responsibility off my shoulders and is always in my corner. That's a really lovely feeling.

And I can't thank Carolyn Mays enough for being a gentle and constructive editor. I always think that having edits done is the same as having your English homework marked at school, and although I liked all my English teachers, Carolyn is something special. Carolyn and Francesca make a great team, and I feel in very safe hands with them both.

Special thanks must go to my writing friends, who are spread far and wide across the world, but in particular Sue Kittow, Jo Simpson and Kerry Birds, who always seem to know how to say just the right thing at all times.

I also need to thank all my non-writing friends who are very patient with me, respect my deadlines and are still my most ardent supporters.

To my immediate and extended McParkes clan. Thanks for all your love, support, encouragement and patience in giving me the space I need to write.

Extra special thanks to Mr McP for all the legal advice, some of which I did take on board, I promise. His legal skills are surpassed only by his strong tea-making abilities, without which I would probably have died of thirst.

And of course, to all my lovely readers and book bloggers, who support me and my books. I have been delighted by how many of you enjoyed the first two Olivia Wells Mysteries and have invested in the characters' lives and storylines. Your appreciation confirmed my belief that Olivia and friends deserved a series, and here we are with book three. There's more to come, I promise.

At this point, I'd like to mention the late, wonderful neurologist Dr Roderick Hughes who diagnosed my Multiple Sclerosis when I was 27 – I will forever hold him in the deepest affection, because in my darkest moments he always gave me hope. And he was always right! I'd also like to thank the team of MS specialist nurses at my local hospital, who are funded by the MS Trust, and keep me on the straight and narrow today.

Finally, as always, to Margot and Geoffrey, who have watched me write every single word of this book, listened to all my worries and woes and never once doubted me. Every writer should have dogs as writing buddies.

About the Author

Jane McParkes has wanted to be a crime writer ever since she discovered *The Famous Five* as a small child. Her dream was fulfilled in 2023 with the publication of the first of the Olivia Wells mysteries, a series of cosy Cornish crime novels with a green twist.

To keep up with Jane's new releases, special offers and behind the scenes of her writing life, sign up to her newsletter at www. janemcparkes.com and follow her on Facebook, X, and Instagram, all **@JaneMcParkes**